# HOW TO PROTECT A PRINCESS

New York Times & USA Today Bestselling Author

# CYNTHIA EDEN

# CHAPTER ONE

*Step One: Set the ground rules early on. Clear communication is key. You're the muscle. She's the target. Simple. Easy.*

"My name is Constantine Leos, and I'm your bodyguard."

The beautiful blonde who'd been swiping a rather shady-looking white cloth over the top of the bar paused at Constantine's announcement. He kept his shoulders back and his arms loose at his sides. This was supposed to be an assignment that he didn't fuck up, and he was going to stick to the Wilde rules on this one. Okay, fine, so maybe Wilde—the security firm that now employed him—didn't exactly have a set of rules when it came to this precise situation. So Constantine had decided to improvise.

Slowly, the blonde tilted back her head. Deep, dark chocolate eyes—warmed with flecks of gold—locked on him. Her bow-shaped lips curled in the faintest of smiles as she nodded. "Does that pickup line often work for you?"

Voices rose and fell behind him. It was a Friday night, and Sal's, the bar in Baton Rouge, Louisiana, was certainly hopping. Plenty of people were hooking up in the bar, no doubt about it, but Constantine hadn't traveled across multiple states and enjoyed the comfort of his boss's private jet just so he could hit on a pretty blonde. "It's not a pickup line. It's the truth." He turned his head and cast an eye around the packed place. "Too many people are here. I don't like it." Talk about a logistical nightmare.

"Then, ah, if you don't like it, you should probably leave. There are lots of less crowded places in the area." Gravely polite.

His attention shifted back to her. "I'm not going to leave without you."

She took a tiny step back. He saw her hold tighten on the off-white cloth. The smile slipped from her lips. "I don't intend to go anywhere with you. My shift doesn't end until 2 a.m."

Constantine's head shook. "Bad mistake. You never, *ever* tell a stranger when you're getting off work. I could be planning to stay around and wait out back for you. You come out on your own at 2 a.m., and then I could grab you."

Her eyes flared with alarm even as a gasp tore from her.

*I am screwing this up.* "Not that I intend to do that, of course," Constantine rushed to reassure her because he certainly didn't want her terrified of him. Her terror would just make things awkward. "I'm your bodyguard. My job is to keep you safe." There. She should be feeling better.

She backed up a little more. Constantine noticed that she'd dropped the cloth. "Right." Now she smiled again, and the smile took the woman before him from being pretty to absolutely stunning. Unforgettable. It was the most charming and warm smile he'd ever seen in his life, and Constantine found himself leaning forward because he wanted to get closer to her as—

"Johnny, gonna need you to escort this guy out." She pointed straight at Constantine.

But, wait, Johnny—who the hell was Johnny?

A beefy hand closed around Constantine's shoulder. *Ah, that must be Johnny.* Constantine lifted a brow as he turned to face his new friend. "There a problem?" It was his turn to be gravely polite.

"Yes." Johnny's eyes appeared as angry, dark slits. "You're the problem. Either you take your ass out of here on your own, or I will escort you out." His grip tightened on Constantine's shoulder. "You really don't want me escorting you out. Trust me on that."

Johnny obviously had confused Constantine with someone else. Someone who could be intimidated. Sure, Johnny might have about sixty pounds on him, but that weight wasn't muscle, and Constantine had never, ever backed away from a fight. He didn't typically start fights, but he always finished them. "I'm not done with my conversation." Again, he tried for politeness even as his patience waned.

"Oh, but you are done," the bartender told him, her voice still pleasant and warm and—oddly—sliding over his nerve endings in the best possible way. "Once you said you'd be stalking me after work, that was your ticket for the door."

He hadn't said those exact words. His head angled back toward her. After all, she was his assignment. "Princess..." Deliberately, he said the magic word.

Her long, thick lashes flickered. "Excuse me?" Not so pleasant and warm. Sharper. A little scared.

"I never said I was your stalker. I said I was your bodyguard. There's a big difference."

She swallowed. "Do enlighten me."

Fair enough. "A stalker would probably want to wear your skin."

"*Jesus.*" Johnny's hold turned punishing. "You are a freak. You're getting out of here, now." He jerked on Constantine's shoulder.

Since he didn't like being jerked around—not a favorite hobby at all—Constantine grabbed the guy's wrist and twisted. The movement would appear deceptively simple to any onlooker. He'd trained for it to look just that way. But in reality, there was nothing simple about the pain that would be sliding all the way from Johnny's thick wrist, up his arm and to—

"*Owww! Dammit, that hurts!*" Johnny hit his knees on the floor near Constantine.

His response was fair. The move was supposed to hurt. "You shouldn't put your hands on people." He let Johnny go.

The bouncer immediately surged toward him.

Constantine didn't even tense.

Johnny went nose to nose with him. Seriously, nose to nose. Invading personal space much? Someone needed to learn appropriate boundaries. "Back up or you'll be on your knees again." A polite warning seemed appropriate given the circumstances.

Johnny licked his lips, glanced over at the gorgeous bartender, and took a quick step back.

"Smart choice," Constantine applauded.

"Seriously?" Disgust coated the word as it came from the woman. "I thought you were the badass bouncer, Johnny!"

"Look, Jules," Johnny hurried to say, "I'm just taking a minute for us to all calm down. Just a calming beat, ya know?"

"Jules?" Constantine forgot the bouncer and focused completely on her. "You prefer that to Juliet?" He could see where she might. Jules was a lot less formal, but...she *was* formal. Pretty much as formal as one could get.

Because the woman standing behind the bar and glaring at him was an honest-to-God princess. An exiled one, but still actual royalty.

"How did you know my name is Juliet?" Fear flickered in her eyes. He hated the fear. His job was to make sure she wasn't afraid.

Trying to buy a little time because clearly, he had not handled the initial meet and greet well, Constantine tugged at the sleeve of his suit coat. Most of the other people in the bar were wearing jeans and sweatshirts. But he'd come in with his tailored suit and black tie. What could he say? He loved his suits.

But back to the matter at hand... "I'm your bodyguard." She just kept getting stuck on understanding that point. "That means I know everything about you." A deliberate pause and then... "Princess."

Her gaze jumped to Johnny, then back to Constantine.

Right. More of an introduction would be in order. He extended his right hand toward her, holding it above the bar. "Constantine Leos, at your service, and I can assure you, I come with incredible references. I work for Wilde, perhaps you've heard of the protection firm?" He kept his hand outstretched even though she'd made no move to touch him. "We tend to specialize in high-end cases just like—"

She grabbed his hand. A warm, soft touch. He rather liked her touch. A surge of electricity danced across his fingers right before she—

Squeezed. "Stop talking," Juliet ordered. Juliet Laurent, age twenty-five. A woman who worked her nights as a bartender and spent her days working to finish up her master's degree at LSU. She wanted to be a psychologist, and he could see where she'd enjoy working at the bar as she finished up her studies. After all, everyone knew customers willingly spilled their guts to bartenders all the time.

He'd made it a point of learning all he could about Juliet, and, honestly, what he'd learned had impressed the hell out of him. But now wasn't the time to talk about that background info. Now was the time to get moving. "I don't have much of a lead." He could feel Johnny watching them. He ignored Johnny and leaned closer to her. "Your secret is about to come out in a very big way."

She leaned toward him, too, sliding her upper body across the bar. "I have no secret."

"Liar." The word came out as an endearment.

Her mouth tightened. "I want you to walk out of this bar. I want you to walk out of my life. And I never want to see you again."

"Never?" he repeated. "What a loss that would be for you. I've been told that I can be quite charming." Under the right circumstances. These were probably not those circumstances.

"Never," she snapped. "You have the wrong woman."

"No, I don't."

"I haven't hired you. I don't need you. Leave." Her breath came faster.

The fear in her eyes had deepened. Hell. So much for an easy first meeting. She obviously was not in the mood to cooperate. Not that he could blame her. The woman's life was about to implode. Because time was of the extreme essence, he'd had to kiss tact goodbye and get straight to the point.

But if she didn't want him by her side...

Then he'd have to slide into the shadows. "They are coming." She needed to be prepared. "You don't have much time."

She snatched her hand away from him. "You have the wrong woman."

No, he didn't. But Constantine inclined his head toward her. "You're going to need me."

"I will not."

"We'll see." With one last look, he turned away. Constantine took a step forward, then stopped. He pointed at Johnny. "Better keep an extra close watch on things tonight. Something tells me the scene will get wild."

Johnny's thick brows climbed. "Wild how?"

"You'll see." Time to regroup. Whistling, Constantine walked through the crowd.

***

*No, no, no, no, no.* This could not be happening. Could. Not. Be. Juliet Laurent's heart drummed too fast and hard in her chest as she watched the tall, dark, and dangerously sexy stranger cut his way through the crowd.

He knew her secret. A secret she'd only learned herself in the last six months. The man had to be trouble.

"Why can't the crazy ones just stay in New Orleans?" Johnny grumbled. "Why do they have to haul their asses up here?"

She swallowed. Twice. Her throat had turned so dry that the movement hurt. "Crazy. Yeah, that's what he was." If only.

*Wilde.* That had been the name of the protection firm that the so-called bodyguard had dropped. Most people had heard about Wilde because the agents were in the news every other day. They protected celebrities. The mega-wealthy. And even...royalty.

*I am doomed.* She grabbed for the black apron that she'd tied around her waist earlier that night. It took her three tries to get the damn thing off because her hands shook so much. Every instinct she possessed screamed for Juliet to run. To burst out of that bar, to jump in her Jeep and to get as far and as fast away as possible.

But...

*Where would I go?* This was home. This was her life.

"Jules?" Johnny frowned at her.

Juliet realized she'd slapped the apron down on the bar top and her hand now gripped her keys. But she couldn't run off in the middle of a shift. That would be irresponsible. Sal, the owner, had always been good to her.

*And there isn't any place to go.*

The guy...Constantine...he'd vanished. He—he could have just been trying to scare her. To rattle her. Before her mother died, hadn't she warned Juliet that opportunists would pop up? That people who'd want to use and manipulate her might appear?

She didn't know Constantine. She sure as hell couldn't trust him. In fact, when it came to her deep, dark secret, Juliet trusted no one.

"I'm fine," she finally said. A total lie, but who cared? With fingers that still trembled, she tucked her keys back into the pocket of her black pants. And, once more, she put on her apron. "If you see that man again, you warn me, got it?"

An immediate nod from Johnny. "Can you believe that shit about wearing your skin?"

Juliet flinched. *Can you believe that shit about him calling me a princess?*

"Sorry," he mumbled. "Don't you worry. I won't let that jerk get anywhere near you. You're safe here."

Safe. Sure. She was safe. Safe in her comfortable, normal life with her comfortable, normal routine. Juliet went back to making drinks, and she tried to forget about the stranger who'd just burst into her life, claiming he was there to protect her.

The truth was, though, that she didn't think protection had been his real plan. She feared he'd been in the bar to wreck her world.

***

Closing time. A few stragglers remained, as they always did at the end of the night, but Juliet knew the manager would take care of them. Rides had already been called, and she'd cleaned up the bar and shut down the register. Her apron hung inside her locker, and she slung her bag over her shoulder before slamming the locker door shut.

Tips had been insane that night. One of the reasons she kept bartending when she could have found something else? *Money.* You just couldn't beat the schedule and the money she was pulling in. Soon, though, she'd be getting her master's and her plan was to hang up her own shingle with her counseling business.

*Soon.*

"Night, Jules!" Johnny called out as he ducked out of a small storage room and back toward the front of the bar.

She clutched her bag a little tighter and eased out the back door. Her trusty Jeep waited in the employee lot. Just about thirty feet and she'd be in that baby and safely on her way home. The door swung closed behind her with a distinct *clank*, and Juliet took a quick step forward.

*You never, ever tell a stranger when you're getting off work. I could be planning to stay around and wait out back for you. You come out on your own at 2 a.m., and then I could grab you.*

The stranger's words whispered through her head, and her pace picked up even more. She didn't see anyone else behind the building. Only employees were supposed to park in this lot, and it was quiet. Well-lit. No sign of the dangerously attractive guy...

A rustle.

A whisper.

A click?

Juliet stilled. Maybe five feet from her ride. That was the distance that separated her. Her hand drove into her bag and her fist came out holding the keys. She hit the button to unlock the Jeep, and the taillights flashed at her as she bounded for her vehicle.

"Juliet Laurent?" A woman's voice. Polished. Poised. And, oddly enough, coming from the direction of the dumpster.

Juliet spun around. Sure enough, a woman had just stepped from behind the shadows of the dumpster. She wore a loose blouse, a pencil skirt, and high heels. She also wasn't alone.

A man was with her. A man who had a camera hoisted on his shoulder.

"I'm Vicky Skye with Channel Four News." The woman rushed eagerly forward. "Are you Juliet Laurent?"

The cameraman followed her.

"*Princess* Juliet Laurent?" The reporter motioned to her cameraman and the light over his lens blasted into Juliet's face. "Tell me, why is the heir to a European kingdom working at Sal's in Baton Rouge?"

Juliet could feel all the blood rushing from her head. Her body swayed even as her stomach rolled sickeningly.

Before she could answer, the screech of tires shattered the night. Her head whipped to the right. A large, black van barreled to a stop, blocking the lane that took vehicles both in and out of the parking lot. *Blocking my escape.*

"Dammit, that's Channel Seven," Vicky groused. "Biting at my heels as usual."

The van's side door rolled open, and three people jumped out. Two had cameras.

Juliet stumbled back.

*Honk.* Loud, jarring.

Her keys slipped from her hand and fell to the ground. Another vehicle had just pulled up behind the van, but since the van was blocking the lane, that driver was trapped.

*Honk.* Long and angry. The driver blared his frustration right before he abandoned his vehicle. He came running for Juliet, too, but he wasn't holding a fancy camera to film her. He just used his phone.

Everyone was closing in on her. Shouting questions.

"Are you really royalty?"

"Why have you been hiding?"

"Do you intend to head back to Lancaden?"

*Lancaden.* A small dot on the map. Barely noticeable. Meaningless to most. Certainly not nearly as famous as Monaco, its neighbor. But the name utterly terrified her. Juliet's head moved in a frantic shake.

"So you're abandoning your people?" Vicky pounced. "Turning away and never looking back?"

All the lights were on her. They were filming. Watching. Questioning. Blowing her quiet life to hell and back. She dropped to her knees as she tried to find her keys.

The reporters closed in even tighter.

"Don't you care about your people at all?"

Where were the damn keys? Her hands clawed against the cement. "I'm American." Her voice came out sounding too hoarse. Too scared. "Born in a hospital right here in Baton Rouge." She'd never set foot in Lancaden, for good reason.

When the people there wanted to kill you, you knew to avoid the place. Hadn't her mother told her Lancaden was dangerous? One didn't rush straight into danger.

"Are you dating anyone?" This question came from the tall male with the camera. He leaned over her. Kept filming. "Who's the lucky partner for a princess?"

She threw up her hand because his camera was inches from her face. "Get back!" The keys had vanished, and she feared someone had snatched them up or kicked them away. After all, without the keys, how could she escape?

But it wasn't like she could drive out of the lot, anyway. Not with the van blocking the lane.

Juliet shot to her feet. She'd go back inside Sal's. Stay there until the reporters left. Except when she tried to get to the bar's back door, they stepped in her way. They surrounded her and kept filming and—impossibly—*more* people had appeared. More people filming with phones. The questions became a non-stop blast as they fired at her.

"Stop, please!" Juliet tried to dodge her way through the throng. "I need to get back inside!"

They closed in tighter. Terror clawed at her because the group was too thick. *How* had this happened? Where were all these people even coming from? Their bodies jostled into her. The filming continued. Phones were all around her as she spun in a frantic circle, trapped.

*"Poor lost princess..."* A low rasp.

Her breath caught. "Who said that?"

More questions blasted at her. A hand grabbed at her arm. Fingers bit into her skin. "Stop!" Juliet cried.

But they weren't stopping. She couldn't break free. The cameras were catching every terrible moment, and there was no escape. She couldn't even get back to the bar because they blocked her and pushed her, and she was terrified. Tears pooled in her eyes.

A growl pierced the night. A loud, rumbling growl that sounded like something that might just come from one very pissed-off dragon. She could even smell smoke drifting in the air.

No, not smoke. Exhaust. And that growl was coming closer. Getting even louder.

"What the hell?" Vicky jumped back and so did her crew. A few others followed suit because a motorcycle had just rolled right up to the scene.

The driver had a black helmet over his head, but she recognized the expensive suit that he wore.

*Constantine.*

He paused the motorcycle near the throng of people as he shoved up the visor on his helmet. "Need a ride, princess?" His hand extended toward her.

Juliet didn't hesitate. She flew toward him and grabbed his hand like the lifeline it was. "I've never been so happy to see someone in my entire life!"

His mouth kicked into a half-grin. "Remember that."

She jumped on the motorcycle behind him. Let go of his hand, but gripped his waist.

He took off his helmet and put it on her head. "Hold tight."

She already *was* holding tight.

But when he spun the motorcycle around, she grabbed on to him even tighter. Juliet could have sworn that she heard the rumble of his laughter, but the growl of the motorcycle's engine swallowed up the sound in the next instant. The motorcycle surged around the parked van—with its still open driver's door—and around the vehicles lined up behind the van. As soon as he hit the street, Constantine drove fast and hard, and when she looked back, she saw that reporters were chasing them.

And still filming.

So much for her quiet, normal life. She kissed it goodbye even as she held tight to...her bodyguard? "Thank you," she breathed against him, not sure if he'd even hear her words.

But he *had* heard her because Constantine said, "No problem. Protecting and saving is part of the package deal."

# CHAPTER TWO

*Step Two: Expect the unexpected...in other words, always be ready for anything. After all, isn't that why you get paid the big bucks?*

Her hold was tight, and her body pressed intimately against his. They'd been driving for about fifteen minutes, and Constantine was sure he'd lost the tails that had been on them. Yes, two rather clever bastards had been waiting in vehicles across the street from Sal's bar. They'd zoomed onto the road as soon as they saw Constantine and his passenger.

"Lost them," he said, not without a hint of pride. He rather enjoyed ditching unwanted company. He and Juliet were in the lot of an old grocery store, no other vehicles were nearby, and he shoved down the kickstand because they needed to take a minute and talk. He turned his upper body toward her. "You can let go now, princess."

"Please stop calling me that." Weary. She released him and pulled off the helmet.

It was too dark for him to be able to see her expression clearly. The darkness helped them to hide from anyone who might be looking for them. But he would have liked to have seen her. *Because I just like looking at her.* An uncomfortable truth he'd revisit at a later time. Back to her question... "Why stop calling you that?" Constantine was genuinely curious. "It's what you are."

"I'm not a damn princess."

"Um, I think there is a whole load of bureaucrats with paperwork from Lancaden who would disagree with you on that one."

"I'm Juliet Laurent. I'm a graduate student and a bartender."

"Sure, but you're also a princess."

"Would you *stop?*"

Probably not. "If you weren't a princess, I wouldn't be here right now. You wouldn't be here. The throng of reporters wouldn't be searching the city for you even as we speak." All valid points, at least in his opinion.

"My name is Juliet. Just call me that, please?"

*Please.* That one word hit him oddly hard. "Sure." Too gruff. "You're Juliet, and I'm Constantine." Con to his friends, but he didn't mention that part. Those friends tended to be on the rather shady side, and they'd no doubt scare the princess to pieces.

"How did you know those reporters would be at Sal's?"

He waited a beat as he tried to figure out the best response. Finally, Constantine decided to go with, "Like I said in the bar, your secret is out. It was only a matter of time before the press closed in."

She sucked in a sharp breath. "But how did they know? How did *you* know? I haven't told a soul." A humorless laugh escaped her. "I didn't even know until my mom was on her deathbed. At first, I thought she was joking. She was so pale and weak in that hospital bed, holding my hand and telling me that I could've had this whole other life and I—I didn't understand why she'd be joking when I was crying, when she was dying, and everything was falling apart." Her lips pressed together.

He shifted his body toward her more. Constantine had the strongest urge to wrap his arms around her. Comfort was not exactly his strong suit, but with her, he wanted to try. A fucking odd reaction.

"I overshared, didn't I?" A sniff. She swiped at her left eye, as if wiping away tears. "I don't normally do that."

"Not exactly a normal night." His hand lifted and brushed over her right cheek. A tear drop had fallen there, too. "My employer was contacted by the counsellor of Lancaden." The guy who was ruling temporarily since the king had taken a turn for the worse with his illness. "There was a bit of, uh, recent drama, that led Wilde back to you."

"I don't understand."

He needed to tread carefully. Juliet might not know all about her family's dark past. And he hated to just spring it on her, so, for the moment, he went with an abbreviated version of events. "Not too long ago, the agents at Wilde recovered a ring that led us in your direction. When the counsellor came calling, we knew where to look for you, because of that ring."

"Wait, back up." She straightened her shoulders even as she kept sitting on the bike with him. "You knew where I was *before* this counsellor guy reached out to you?"

A nod. They had.

"And you...you weren't going to say anything. You weren't going to approach me."

Wilde hadn't been hired to protect her then so... "We weren't going to interfere with your life. You were discovered during the course of a different investigation entirely." One that had involved someone very close to Constantine. Again, not anything she needed to know. "But then the king's health took a sudden, hard turn, and you became very, very in demand. Our client came calling with an offer that we didn't refuse."

She stared at him.

"You know you're the next in line to rule." No way she didn't realize that part. "If the king dies, you get the crown." Shouldn't that thrill her? Not the king's death because yeah—morbid. Not exactly joyful. But getting a crown? Getting a fairytale life handed straight to you on a shiny platter? Wasn't that a dream?

"I..." Her voice dropped to a whisper. "My mom had nothing to do with that world. My grandmother fled the country. *I* was born here. There's no way I'm next. I *can't* be next." She seemed horrified. Not thrilled.

But her joy or her horror wouldn't change things. "Oh, but I'm afraid you are next." He was staring at the woman who was supposed to be a queen. And she was shaking in the cold. Dammit. He hopped off the bike.

"What are you doing?"

He took off his suit coat. Not much protection, but better than nothing. He held it out for her. "Slide your arms in the sleeves."

"But..."

"Just do it, prin—uh, Juliet."

"But then you'll be cold."

So what? He'd been cold plenty. "My job is to protect you, not have you worrying about me feeling a chill. Arms, Juliet. Into the sleeves. Now."

She didn't extend her arms. "Has anyone ever told you that you can be very bossy?"

"Sure. Lots of people have mentioned that trait." He gave up waiting for her and slid her left arm into the sleeve. Before he could reach for her right, she grudgingly extended it. In moments, he had her covered in his coat. It swallowed her, but at least it would be better protection from the cold. "That will hold you until we get to the hotel."

"Excuse me?"

"The hotel." Constantine shot a quick glance around the parking lot. Still no sign of other cars, but it was time to get rolling again. "Not like we can go back to your place." He slid back in front of her.

"Why not?"

"Lock your arms around me."

She didn't lock her arms around him, but her fingers pressed against his waist. A tentative touch that felt butterfly light. "Why can't I go home?" Juliet pushed. "It's been a rough night, and I would just like to collapse in my own bed."

"No worries, you can collapse in my bed." The mental images that statement stirred...not of her collapsing and falling asleep, but of gorgeous Juliet *being* in his bed, with him.

*Nope. Shut it down. She's the client. Hands the fuck off.*

He started the motorcycle, revved the engine, and tightened his hold on the handlebars. "What I meant, of course, was that you can collapse in the hotel bed."

"You haven't told me why I can't go home."

"You can." If she insisted on it, he wouldn't stop her. Not like he could kidnap a princess. That would be a serious international incident, even if she was claiming to be American and not the heir to the Lancaden crown. "But be warned that the reporters will have figured out where you live. If they knew where you worked, then doesn't it stand to reason they have your home address, too?"

"Dammit."

"Um, yes. Dammit. So you can go back to your home, where they are probably waiting already, or you can come with me, get some rest, and then we'll plan our next move when the sun is up." Though, technically, he already knew what the next move was supposed to be.

He was supposed to get her sweet ass on a private plane and deliver her to the counsellor of Lancaden who would meet them at the Wilde office in Atlanta. After that meeting, Juliet would be off to Lancaden. That was his job—protect her until he delivered her to the counsellor. Then Juliet flew to her castle. An actual fucking castle. Wasn't that a kick in the nuts?

"Just for tonight?" Hesitant. "I can go home tomorrow?"

Should he shatter all her illusions right then and there? Because Juliet had to realize that her life would never be the same. He turned his head to look over his shoulder, fully prepared to dish out some harsh reality.

And he caught her swiping at her cheek again. Hell. "Let's just focus on tonight," he muttered. "You tell me where you want to go, and I'll take you there."

A quick nod. "Tonight only. Yes." An inhale. "A hotel would be better, I think. I just don't want to deal with the reporters. They were crowding in and shoving, and I felt like I couldn't breathe."

His gut clenched. "Some bastard shoved you?"

"I couldn't get away. They were closing in and then—" A long exhale this time. "Then you were there. Thank you for saving me."

"I should have been there the whole time. Don't thank me for screwing up the first day on the job." No way should he have walked out of that bar without her. "No one is gonna shove you again, got it? I will be between you and everyone else. You won't get hurt. You will be protected. I guarantee it."

Now it was time to do his job and get her out of the open. "Put the helmet back on." Because she hadn't.

Her hands fluttered and she got the helmet on.

"Arms around me." An order. He didn't want some light touch. He wanted her holding on tightly.

He faced forward and felt her arms slide around him. "Good." The motorcycle growled as they got the hell away from that parking lot.

\*\*\*

When Constantine had said they were staying at a hotel, she'd expected your typical double room. Maybe four hundred square feet of nice and clean space. He'd sleep in one bed, she'd crash in the other—*after* she called the Wilde firm and verified Constantine's identity.

But he didn't take her to just any hotel. He took her to the fanciest place in the city. Constantine didn't pause at the check-in desk, but instead he went straight to the elevator, pulled out his keycard, and slid it over the security pad so that he could access...

"The top floor?" Her shoulders hit the back wall of the elevator. "That's where the suites are." The really, really big suites. She knew this hotel. She'd worked at the bar once upon a time.

"Yep. That's where they are."

Mirrored walls surrounded them. The elevator seemed oddly small, tight, but that was probably because Constantine took up so much room.

Classical music played from the elevator's speaker. "A suite on that floor has to be really expensive."

"Um."

She wet her lips. "I would imagine that it's expensive to pay for a Wilde bodyguard, too."

His head angled toward her. Originally, she'd thought his eyes were a light blue, but now she saw they were more gray. He winked in response to her statement. "Well, we don't exactly come cheap."

No, she hadn't thought he did. "I can't pay—"

The elevator dinged. The doors slid open.

"You're not paying. The king is, by way of the counsellor. Don't worry, we'll go over all the details in the morning."

She was worrying. A lot. Because the words he'd just said had raised a million red flags for Juliet. Her back remained pressed to the rear wall of the elevator. She still wore his coat, and it warmed her. His crisp, masculine scent clung lightly to the fabric. "I think, before we do anything else, it would be a good idea to verify your identity."

The doors started to close. Constantine threw up a hand and the motion sensor immediately opened the doors fully again. "Before we go inside the hotel room together, you mean?" His broad shoulders rolled in a shrug. "Sure, let's do that. Though, you want to step into the hallway to make your call or do you feel like hanging out in here longer?"

Tight spaces always made her tense a little, so she shoved away and took some quick steps forward. Once in the hallway, she pulled her phone from her purse.

"It's after hours." He'd followed her into the hallway. The elevator doors closed behind him.

"You'll get the operator, so why don't you just cut through the BS and speak directly to the man in charge?" With a shrug, he reached into his pocket and pulled out his phone. His fingers tapped on the screen, and he turned the phone toward her. "Just ask Eric Wilde all of your questions."

Eric Wilde's image filled the screen. She recognized him from the photos she'd seen on the news. As she stared at the screen, Juliet saw the call was connecting and—

"*Constantine.*" A man's warm, deep voice. "Did you make contact with the target?"

Her stomach twisted. Is that what she was? A target?

"She's standing right in front of me, boss," Constantine responded, tone almost cheery. "And I don't think she liked being called a target, FYI."

Nope, she had not, and her expression must have given her away.

She heard what could have been a throat clearing. "My apologies. Ms. Laurent? This is Eric Wilde, and you are in safe hands."

Her gaze darted to Constantine's hand as he gripped the phone. A strong hand. With long, tan fingers.

"He will protect you and make sure you get transported—"

"Yeah, she's wanting to verify my identity," Constantine cut through to say.

Juliet blinked. Wait. Had Eric just said *transported?*

"I've transported her to a secure location," Constantine added smoothly. "No worries on that score. The press found Juliet at her job, and I've got her at the hotel tonight so I can better monitor security. Before she goes into the suite with me, she wants to know I'm someone she can trust."

Her gaze lifted to find him staring straight at her. His eyes were so deep. Intense. Seeming to see through her. "I just need to know that he's one of the good guys," she managed to say.

Constantine's expression hardened. "Good guys don't get shit done."

"Ahem. Uh, Constantine?" Eric's voice sharpened.

Constantine ignored him. "The boss isn't going to tell you I'm good."

Her hands curled at her sides. "Why not?"

"Ms. Laurent," now Eric was back to sounding smooth, "I can assure you that—"

Hadn't he already assured her of something else a few moments ago? She shook her head, brushing his words aside as she kept her focus on Constantine. "You're not good? If you're not good, then what are you?"

"He's great," Eric praised. "Great at his job. Be certain that he can protect you in a way that no other—"

"In a way that no good guy can," Constantine stated flatly. "Good guys hesitate. They don't like to get their hands dirty." He stepped closer to her. "That's why you need someone like me. I'm not scared of the dirt or the blood or any damn thing else. I will do whatever it takes to make sure you're safe. You are the only priority for me."

Her heart seemed close to bursting out of her chest. "So, what are you telling me?" A nervous laugh bubbled from her. She hated nervous laughter, but it always emerged from her. The sound seemed to linger in the air. "That you're some sort of—of bad-guy bodyguard? Is that even a thing?" It couldn't be a thing.

"I don't know." His head tilted as he studied her. "Are you telling me that you're some sort of long-lost princess who has been hiding out in Baton Rouge her whole life? Is that a thing?"

Her eyes narrowed. "Are you being funny?"

"No!" From Eric. Loud. "Am I on speaker? *Constantine,* get me off speaker. Give the phone to Ms. Laurent, and stop, ah, stop your *particular* brand of reassurance for the moment."

At first, Constantine didn't move. He was so close that if he just tilted forward a few inches...

*He could kiss me.*

Wow. Where in the world had that thought come from? She did not want to kiss this—this stranger. She was not that hard up.

Wait...

*How long has it been since I had a date?*

Maybe she *was* that hard up. Or maybe Constantine was just unnaturally sexy. Either way...

He smiled at her. He didn't have dimples. He had sort of like dents in his cheeks. Sexy dips that didn't go too deep. His smile was wide and warm, and it looked so oddly charming even though he *still* somehow managed to look darkly dangerous even as he grinned in that appealing way.

"Here." He put the phone to her ear. His fingers brushed over her cheek. "I turned it off speaker for you. You and Eric can talk privately."

Her hand reached up to take the phone, but she wound up just wrapping her fingers around his. A surge of awareness skittered down her spine.

And he saw it. Understood it. Because they were standing *so* close in that hallway, with the lights on overhead, he could see everything clearly, as could she. His pupils flared a bit, and he gave a slight nod.

"Ms. Laurent?" Eric's voice. "Ms. Laurent?"

"Yes. I'm here." Here and still basically holding Constantine's hand. She needed to stop that. Juliet took a step back.

Constantine's hand slid from beneath hers.

She could breathe better. Maybe. "Look..." Time to focus. "He called you. I have no idea if I'm even speaking to the real Eric Wilde or not. This call isn't exactly the reassurance that I need." Maybe they should do a video call? Wouldn't that be better?

"I will have the lead detective from the Baton Rouge PD at your hotel room within fifteen minutes."

"Come again?" But, no, she couldn't have misheard. The connection was crystal clear.

"She will come inside and verify that Constantine works for me. I'm sure you've seen Raven Douglas's photo before, so you will know who she is. She can back up everything Constantine has told you." A short pause. "When we realized we needed to make contact, I reached out to Raven as a precaution. I wanted her in the loop."

So now there was a loop? Wonderful. But having a cop come in and reassure her—face to face—about Constantine was way better than a video call. Especially someone local that Juliet had seen working and knew was well respected. *Well respected, if a bit scary.* Because Raven had a reputation in Baton Rouge.

"Constantine is former FBI," Eric revealed.

Her shoulders stiffened. Her gaze had fallen to the floor, but at that new revelation, her stare flew right back to Constantine's face. "He is?" Then why the ramble from him about not being a good guy?

"I'm very lucky to have him as part of my team, and while some of his methods may be unorthodox, you can count on him. I think he'd walk through fire to protect a client."

She wet her dry lips. "I certainly hope that's not necessary."

A faint laugh. "It shouldn't be." Clearly, Eric meant to sound reassuring and friendly. "Just know that Constantine has my full backing, and Raven will be there soon. You can trust both of them."

"I can't pay for his services." How long was she supposed to need a bodyguard? A day? A week? *Forever?* No, no, definitely not forever. A bodyguard would get in the way while she was attending classes or working at the bar or—

"And you probably haven't turned on a TV in the last little while." He still sounded reassuring, but his words had her tensing. "But you need to know that your cover is blown."

It hadn't exactly been a cover. More like, it had been her real life.

"And you're lighting up social media," Eric added.

Her lashes fluttered. "Thank you for telling me."

"Stay at the hotel for the remainder of the night. Get some rest before you meet the plane tomorrow."

"A plane?" That was crazy. "But I'm not going anywhere."

Constantine reached for the phone. "We should get into the suite. Granted, I've made certain no one else is on this floor..."

He'd cleared out the entire *floor* for them? All before she'd even agreed to stay with him? The knot in her stomach seemed to double in size.

"But I'd feel better if we were secure inside while we wait on Raven."

She let go of the phone.

Constantine brought it to his ear. "We'll talk soon, boss," he promised.

She thought that Eric said something in response, but she couldn't quite make out his words.

Constantine shoved the phone into his pocket. Then he pointed to the end of the hallway. "The presidential suite awaits."

***

She hadn't come home. He stood in her bedroom, the knife gripped in his hand. He'd been waiting on her. He knew her routine, had it down *perfectly.* By two-forty-five at the latest, Juliet should have returned to the small house that she rented on Second Street. She should have typed in her security code—0814, for her mother's August birthday—and crept into the dark house.

She would have gone to the kitchen first. Gotten a glass of water. Then strolled to the bedroom.

*Where I would be waiting.*

He knew her routine. He knew her. After all, he'd been watching and planning. Looking for the perfect time to make his move.

But he was in her bedroom, the knife gripped in his hand, and *she* wasn't there.

He drove the knife into her pillow. Hit it again and again as he sliced deep and feathers drifted into the air. He lifted the knife once more and drove it into the mattress. The mattress where Juliet *should* have been, but the bitch hadn't come home. She'd left him waiting, after all his careful planning, and she was not—

*Voices.*

A rumble that teased his ears at first, but then grew louder and louder. Leaving his knife embedded in the mattress, he whirled for the bedroom door.

What in the hell? He bounded down the hallway, moving unerringly in the dark because he knew every inch of her house. Knew where every single piece of furniture was placed. He didn't so much as bump into an end table as he made his way to the window and eased back the curtains to see the crowd of people outside. The cars. The lights.

The cameras.

A bitter smile curved his lips. Now he knew why Juliet hadn't come home to him. It would seem he wasn't the only one who knew her secret any longer.

The truth was out. Now they would all be hunting her.

# CHAPTER THREE

*Step Three: Put proper boundaries in place. No emotional connections can exist. She's only a job. Nothing more. When the job is done, you will forget her, and she will forget you. Case closed.*

"Did we really need such a huge suite?" Juliet stood near the L-shaped couch, still wearing Constantine's coat, and she managed to appear both incredibly delicate and hauntingly lovely.

It was the lovely part that was gonna be the problem. He took a step back from her. *What is my deal?* He worked with beautiful women all the time. He'd dated a fantastic assortment of women over the years, and he'd enjoyed them all. Control wasn't a typical issue for him. But something about Juliet had him feeling way too off center.

His gaze cut to the tall windows behind her. During the day, the view of the mighty Mississippi would be something to behold, but right then, all Constantine saw was darkness. "This suite has the best security," he said because he had to make some sort of reply to her question. Could he have gone smaller? Yes, he could have. So small that they could have shared a bed.

*Nope. Shut down that mental image.* "You have your own room." He pointed to the right.

"You'll find a king-size bed in there. Supposed to be the softest mattress money can buy. You can drift off and have sweet dreams all night long." Or, for the few hours of night that remained.

"I'm more worried I'll have nightmares instead of sweet dreams." She bit her lower lip. "Where will you be sleeping?"

He looked meaningfully at the couch behind her.

"There's not another bed you can use?"

"There is." A whole other bedroom. "But I want to be between you and the door. If someone does manage to get past the hotel security and up to this floor, to this suite, then the bastard will have to deal with me before he can so much as look at you."

She rocked forward onto the balls of her feet. "You really think a reporter would be that desperate for a story? Desperate enough to break into this suite and fight past you just to snap some pics of me?"

Juliet didn't understand the situation. Slowly, he closed the distance between them. "I'm not just talking about some member of the press." He pulled his phone out of his pocket and opened one of the social media apps. A few scrolls and...Constantine turned the phone toward her. "As of now, you're a celebrity. A real-life princess. That title can come with plenty of perks, but trouble will also follow you."

Her eyes widened as she stared at the screen. "I'm on my hands and knees on the ground in that pic." A shudder. "They surrounded me. I was just trying to find my keys and I—" She looked at him, not the phone. "I couldn't find them. They must have accidentally gotten kicked away by someone, and if you hadn't appeared, I don't know how I was going to get out of there."

His jaw locked. "You won't be in that situation again," he vowed. "And I'll find your keys. We'll go back for them when it's light outside."

"Before we meet the plane?" Her head tilted to the right.

Ah, so she had caught that part. Probably because it had been hard to miss since Eric had just blurted out that line.

"What plane are we meeting?" Juliet pushed.

Time for a bit of truth. "We need to fly to Atlanta so you can meet with Eric. A representative from Lancaden will also be there to speak with you."

"And then?"

"Then the representative will want to fly you home."

"I am home." A hard, negative shake of her head. "I don't mean this hotel suite. Clearly, I don't. I mean Baton Rouge. This *is* my home. Not some place across the Atlantic Ocean with people I've never met."

"Maybe it's time you meet them."

"Or maybe it's time I don't." Two fingers lifted to rub against her temple. "My mother was terrified of that place. She told me she'd kept the truth from me for so long because she never wanted me going there. She said it was too dangerous, but I had to know who I really was before she passed. I had to know so I could protect myself."

"Protect yourself?" Hello, red flags. They were flying high. "From what?"

"I don't know." Frustration seethed in Juliet's words. "She just didn't want me to go there. Told me she'd stayed safe all these years and that I should stay away, too. She said people in Lancaden would want to kill me." Her hand fell. "Then she died so it wasn't like I could ask her other questions. And you probably already have some full, shiny dossier on me so it's not like you don't realize this but...I never knew my father. When I asked about him as a kid, I was just told he was dead. A tragic boating accident."

His gaze cut away from her. One line in particular that she'd said kept replaying through his head. *She said people in Lancaden would want to kill me.*

Not gonna happen. *Not on my watch.*

"Constantine?"

He pushed down the rage that had filled him at the thought of someone trying to kill Juliet.

"Do you have some kind of fancy dossier on me? Did you dig into my life?"

Technically, a whole crew of agents had done the background work on her. "I did review a dossier on you. The material inside confirmed that your father is deceased. The file also confirmed that you are the closest relative that the king of Lancaden has and that's why the crown is supposed to go to you when he dies." Constantine's stare tracked back to her. "The counsellor doesn't want you hurt. If he did, he wouldn't have hired Wilde to protect you."

"I suppose you're right about that." Her shoulders sagged. "Do I even want to know how much your daily rate is?"

"Probably not."

She winced. "That high? Wonderful." A long sigh. "At least tell me this, am I the first princess you've protected?"

"Yes."

"Who do you usually protect?"

"Rich pricks. Spoiled celebs." He shrugged. "Rather thought you'd be along the same vein."

Her gaze sharpened. "Say again?"

He was sure she'd heard him. "But you're not," he added as his gaze slid down to take her in. To study her. "You are not what I expected when I first saw your picture."

She reached out and touched his hand.

A surge of awareness pierced through him. *Yep, there we go. That problem again.*

"What did you think when you first saw my picture?"

"You were pretty." No, pretty was way too tame a word. His buddy Remy was the artist, he would have come up with all kinds of flowery descriptions for Juliet. But Constantine had just stared at her picture and thought...

*Unforgettable.*

But, no, that wasn't entirely true. He was lying to himself. Because when he'd first seen her, the *very* first thought that had flown through Constantine's mind had been...

*I want her.*

His phone vibrated. He still gripped the damn thing, so he flipped it over and read the text.

"Hotel security is escorting Raven up. She can answer all your questions."

Talk about a fast trip.

After firing off a response, he shoved the phone into his pocket.

"Here." She shrugged out of his coat and handed it back to him. "Thank you for the loan. And for saving me earlier tonight. You were a real hero when I needed one."

He took the coat. His fingers slid over hers. "Don't make that mistake."

Her brows lifted. "What mistake would that be?"

"Thinking I'm a hero."

"Oh. Right." What could have been hurt flashed across her face. "I'm just a job. You rushed in on the motorcycle because you are being paid to keep me out of trouble."

"I'm being *paid* to keep trouble away from you," he corrected her gently. "But that's not the mistake I was talking about. I'm not hero material. Heroes, good guys—I told you already, they just can't get shit done."

She smiled at him.

*Fuck me.*

Then she winked. In spite of everything that had happened that night, the woman winked at him.

*I am done.*

"I think you're protesting too much, Constantine. You're my hero. Deal with it."

A rap sounded at the door.

Her nose scrunched. "Time to meet the head cop in charge. I should tell you, she makes me nervous. I've seen Raven Douglas in news reports, and she's fierce."

"You're a princess." No one should intimidate her.

"I'm a bartender with a ton of college loans."

He dropped his coat. Took her hand and tugged her toward the door. "No one should make you nervous. You should make other people nervous." Princess or not, she didn't need to worry about being intimidated by anyone. He checked the peephole and saw Raven glaring back at him. One of the hotel security guards stood a few feet behind her.

Constantine swung open the door.

"I was in bed," Raven announced in an aggravated tone. "Because it's the middle of the night. Sane people sleep at this hour. People who have to be up at six a.m. so they can go hunt down murderers sleep at this hour." She put her hands on her hips and craned her head so she could see Juliet. "Am I supposed to curtsy to you or some shit? Bow?"

"No, uh—" Juliet began.

"Because I don't do that crap. If you're expecting it, prepare for disappointment." Raven pointed at Constantine. "He's Constantine Leos, an agent with Wilde. Apparently, he's also former FBI, and he has lots of weird ties to *both* the Feds and the CIA."

Constantine raised a brow. "How do you know that?" That particular info wouldn't have been included in the Wilde intel.

"Because I know how to dig. And when I get a call from some bigwig, out-of-state guys telling me to play nicely..." She gave him a wide smile. One that wasn't particularly *nice*. "I get curious. Curiosity is a terrible weakness that I have. Just terrible." Once more, she turned her attention to Juliet. "He's who he claims to be. Any other questions? Or can I go back to my beauty sleep now?"

Raven was, indeed, the no-BS detective he'd been told to expect. He darted a glance at Juliet. A faint red stained her cheeks.

"Thank you for coming by," Juliet said, voice soft. "I'm sorry that you were taken out of bed, and I very much appreciate you giving me the reassurance that I can trust Constantine."

He looked back at Raven just in time to see the flash of surprise cross her face. "I know," he said, sighing. "It's going to be a problem. I'm hoping she can adapt quickly."

Raven's brows climbed. "They will eat her alive if she doesn't." She shook her head and pointed at Juliet once more. "Being fucking sunshine and rainbows won't do anything but get you stomped on in this world. You already came close to getting stomped once tonight, didn't you? Because, yes, I saw the video. They had you on the ground." And, surprise of surprises, sympathy flashed in her eyes. "You didn't deserve that. That particular pack of reporters can be real bitches. Don't be afraid to kick their asses."

"Sorry." Juliet inched closer. "Did a *cop* just tell me to kick someone's ass?"

"Figuratively, of course." A smooth reply. "What I meant was...let them know who is in charge. If you don't, it will be your funeral." A curt nod. "Night." With that, she turned and marched back down the hallway.

The rather bemused security guard followed in her wake.

Constantine shut and locked the door.

"She is exactly what I expected." A rush of words from Juliet. "Actually, she might have scared me even more in real life." A pause. "I'm not sunshine and rainbows. I just try to be polite, and I don't think that's such a bad thing. My mom and grandmother raised me to be polite to everyone. Said it was necessary—"

"Princess training. Right. I get it."

"No, it wasn't princess training. Being polite isn't reserved for random people with ties to royalty."

She was hardly random. "You'll have to deal with a ton of asshats. Being polite is probably like wearing armor in that world." He considered the matter. "You want to tell someone to fuck off, but I bet your mom and grandmother trained you so that when you *really* want to tell people to fuck themselves, you probably say something super sweet like... 'I hope you have the most magnificent day.'" He'd been teasing, hoping to ease some of the stress from her expression but...

Her eyes widened.

*Fuck me.* "Are you serious? When you get super mad, your mom trained you to say—"

"Not my mom. My grandmother. She was the one who, ah, suggested that I just substitute some words in my head. She thought it would make me feel better, help me get frustration out in a difficult situation. And I don't say for people to have magnificent days. That's not me at all."

*Do not change expressions. Do not.* "What do you say? Like, if you're talking to a real prick who is getting on your last nerve, what will you tell the guy?"

"If he's a real prick..." Juliet cleared her throat. "Then I say something like, 'It's been a rare pleasure to meet you.' The words start with the same letters, but, of course, they're very different. Just a silly little game my grandmother taught me when I was a teenager." A wan smile curved her lips. "Like our secret code. I got into the habit of using it, and I still do to this day."

*Real prick. Rare pleasure.* He wanted to burst into laughter, but pressed his lips together instead.

"Actually..." Her stare darted to the closed door. "My grandmother reminded me a whole lot of Raven Douglas. You didn't mess with her. At all."

No, you didn't. Because while Juliet didn't know it, he had quite a bit of information on her dearly departed grandmother. Like the fact that the woman had once hired an assassin to try and take out the king of Lancaden.

Hardly the heart-warming story to share at the moment, however. That ill-fated assassination attempt had wound up causing Juliet's grandmother to be exiled. She'd fled far and fast and had been hunted by a whole lot of people who wanted her dead over the years.

Lucky for her, she'd been hard to kill.

"I should go to bed." Juliet took a few steps toward the bedroom door, then stopped. "You're going to be on the couch? You're sure that's okay with you?"

He'd slept on far worse. Constantine strode for the couch and went ahead and made himself comfortable. "I'll be just feet away from you," he assured her. "So if anything happens, if you need me, I will come running."

"Thank you."

"It's what I'm here for."

"Right. Your job." She shuffled into the bedroom. The door quietly closed behind her.

*It's what I'm here for.*

Protecting her was supposed to be the job. Fantasizing about her, wondering how she'd taste and feel against him—not on the agenda. Not.

He tilted his head back against the cushions. His eyes squeezed shut. An image of Juliet immediately filled his head. Hell. He was such a fucking idiot.

\*\*\*

"I'm not getting on a plane to Atlanta."

Constantine paused in the act of buttering his toast. He crooked one brow at her. "Want to tell me why not?"

She could think of a hundred reasons, but she'd start with... "I'm not getting on a plane when I have no clothes. Last night, I was flustered." A nice word. It sounded way better than *utterly terrified*. Though that was what she'd been. "I wanted a safe place to fall."

"You can fall with me anytime."

Those words seemed to pierce right through her. Her breath caught.

He went back to buttering his toast. As if his seductive rumble hadn't just shifted her whole world. "If clothes are the issue," Constantine said, "we can make a pitstop by your place. Or we can go pick up new things."

"No." No buying new stuff that someone she didn't know had paid to purchase. "My place. I definitely need to go there and change."

His strong, white teeth bit into the toast. After swallowing, he told her, "Reporters will be waiting, but if this is your decision, then I'll handle them." His gaze seemed to see past her. "We'll pick up clothes, pack your bag, and then head to the airport. The private plane had a delay, Eric already texted me about it. We won't be able to fly out until noon so we should have plenty of time to get everything done by then."

She wanted to eat, but the lead in her stomach made the task hard. "I have a job. I'm supposed to work at Sal's tonight. Not like I can just rush out and abandon my responsibilities." Reason two why she couldn't get on the plane.

He chewed some of the toast. Chewing toast was not supposed to be a sexy act, not at all. Eating was normal. Everyone did it. But his gaze was so deep and sharp, and she couldn't quite look away from him and this was weird, and she probably hadn't gotten enough sleep and—

He took a sip of his orange juice.

*Get a grip, woman. So an attractive man is having breakfast. That is not a reason for you to lose your mind.*

"You get that your job at Sal's is over, don't you? If you're working the bar, the place will get slammed with reporters and curiosity seekers."

Her fingers trembled a little as she reached for her own orange juice. "Sounds like that might give the bar a boost in customers."

"Um. Sounds like it would be a living hell for you."

He wasn't wrong. She let go of her orange juice glass, not having taken even a sip.

"Why don't you call your boss? Ask for a few days off?" His voice seemed so mild. "We'll go to Atlanta, you can at least talk to the rep from Lancaden, and if you don't like what he has to say, then you can tell him to fuck off. Or, you know, switch words on him and tell the guy to go have a 'fabulous outing' or something."

"I..." Her breath stuttered. "You wouldn't have a problem with that?"

Constantine shrugged.

"But the Lancaden counsellor is the one paying you."

"Yeah, but it's your life." He held her gaze. Waited.

Her mind scrambled. *Go to Atlanta?* Actually see the people—one of the people, anyway—that her mother had always warned her about?

Or...the other option...

Stay in town. With the reporters. With a job that—dammit, Constantine was right—her job was probably long over. She couldn't just head back into the bar because reporters would swarm her. As far as her classes were concerned, she had a bit of luck there. She'd finished up her last in-person class recently, and she only had a seminar to do online, but that seminar was scheduled for several weeks away. Everything else could be completed online.

"What do you have to lose just by hearing the man out?" Constantine asked her. "I promise, I will fly you right back here if that's what you want."

Her lips thinned, and she nodded.

"Good choice." He pushed the plate of eggs toward her. "You might want to protein up. When we're done with breakfast, I'll sneak you past the reporters." His gaze drifted over her. "Gonna need a bit of a disguise for that to work, but don't worry, I have a plan."

She was starting to think that he always did.

\*\*\*

Her disguise had turned out to be an oversized sweatshirt and jogging pants, a baseball cap that hid her hair and hung low over her forehead, and sunglasses. Hardly deep spy getup, but as they walked through the lobby, no one even glanced twice at her, so Juliet figured the attire must be working.

She'd twisted her hair into a quick knot and slapped the cap on top of it. The clothes were huge on her, but she knew that was the point. Though she did think the outfit would blow around like crazy on her once they got on the motorcycle.

But when they exited the hotel, a motorcycle wasn't waiting for them. A valet attendant stood near a small, black car. A Benz. Constantine's hand was a steady reassurance at the base of her back as he guided her toward the vehicle. She didn't ask him any questions, not with the valet guy watching, so she slid inside, kept her head averted, and when the door closed on her side of the car, her breath expelled in a relieved rush.

Constantine climbed into the driver's seat. She caught the careful handoff of a cash tip between him and the valet, and then they were on the road.

"What happened to the motorcycle?" Juliet finally asked after too many miles in silence.

"My partner is taking it." He cut a glance toward the rearview mirror. "He's tailing us with it right now."

Immediately, she whipped around. The bill of her baseball cap bumped into the seat. "You have a partner? Since when?" She hadn't seen any sign of a partner. She still didn't. There wasn't a motorcycle tailing them. "I don't see him."

"That's because he's good. If you did see him, then we'd have a problem." Casual. Easy. "As to the 'since when' question...typically, Wilde agents are always assigned partners. I'm lead agent with you, so I'm the one you get up close and personal with, while Holden is the backup. He watches both of our asses from a distance. If something happens to me, he'll step in to make sure you're protected."

"Why would something happen to you?"

"It won't. Just if it did."

"It won't," she said, definite. *Because I don't want anything happening to Constantine.*

"Watch it, princess, or I'll think you're starting to care about me." A light tease.

She still didn't see the motorcycle. Juliet turned to face the front. "I don't want anyone hurt."

"Ah, so I'm not special. Got it."

"I didn't say that. I think you're quite special." An instant response. "Very unlike anyone I've ever met before."

"Same, princess. Same."

They were almost at her house. "I thought you weren't going to call me that anymore." She could see the line of cars. Oh, damn. "We are not going to be able to get past them."

"Sure we will. I told you before, I have a plan." That easy confidence again. Nothing seemed to ruffle Constantine. Nothing at all. "We'll park down the way a bit, and when they get distracted, we'll slip in the back of your house."

Her fingers tapped against her thighs. "What would distract them?"

After parking the car, he sent her a beaming smile. "Oh, I don't know..."

Yes, clearly, he did know.

"Last night, a stud on a motorcycle whisked in and saved you from the scene behind the bar, carting the lovely princess off into the night."

"A stud?" she repeated, scrunching her nose.

"Reporters are trained to note details. I'm sure they will remember the bike. Especially when it comes roaring down the road in five, four, three, two..."

*Roar.*

Sure enough, the Harley had just rolled down the street. The driver wore his helmet with the visor pulled down over his face. But the driver wasn't alone. A woman held tightly to him as she sat behind him on the seat. A woman who also wore a helmet, but her long, blond hair tumbled down her back, and the sight of that blond hair seemed to be the equivalent of waving a red flag at the assembled crowd.

The motorcycle paused a moment while the driver looked at the small house. And at the reporters. Then the engine roared again, even louder.

And the motorcycle took off.

The reporters rushed to follow. Most jumped into their vehicles, but some even ran down the street on foot after the driver.

"And that," Constantine said, sounding smug, "is how you make a distraction. Let's go grab your bag."

# CHAPTER FOUR

*Step Four: Be good to the client. Be a fucking nightmare to the rest of the world. Because when everyone else fears you, they'll stay the hell away from her.*

They went in the back. The reporters had acted just as Constantine had anticipated. He'd needed to come up with the plan fast, too, especially once Juliet had proved adamant on going back to her place.

But, really, all he'd needed was a woman with blond hair who didn't mind making some extra cash. And, luckily, a lady named Kara Carlisle had been performing at the hotel, singing the blues at night, and Holden had offered her some cash for an hour's worth of work.

*Done.*

"It will just take a moment," Juliet promised as she hurried down the hallway. "I'll grab my stuff and be right back."

Nodding, he glanced around. Bright colors in the kitchen. Deep blue in the den. Books scattered around. Textbooks, counseling journals, romances. A yoga mat waited in the corner of her den and—

*"Constantine!"* A sharp, scared cry.

He ran to her, cursing himself because he shouldn't have let her out of his sight. A reporter could be waiting inside her home. He should have considered that possibility sooner. "Juliet!" A roar of her name as he burst into her bedroom.

But no reporter lurked in there with her. Juliet stood, alone, near the bed, with horror stamped on her beautiful face. He took in the scene with a fast sweep of his gaze and noted the white feathers around the bed. Feathers on the floor, a few that danced in the air because Juliet was now rushing toward him, and she'd caused the feathers to stir up.

She grabbed his arm. "Someone—" A frantic bob of her head. "Someone was *here* last night."

He took her hand. Locked his fingers with hers. Brought her with him closer to the bed so he could get a better look. What he found had rage blasting through every cell in his body. *Sonofabitch.* He knew slash marks when he saw them. Marks left by a knife could be very distinct, of course, but it was the actual *fucking knife* that had been plunged in her mattress that was the real damn clue.

Some bastard had broken into her home. Had slashed her pillows, sending feathers all over the fucking place, and then, the prick had driven the knife into her mattress.

*What would he have done if Juliet had been in this bed?*

"Who would do this?" Juliet whispered as her body slid ever closer to his. "Why?"

Constantine didn't know. But he would absolutely find out, and the bastard would pay.

*You don't get to scare her. You just made the worst mistake of your life.*

\*\*\*

"Two meetings in twenty-four hours. Not exactly what I was expecting." Raven Douglas strode into Juliet's house with three cops at her back.

"Hardly what I expected, either," he returned curtly. Rage still coursed through his blood. Every single time he realized what *could* have happened the night before...

His gaze darted to Juliet as she huddled on the couch. The last twenty-four hours had not been the best for her. Understatement. She looked far too pale and breakable to him. The oversized clothes hung on her, making her seem even smaller and more vulnerable. The baseball cap had been tossed on the cushions near her, and her thick, blond hair tumbled over her shoulders.

"I'm sure you destroyed *my* crime scene," Raven said, and there was no missing the possessive *my*. "It would have been great if you had backed out and stayed out until my team could get in to analyze and collect evidence. Normally, of course, a small B&E won't get the massive rollout that you're about to see." Her lips tightened. "But, hey, we're dealing with a princess, so the city thinks she gets priority."

"It's not a B&E." Juliet's voice. Emotionless. Clear. Oddly calm given the circumstances. "From what I could see, nothing was taken."

A furrow appeared between Raven's brows. She glanced from Juliet back to Constantine. "The dispatcher said—"

"Don't know what your dispatcher said," he managed through clenched teeth, "but the perp didn't take anything. Instead, he *left* something behind."

The furrow smoothed away. "Show me."

Immediately, his focus shifted to Juliet.

"Stay with her," Raven ordered the cops.

They sidled closer to her. One of the cops, a young guy with tousled, dirty blond hair, stared at her with clearly star-struck eyes.

*Watch it, buddy.*

"I'm Jacob." He smiled at her. "You need anything?" he asked her, voice tender.

"She needs you to do your fucking job and make sure no one else gets into this house," Constantine blasted.

Juliet flinched.

Hell. "Sorry." A curt apology. He wasn't pissed at the young cop—okay, fine, Constantine was—the guy needed to stop eye-fucking Juliet. Constantine was mostly enraged at himself. *The bastard was in her house.*

"You're seriously pissed," Raven observed.

He spun on his heel and marched down the hallway toward Juliet's bedroom.

"Guessing this is gonna be as bad as I am now fearing," she muttered as she followed behind him.

He stopped near the open bedroom doorway. "I know how to preserve a crime scene." He could do it in his sleep. "As soon as I realized what happened in there, I backed Juliet out. I never touched anything inside the bedroom, and she swears that she didn't, either. That as soon as she saw the bed, she froze."

Pulling on gloves as she strolled over the threshold, Raven nodded. "Yep, the sight of a knife can make anyone freeze." She edged closer to the bed. "Someone did a whole lot of slashing. Wonder what the pillow ever did to him?"

"You think this shit is amusing? *What if Juliet had been here?*"

Raven turned her head toward him. "I get that my manner is abrupt. Most people can't stand me, and that's cool. I can't stand most people." Her chin lifted. "But sometimes, you have to use humor to help you cope or the world will tear you apart. Even if it's piss-poor humor, you use it. Mr. Former FBI, are you really gonna act like you've never done the same at a scene?"

He had, but this was different. Because this was Juliet.

"I'm guessing your girl has no security cameras outside."

"No," he rasped.

"Considering who she is, don't we think that's a major mistake." Not a question, but a statement as she strolled carefully around the room, observing, not touching.

"We do." A rumble.

"Um. I'll take that to mean you're rectifying the situation immediately."

"I'm taking her out of Baton Rouge. We were supposed to leave at noon, but I'm guessing that flight time needs to be backed up until you're done with your questioning."

"You guess correctly." She returned to the doorway. "I'm assuming you already looked for signs of forced entry?"

"You assume correctly." His hands remained loose at his sides even as the fury kept burning within him. "No sign that the locks were picked."

"Interesting." She swept another glance around the room. "This whole situation begs the question...did her bed get sliced *before* the news broke that she was a missing princess? Or after? Are we looking at someone who is just after Juliet Laurent? Or someone who could be developing an obsession with our newfound royal?"

"I think we're past the 'could be' part on the question of obsession. We passed that point with the fucking knife."

Her brows rose. "You're sounding very, very angry about all this."

"How the hell am I supposed to sound? Thrilled?"

"Just thought you bodyguards were all unemotional. It's not personal, right? Just business. Isn't that a slogan or something?"

No, it wasn't. He stared at her. "It's my *personal* responsibility to see to Juliet's safety. If I hadn't taken her with me to the hotel last night, the bastard could have gotten to her."

"Then I guess it's a good thing Juliet has a *personal* hero on her side, yes?"

Time to get back to Juliet. But first, "She lost her keys behind Sal's last night. When the reporters swarmed, she thinks that someone accidentally kicked them away. But, seeing as how there is no sign of forced entry here..."

"You think the reason the locks don't show signs of forced entry is because our perp had a key?" She nodded. "Certainly a possibility. In that case, it's more about the princess, and not the person she is."

"I disagree. You can't separate the two. Juliet is the princess, and the timing of this attack is shit." He spun and marched back into the den.

Juliet hadn't moved from her position on the couch. Jacob still hovered near her, making his moony eyes at her. But Juliet's gaze went straight to Constantine.

He crossed to her side. He made a shoo motion with his hand at Jacob, and when the cop stepped aside, Constantine eased onto the couch next to Juliet. When her body brushed against his, a little of the tension slipped from him.

*She's safe. No one is going to hurt her. Not on my watch.*

"Search the area." Raven's voice. She'd followed him back to the den, but she was speaking into her phone. "Every inch of the parking lot at Sal's. We're looking for missing keys. Bag and tag if they're located." She hung up her phone.

"Nothing like this has ever happened to me before," Juliet whispered.

His head turned. She gazed at him, and there were tears in her eyes.

"I'm scared," she admitted.

"You don't have to—"

"Ms. Laurent," Raven began as she settled into the chair across from them. "I need to ask you a few questions."

She'd cut through his rasping words of...*You don't have to be scared because I am going to find the sonofabitch and rip his balls off and shove them down his throat.* Constantine sucked in a deep breath. Those probably wouldn't have been the best words to say in front of the cops.

Juliet's head swung toward Raven. She nodded in response to the other woman's words. Her hand also reached out and caught Constantine's.

Surprised, he glanced down. Did she even realize she'd just touched him?

"Are you currently seeing anyone, Ms. Laurent?" Raven asked.

"Just call me Juliet. And, no, I'm not."

Raven's gaze darted down to Juliet and Constantine's joined hands. "I see." A brief pause. "When was the last time you were in a relationship?"

"Ah...six months ago?"

"Seven," Constantine answered.

Juliet's head whipped toward him. "What?"

Hell. He'd clamped his mouth shut, but it was too late.

"How do you know that?" Juliet asked him, but then he saw understanding dawn in her dark gaze. "Oh." She lifted her hand from his.

"A dossier." Raven seemed pleased because she'd obviously reached the same conclusion Juliet had. "I was hoping Wilde had been as thorough as the rumors say. I'm guessing you've done full background checks on all her previous lovers?"

He saw the red stain Juliet's cheeks. *Fuck me.* "Yes." A hiss.

"And did any red flags appear? Anyone who should be gaining the focus of the Baton Rouge PD?"

One asshole did come to mind. The professor she'd broken up with seven months ago. "Christian Hale."

"Chris?" Adamant, Juliet shook her head. "He's a tenured history professor. Well respected in his field, there is no way—"

"Even tenured professors can get assault charges filed against them."

Her mouth dropped open. "What? When?"

"Seven years ago. But don't worry, his judge daddy made the charges vanish. Wilde just happens to be good at digging into the past." He rolled one shoulder in a shrug. "Wasn't one of the reasons you broke up with him because he made you feel uncomfortable? He seemed to always be around and you wanted space?"

She stared at him with stunned eyes. "How did you know that?"

"Because I'm Wilde, and we're thorough." That was an understatement. The Wilde techs could dig up anything on anyone. And to think, once upon a time, he'd thought that the FBI had serious reach. That reach was nothing compared to the organizational ties that Eric Wilde possessed.

Constantine had never expected to join Wilde and become a Wilde agent. Then again, he'd never expected for his FBI associates to turn on him, to be left for dead, and to have to rely on a criminal for help. A criminal who would go on to become his best friend. The best friend who would eventually lead him to Wilde.

But that was a story for another time and place.

For now, he had to deal with the bastard who'd decided to break into Juliet's home.

"Is there anything you don't know about me?" she asked, voice husky.

Sure. He didn't know what was going on behind those big, dark eyes of hers right at that moment. Was she furious because he knew so much? Did she feel invaded? Exposed? Too vulnerable? Did she want to snarl and scream?

"Something tells me," Raven noted with a tip of her head, "that the man even knows your bra size."

Thirty-four C.

"He probably knows exactly how long you dated this Christian guy and even the number of times you had sex with him."

Constantine's hand curled into a fist. A surge of sudden emotion caught him off guard. And that emotion? Fucking jealousy.

"Zero," Juliet said, angling up her slightly pointed chin. "And I don't care what Constantine's report says, that number is the truth. That's why I know Chris isn't behind the attack. We didn't date long enough to cross that particular milestone. I hardly think that after all this time, he's suddenly developed some sick obsession that makes him slip into my home and slash my pillow and mattress."

"You never know," Raven returned with a purse of her lips. "I've seen some pretty crazy obsessions in my time. You'd be surprised by how normal—how *good*—some guys can seem. But really, they're hiding a dark side. Good in public, monsters in private. That's why I always look twice at any guy who claims to be good."

Surprise rolled through Constantine. He studied Raven with new eyes. "You and me both." Something they had in common.

"I'll add Christian to my suspect list," she said. "Now tell me about everyone else in your life."

A fierce pounding shook the front door. Constantine immediately surged to his feet.

"Who the hell is that?" Raven demanded as she, too, rose. She motioned to Jacob. "If that is some jackass reporter, send the fool running."

Jacob nodded. He thrust back his shoulders and marched to the door with a pronounced swagger of authority. He yanked open the door. "You are going to need to step back," he began as he raised one hand.

"Yeah, do me a favor?" A drawling voice threw back. "How about step out of my way and let me in to do my job?"

Ah, yes. Constantine had expected this arrival. He glanced at his watch. It had actually taken longer than he'd expected for his backup to arrive.

*"You are talking to a police officer,"* Jacob snapped.

"Right. The badge and uniform were a clue. Got it. Damn, you look young. Now I'm worrying about you being on the streets even as you continue to block my path." The new arrival cleared his throat. "Yo, Con! Tell this guy I'm with you!"

"This is a crime scene." Raven seethed. "The whole house is a freaking crime scene. I want everyone out!"

But if they went out, they'd be sent straight into the path of the reporters. Wasn't that the whole reason she'd had their sit-down inside? *In the crime scene?* Because, yes, clearly, the whole house was a crime scene. It had been the entire time they'd been chit-chatting. But the sharks—ah, reporters—were clustered outside, and Constantine had kept Juliet inside, on the couch, for her safety and privacy.

He'd thought that Raven had been keeping them inside using the same reasoning. Yet now, apparently, her plans had changed. And Constantine suspected why. "You think you're going to draw the bastard out by parading her around that pack?"

Raven blinked. Her hand pressed to her chest. "Why, that's a great idea. Thanks for suggesting it."

"*Con!*" Came the annoyed yell from the doorway.

*One fire at a time.* He couldn't put them all out at once, so he'd start with the fire doing the yelling. "That's my partner." At the moment. A situation that still didn't feel natural. "Holden works for Wilde, too. If we're taking her out into that swarm, I want him on one side of her and me on the other."

Frowning, Jacob glanced over at Constantine. "You sure he's with you?"

"Unfortunately, yes." Unfortunate because Holden was a bit of a loose cannon. The man did *not* blend well as a rule. In fact, he was so very different from Constantine's usual partner that Constantine kept having to readjust expectations.

Holden pushed his way inside. "What the hell happened in here? I got the nine-one-one text from you and hauled ass right after dropping off our actress." His gaze swept over Juliet as she continued to huddle on the couch. "She looks terrified but unharmed."

Juliet's head lifted.

"Aw, jeez," Holden groused. "Not terrified. She looks more like someone stole her favorite puppy." He strode toward her and patted her on the shoulder with his bear-like hand. "There, there."

His first pat had almost knocked her off the couch.

Constantine caught his partner's hand before Holden could do more damage. "Some asshole broke into her home and left a knife in her bed."

Holden's face hardened, a subtle change around his mouth and green eyes. "You don't say." Low but seething with a hard anger.

Raven clapped. When all attention flew her way, she directed, "I want everyone out, now. Let's get this party moving."

He would hardly call it a party, but maybe Raven didn't attend a lot of fun events.

"I'll continue questioning down at the station, and when I'm done, you can catch that plane that will take you out of my city." She gave him and Juliet a hard grin. "I think a little distance is exactly what the princess needs right now."

In other words, she wanted the princess—and the trouble that was surrounding her—out of Baton Rouge. Fair enough, Constantine also wanted Juliet far away from trouble.

Constantine scooped up Juliet's ball cap. He slid it onto her head and tucked her hair under it as best he could. "I'll be beside you," he promised her as he caught her hands and pulled her up to stand in front of him.

"So will I," Holden said. He shoved his hand toward her. "Holden Blackwell, at your service, ma'am."

She extended her hand and had it immediately engulfed by his. "Juliet Laurent. But I guess you already knew that?"

"Pretty much everyone in the US knows your name at this point. And the fact that this shady business just went down at your place? Your story is gonna explode even more." He raised his brows. "Consider yourself warned."

Holden was still holding her hand. So Constantine physically separated their hands and pulled Juliet closer. "She's warned," he groused. "Now let's get the hell out of here." He turned toward Juliet. The scene outside wasn't going to be pretty.

But going out the back door wasn't an option. The cops were leading the show, and they wanted them parading out front.

"You will stay with me every step of the way." An order, not a question. "I'll be with you and so will Holden. Don't answer any questions, I don't care what they say. We're gonna get you clear, and you will be safe," he vowed.

"It's a feeding frenzy out there." From Holden. "Had to fight my way through the throng. Those sharks definitely smell blood. Hard not to, though, when the cops came in with sirens blaring." He snorted in disgust. "Guess the idea of attempting a *low profile* just couldn't happen for the PD?"

"It's time." Raven's voice hummed with impatience. "I want her at the station, now."

And so they went. The cops led, and yeah, it was a fucking feeding frenzy, just as Holden had warned. As soon as the reporters—and just general, gaping bystanders—caught sight of Juliet, they surged forward like a tidal wave getting ready to slam into a shore.

"Get the hell back!" Holden thundered.

Some of them retreated because Holden did possess the wonderful talent for intense intimidation. Probably because he looked like a crazed MMA fighter right then—or maybe because he *had* been an MMA fighter back in the day and he still knew how to cower his opponents with ease.

Constantine kept his arm around Juliet's shoulders as they pushed through the crowd. Cameras followed their every move. Questions blasted into their ears.

*"Why were you hiding, Juliet?"*

*"Are you going to take the crown?"*

*"How does it feel to know that your grandmother tried to commit murder?"*

Fuck.

Juliet stumbled. Her head whipped up and turned toward the reporter who'd just asked that question. He flashed a wide grin at her. "Jeremy Knight, from *Insider Confidential*. How does it feel to know that your grandmother hired a killer to assassinate the king of Lancaden?"

"No," her voice was breathy, shocked, and all too clear for everyone to hear because a tense silence had descended over the crowd. "That's not true." She looked back at Constantine. "Is it?"

*Yes, princess, it is.* "Don't answer their questions," he growled instead. "Remember that rule?"

"But—"

Jeremy Knight leapt forward, with his hand outstretched as if he would touch Juliet. In a flash, Constantine had Juliet behind his back. *"Get the hell back."* Deadly. Ice cold.

Jeremy froze. "I have questions."

"Good for you. I have no fucking patience and a strong desire to kill on most days." He smiled. "Guess we both have issues, huh?"

*"Did you just threaten me?"*

No, he'd used very careful wording because this wasn't his first ballgame.

Juliet's fingers pressed to his back.

"Move," Constantine snapped to the bastard in his path.

"Uh, you gotta step back," the cop, Jacob, mumbled as he pointed to the side so that Jeremy would presumably know where to go. The cop was being too polite by far.

"Move or I will move you," Constantine ordered.

A muscle flexed along Jeremy's jaw, but he moved. Good life choice.

And Constantine was done with this shit. *Parading her around for them? The fun is over, Raven.* "Clear the path, Holden," Constantine ordered.

"Clearing," his partner returned.

Constantine swung around to face Juliet. Juliet who had her head tipped back and who stared at him with wide, stark eyes. Stark because that prick reporter had just thrown a terrible family truth right in her face, and, clearly, she'd had no clue about her grandmother's murderous past—or, rather, her attempt at a murderous past.

"You hold on to me," he directed.

"Constantine?"

He swung her into his arms.

Holden made sure the path stayed clear.

Holding her tight, keeping her against his chest as she curled her arm around his neck, Constantine carried her through the pack and to the waiting patrol car.

# CHAPTER FIVE

*Step Five: Stay out of her personal business.*
*Her pain isn't yours.*
*Repeat that shit mentally enough times, and you*
*might believe it.*
*Ah, screw it. You won't.*


"I've never flown in a private jet before." Juliet perched in the seat with her hands curled in her lap. "Actually, this is my first time to fly at all."

They hit a patch of turbulence. God, she hoped it was just turbulence. Her hands flew up and clamped around the armrest. *Be turbulence.* *Be turbulence.* Her gaze darted to the window. Night had fallen, and she couldn't see anything but darkness through the small bit of glass.

The cops had kept them at the station for seemingly forever, and all she'd wanted to do was run away. Before, she'd balked at the idea of hopping on the jet and going to Atlanta. But after what had happened at her rental house...

*Getting out of town for a few days while the cops hunt that jerk? Great idea. Masterful plan. Brilliant.*

"It's all right." Constantine sat across from her. His low voice sent her gaze jumping back to him. While nerves had her stomach twisting and diving, he appeared perfectly calm. "The pilots have everything under control."

Holden was one of those pilots. Or, at least, he was up in the front with the pilots. She hadn't seen him since the plane took off. It was just her and Constantine in the back. They were sitting in the lush seats, and his knee would occasionally brush against her leg. For some reason, that occasional brush felt oddly intimate to her.

*Because you have been without a man for clearly too long.* If the brush of his leg felt intimate, she had problems.

*Problems.* Right, yes, she did.

The plane stopped the alarming shaking, and she could breathe normally again. "He was lying."

Constantine crossed his arms over his chest.

"The reporter," she clarified because it was probably important to say which "he" she meant. "From *Insane Confidential.*"

His lips quirked. Those wonderful, distracting slashes appeared in his cheeks. "I think it was *Insider Confidential.*"

"Um, yes. He was wrong."

Constantine's smile slipped.

"I knew my grandmother very well. She could be demanding. *Exacting.* But she was hardly a killer." A would-be killer. The reporter had said that she'd *attempted* to kill the ruler of Lancaden. But the ruler...God, this part was crazy. *Crazy.* Because the ruler back then—it was the same person who ruled now. Her grandfather.

A fact that still boggled her mind.

"The king was divorcing her at the time. He found out that she was cheating on him and that she was pregnant." Constantine's voice held no emotion. "She swore the baby was his."

*The baby*...Juliet's mother.

"But he didn't believe her. And, according to the intel Wilde has obtained, the king was busy with his own extra-marital events, and he had a much younger mistress who was itching to take the crown."

Her lashes fluttered. "He married the mistress."

"Years later, yes. He did. But they had no children. That would be why you are being called home."

"Not home." Goosebumps rose on her arms. She'd been about to say the small house on Second Street was home, but then an image of the knife in her mattress had slipped through her mind. "My grandmother didn't try to kill him." Him. Not saying her grandfather's name. Not actually naming the man who'd denied her mother. *And me.* For so long. Until his deathbed. "I've researched Lancaden. There is no report of my grandmother trying to kill the king."

"It's what is called an open secret. Those in the right—or wrong—circles knew. Those circles have now clearly expanded." His gaze cut to the window. Constantine seemed to be mulling over what to say, and unease—even more unease than she'd already been feeling—slithered through her.

And then his stare returned to her face. "Recently, a very important ring was located."

"What does a ring have to do with—"

He uncrossed his arms. "The ring belonged to your grandmother. It was discovered during the course of a Wilde investigation."

Her tongue slid over her lower lip.

His gaze dropped to her mouth. Lingered.

She expected him to keep talking. He didn't. His gaze did remain on her mouth. "Constantine?"

He swallowed. "I hadn't planned to tell you about the ring now. I'd hoped the truth wouldn't be discovered for a while because I feared it might...hurt...you."

"Being abandoned by your family hurts." She knew her smile held bitterness. "Being told you don't belong hurts. Living your whole life that way? It hurts."

"Yes." A nod. "It does. Some days are real sonsofbitches."

Juliet leaned toward him, pulled by the pain she'd just heard in his voice. Her hand reached out, and her fingers curled around his knee. "I'm sorry." *He knows what it feels like. How I feel.*

Once more, that gaze of his flickered. This time, it moved to her hand as it rested on his knee. Then back to her face. When he looked at her face, she could see some unnamed emotion heating the gray of his eyes. "Why? Why are you sorry?"

"Because something bad happened to you."

His hand moved in a flash and covered hers. She expected him to then remove her hand from his leg. He didn't. His hold tightened around her. "I am the bad thing."

"No. You're the white knight who carried me through the crowd of reporters."

"I'm the asshole who wanted to kick their asses."

"Same thing."

He lifted her hand, but only so he could cradle it with his own. His thumb slid along her palm, and she'd never in her entire life realized that a palm could be so sensitive. He was stroking her palm, and her heart raced faster.

"But I didn't," he said quietly. "Because I never, ever hit first. My dad did. All the time when I was a kid."

Her left hand unbuckled her seat belt and she slid down, moving so that she was closer to him.

"What the fuck?" Constantine shook his head. "Princess, you are not supposed to *kneel.*"

She honestly hadn't realized she was—she just wanted to be closer. But, yes, she was kneeling near him. "I'm sorry. I hate the idea of anyone hurting you."

His eyes squeezed shut. "I knew you were going to be a problem."

She was trying hard not to be a problem. She'd gone along with his orders. She'd gotten on the plane, hadn't she?

"Knew it from the first moment I saw the pic of you. *Problem.*" His eyes opened. "If you don't get back in your seat in the next five seconds, I will be kissing you."

Her breath whispered out.

"Five."

She should get in her seat.

"Four."

Really, she should.

"Three."

But he'd just let go of her hand...only to lean even closer. And they'd already been plenty close. His fingers slid under her chin and tilted her head back.

"Two."

She could almost taste him. The peppermint that she'd seen him take right after they boarded the plane.

"One. You had your chance to run..."

They were on a plane. Not like there was a lot of running room, but she got what he meant. She got—

*Kissed.* That was what she got. Kissed. His mouth pressed to hers, with his lips open. A hot, languid, curl-your-toes and turn-you-on kiss. One that teased at first. Tasted. Tempted.

One that had her hands flying up to lock on his legs because yes, she was still kneeling on the floor of the plane. She grabbed him wherever she could and held on.

At her touch, he growled into her mouth, and the kiss changed. It became rougher. More demanding. Fierce.

*Possessive.*

Not just tempting, but taking, and she was helpless to do anything but respond as the hottest, most consuming need of her entire life swept through Juliet's body. Her mouth opened wider. Her tongue met his. He tasted of peppermint, and she would never, ever be able to have a peppermint again without remembering his kiss.

And he could kiss. Masterfully well. Better than any other guy in her life. He had her aching. Had her pushing nearer to him, and, somehow, she was now between his spread knees. Had he pulled her into that position? She couldn't remember and didn't care. Her hands curled around him, and she kissed him with a passionate force because this moment was incredible. He was incredible.

His hands slid down her back. Pushed over her hips. Almost touched her ass. She wanted his hands on her ass. She wanted his hands everywhere and—

"I think you are taking the term 'bodyguard' a little too literally, man," Holden announced, then he coughed. Twice. "I don't think you actually have to put your hands all over her body."

Constantine stiffened. She felt his muscles seemingly turn to stone beneath her touch. His mouth pulled from hers as his head lifted. Not too far, only an inch or so. He stared into her eyes. "We will finish that."

Juliet didn't even know how to respond, but in the next moment, his hands had moved to her hips. He lifted her up with effortless strength and put her back in her seat. "Comfortable?" he asked politely. A muscle jerked along his jaw.

"Y-yes." Not really. She was pretty flushed and super, super embarrassed that Holden had just caught her between Constantine's legs while she made out with him as if her life had depended on that kiss. Fanning her flushed face with one hand, she forced herself to look over at Holden.

He crooked an eyebrow.

"That wasn't what it looked like," she began, trying to gain control of the situation.

"It was exactly what it looked like," Constantine fired at his partner. "And don't say another word to her about it, Holden, got me?"

Holden lifted up his hands and held them in front of his body. "Easy. Look, I was just being a good partner and coming to make sure the patch of turbulence we passed hadn't rattled the princess. But it's good to know you were making sure she was distracted."

Constantine stood toe to toe with him. The two men were the same height, and while Holden might have more weight, Constantine appeared far more dangerous. There was just something powerful and dark that seemed to swirl in the air around him. A tension that was palpable. "You do not want to say anything I don't like. You do want to rethink every single thought you have running in your head before you open your mouth."

Holden peeked around Constantine. "I bet I can do that rethinking a lot better from the front of the plane."

"Bet you can, too," Constantine rumbled.

Holden saluted and headed for the front of the plane.

Juliet pressed her lips together. That scene had gotten out of control, fast. One moment, she'd been feeling the overwhelming urge to comfort Constantine, and in the next, she'd been about to rip his clothes off.

Constantine's back was to her as he watched Holden walk away. Juliet used that opportunity to focus on her breathing. Or to try and get her breathing back in a nice, normalish pattern.

Constantine swung back to her.

"I was trying to comfort you," she blurted.

His jaw tightened.

Okay. Perhaps that hadn't been the best thing to say.

"You kiss a man to comfort him? That's your usual MO?"

Her flush burned hotter. "No."

"Good to know. Because if that was the case, I'd have to say I never wanted you to fucking comfort any other man again." His head tilted. "Huh. Now that I think about, I still don't."

She had no idea what she should say in this situation. *I just made out with my bodyguard.* "I'm sure we broke rules."

He put one hand on her seat's headrest. Constantine leaned over her. "What rules would those be?"

Her attention shifted to his mouth. She wanted to taste him again.

*Stop this!*

"What rules, princess?"

The title seemed to be a taunt. And an endearment. How could it be both? But it sounded like both when "princess" rolled from his lips. "Rules about...getting involved with the client."

"Technically, some guy from Lancaden is the client. You're the target."

Her tongue swiped over her lips. Being called a target wasn't the best thing in the world. The term grated every time she heard it.

He leaned in a bit more. "I've been making my own rules when it comes to you."

"You have?" She angled her head back and moved a little closer to his mouth. Her eyes started to drift closed because Juliet was pretty sure they were about to kiss again.

"Fuck."

Her eyes flew open. He'd backed away.

So maybe they were not going to kiss again.

"I have been making rules," he gritted out. Constantine returned to his seat. "The most important rule is not to let you get hurt."

She could certainly get behind that rule. Full support.

"If we get involved, I will hurt you, princess."

Shock rocked through her. "Why would you say that?"

"Because it's not going to end well. No fucking way it can. I'm not the guy who rides off into the sunset with the fairytale princess."

Her anger stirred. "That's good. Because I don't remember this being a fairytale."

"I'm not the guy," he repeated.

And she understood that what he actually meant was...*I'm not the guy for you.* "I have a rule, too," Juliet informed him. *Inhale. Exhale.* "It's to not waste kisses on guys who get scared when their partners are close by."

"Scared?" His hands moved to curl around the armrests at his sides.

She inclined her head toward him.

"Princess, there is very little in this world I fear." His lips quirked as his gaze slid down the aisle toward the front of the plane. "I can assure you, Holden isn't on my list at all. I can handle him in my sleep." His attention shifted back to her. "Kissing you was a mistake."

How wonderful. "Every woman in the world loves to be called a mistake." Was that pain she felt? It was. She squeezed her eyes closed just in case that pain might try to sneak into her gaze. "I think I'm going to nap." No, she wasn't. "Wake me when we get there?"

"*Juliet.*"

The *mistake* kept her eyes closed.

"You don't want to get involved with me."

"Right. You're my bodyguard. I'm your target. Check." The term "target" just got colder and colder. "Best if we just maintain our positions. The kiss was a mistake." Her eyes didn't open. "Chalk it up to the stress of the last twenty-four hours." Actually... "*No.*" Her eyes flew open.

And she caught him staring at her with an expression of absolute longing on his face. Savage need. A need so intense and stark that it stole her breath.

Then he blinked, and a mask slid into place. He went back to being the tough, dangerous bodyguard.

Shaken, Juliet took a moment before she spoke again. *Don't stop now.* "It wasn't because of stress. That was a lie. I don't want to lie to you."

His eyes glittered.

"You haven't lied to me, and I want to do the same with you. No secrets." As a general rule, she hated lies. When you found out that your whole life was a lie, the notion of lying to others left a bitter taste in your mouth.

Emotion blazed in his eyes, but she couldn't quite figure out *what* emotion raged so strongly. She just knew that the gray of his eyes had turned stormy.

Juliet soldiered on. "I wanted to comfort you because I'm sorry that you had it so rough when you were a kid." Rough seemed to be an understatement. "I don't like that you were hurt."

His grip on the armrests tightened.

"I know those kinds of actions—what your father did—that can leave scars on a person. You seem fine on the outside, but the pain just hardens you deep *inside.*" Wasn't that why she wanted to be a psychologist? To help people? "I wanted to comfort you," Juliet said again. "But then something changed." She was riding this honesty train even though it was probably a terrible mistake. Too late. No going back now. "I'm attracted to you. I'm sure you get that from lots of women." Because he was gorgeous. "And when we kissed, it had nothing to do with comfort or stress. I wanted to kiss you."

He didn't speak.

Okay. So no big confession from him.

He still gripped the armrests far too tightly. So tightly she wondered if they might snap off beneath his hands.

"I get it," she added when the silence stretched to an uncomfortable degree. "You're not..." A click as she swallowed. "The guy." The guy she should want. The guy she should need. But...

"I'm the guy who enjoyed the fucking hell out of that kiss," Constantine said, voice low and growling. "The guy who can still taste you, and, baby, I want more."

Her mouth dropped open.

"I'm the guy who usually takes what he wants and lets the world burn."

Um, not what she'd expected.

"But I'm the guy who's trying to be different with you. You need a bodyguard. You don't need a possessive-as-hell lover who wants to strip you and fuck you until you scream his name." A pause. One fraught with tension and a dark, simmering need. "Princess, you need protection. You don't need a desire that will rip your world apart."

Her world had already been ripped apart. She was running away from her life. Heading into the night with a man who had a voice that growled and a kiss that consumed.

"So I'll keep protecting you," Constantine vowed. "And I'll make absolutely sure that you stay safe. Because that's my job."

She was the job.

And the desire they felt? Clearly, it wasn't going anywhere. Nothing would happen. A mistake, just as he'd said.

Too bad it had felt like the best mistake of her life.

\*\*\*

"What in the sweet hell was that about?" Holden asked, voice soft, as they stood near the plane.

They'd arrived in Atlanta moments ago. Holden and Constantine had disembarked before

Juliet because Constantine wanted to make sure the area was secure. No way did he want his princess walking into another feeding frenzy.

But the private area was deserted. Just a skeleton crew. No sign of reporters.

"You've been on the job with the woman for one day, and you're already kissing her?"

Constantine's head turned toward his partner.

"Fast," Holden said. "Damn fast. I had no idea you were such a smooth operator. Color me impressed."

"Are you looking to get punched in the face?" Constantine asked, curious.

"You really think you can?" Holden shoved his hands into the pockets of his jeans. "You think you'd get the hit in before I deflected and had your ass on the ground?"

Constantine smiled. "I know I can." And his ass would not hit the ground.

Holden cocked his head to the right. "You *know* I'm ex-MMA, right? We did talk about this over a beer, yes? Or are you one of those guys that forgets shit when he drinks?"

"I don't forget anything." Ever. A talent he had. "And you might be ex-MMA, but you have no idea what I've done in my life."

"You were a Fed." Seemingly bored, Holden surveyed the scene.

A black limo had just pulled up. Their ride. It was too late for them to head to the Wilde office, so Constantine had plans to keep Juliet in a secure location for the night. They'd visit Wilde first thing in the morning.

"Also heard some rumors that you did contract work for the CIA," Holden continued, voice casual. "Were you some kind of spook or something?"

"Or something." Because he'd been forced into taking the jobs with the CIA. When it was either play ball or get tossed into a secret government facility, you learned how to pitch like an All-Star.

The driver exited the limo and stood behind the chain-link fence. Constantine recognized him from Wilde and nodded. *Batter up.* Time to get the show moving. But first, just so he and Holden were one hundred percent clear... "She's stressed. Her whole life was just turned upside down. The kiss was a mistake. The case will continue without issue."

"Was it her mistake or yours? Because you were in your seat. She was in front of you, and it looked like she was—"

"Not another word." Lethal. "It didn't happen, understand? You saw nothing. I'm her bodyguard. I'm staying close."

"Definitely, you are. Super close."

Damn right, he was. Constantine turned and strode toward the plane. Time to transport the princess.

*Fuck me, I can still taste her.*

His hands clenched into fists at his sides.

# CHAPTER SIX

*Step Six: Keep your hands off the princess.*
*Unless the intent is to protect, do not touch.*
*Why is this such a hard concept to understand?*

"Is this...your place?" Juliet's voice was cautious but curious as she stood in the middle of the penthouse. They'd made it to downtown Atlanta. Lights from the city gleamed below and were clearly seen through the floor-to-ceiling windows.

At her question, he shook his head. "It's a safe house, one of many owned by the company." By this point, he knew the reporters would have learned that he and Holden worked for Wilde. They wouldn't know about Constantine's true past though, because all those secrets had been buried by Uncle Sam. They would just know he was a Wilde agent, her bodyguard.

That meant the smart reporters would figure out he'd taken the princess to Atlanta since that was the base of Wilde operations. "If reporters trail us..." It would be easy to bribe someone from the Baton Rouge airport to get the flight plan. "They'll probably look for you at the local luxury hotels." The ones with the best security. "And because they'll be focusing there now, we went off-grid." He pointed down the hallway. "There are three bedrooms here, so take your pick. The security in this place is a dozen times better than what you'll find in any high-end hotel." Of course, it was better. It had been installed by Wilde. "No one will get to you, and you can rest easy." Constantine rolled back his shoulders, feeling the tension in his upper back and neck. "We didn't get to take your clothes with us—"

"Because my home got turned into a crime scene?"

Yep, that would be the reason. "So I had some Wilde staff pick up clothing for you. There should be a bag waiting in the hall. You'll find toiletries, shoes, everything you need."

She glanced down the hallway. "Are you taking one of the bedrooms?"

"I'll be on the couch."

Biting her lip, she swept her gaze back to him. "Because you still want to be between me and any threat that might come bursting in the door?"

"Call it a quirk." He shrugged out of his coat. Tossed aside his tie. Undid the top button of his shirt. "But no one will be bursting in. You're safe." *Go to bed.*

She needed to walk down that hallway. Turn and go to sleep.

Because he still wanted her. Even more now than before. He knew how she felt in his arms. How she tasted. How she made the sexiest little moan when she got turned on.

"Good night, Constantine."

"Night, Juliet." He held his breath, but yes, it was happening. She was heading toward the hallway. Just a few more steps and temptation would be out of his reach. *Keep going. Just a few more—*

She paused. "What happens tomorrow?"

They'd been over this, but he'd review it again. "We go to Wilde at 8 a.m. We'll head up to Eric's office, and there you will find the rep from Lancaden waiting to meet you."

She looked back over her shoulder. "Is that when you tell me goodbye?"

He stiffened.

"Because someone from Lancaden is the client, and I'm the target." Her hair slid over her cheek. "So when you actually deliver me to that waiting representative, is your job done?"

His feet remained rooted in place. "My job is over when Eric tells me it is."

"So you're not just going to walk away when I get in that office?"

"No," he rasped. "I'm not."

She smiled. The sweet, beautiful smile that lit up her whole face. "Good. Because you know what?"

Constantine couldn't tear his gaze away from her smile. *Fuck me.*

"I think I'll miss you when you're gone," Juliet said. The thick carpeting swallowed the sound of her steps as she padded down the hallway. Constantine remained standing in the same spot.

They'd just met. He looked at his watch. 2 a.m. So he'd known her for over twenty-four hours now.

And he knew that when she was gone, yeah, he'd miss the hell out of her, too.

***

"Game face, Juliet."

Her head jerked toward Constantine.

He gave her a reassuring smile, or, as reassuring as she supposed his smiles could be. The grin still looked oddly dangerous. They were riding up the elevator at Wilde. She and Constantine were the only ones in the small space, and she was so nervous that her knees wanted to knock together.

The morning trip to Wilde had been uneventful. It had only been a small drive through the downtown area. The same limo driver had been behind the wheel. He'd taken them inside a private parking garage, and then she'd been spirited into Wilde. No reporters. No curious bystanders.

Just her and Constantine.

Now they were going up to the top floor. She hadn't seen Holden, but she was sure he had to be lurking around somewhere. Soon she'd meet Eric and the representative from her grandfather's country.

This was the part where she'd tell him that she had no interest in ruling. That her life was in Baton Rouge. That—

Constantine's phone rang.

The elevator dinged. The doors slid open. She pulled in a deep breath and started forward.

"Hold on." Constantine's hand flew out and curled around her arm.

As usual, his touch sent a charge of heat zipping through her, but she'd been chilled and the heat felt good.

"The call is from Raven. Let's see if she caught the bastard." His fingers slid away from her. His right hand gripped the phone. And his left—the hand that had just touched her—reached out to press a button on the control panel. The elevator doors remained open.

He put the phone to his ear and kept his eyes on her. "It's Constantine," he answered. "Tell me you're calling with good news."

Juliet couldn't make out Raven's response, but she *could* see the sudden flash of fury that darkened Constantine's expression.

"You found the keys behind the bar—but *what?* How the hell did that happen?" he snarled. "You should've had eyes on her place."

*Oh, no.*

Holden appeared and glanced meaningly at the open doors of the elevator. "Were you planning to exit?" he asked, voice pleasant.

"Fucking hell," Constantine's rage rumbled in his voice. "This is the last thing we wanted to hear."

Holden pursed his lips. "Want to tell me who he's got on the phone?" he asked Juliet, keeping his voice low.

"Raven Douglas," she whispered.

Holden winced.

"Yes, yes, I'm with her. She's safe. She'll stay that way. Let me know when you get the arson report." Constantine hung up and shoved the phone into his pocket.

"I'm sorry," Holden said, sounding anything but sorry. "Did you just say 'arson' during your lovely conversation with the Baton Rouge detective?"

Constantine reached for Juliet's hand. He gave her a quick squeeze.

This wasn't good. "What happened?"

The faint lines around his mouth deepened. "Someone torched your house."

She shook her head. No, that couldn't be right. She'd heard him wrong.

"At least fifteen reporters are on the scene. It happened just a little while ago."

Holden yanked out his phone. Did a few quick scrolls. "Sonofabitch." Not so pleasant or teasing any longer. "Social media is already lighting up."

Once more, Juliet shook her head. "But..." This made no sense. "If reporters are there, then someone saw...someone could have stopped—"

"They saw the fire come shooting out of the windows. They didn't see who started it. They just filmed and are broadcasting now. Raven was calling to give us a heads up so I could tell you before..." He slanted a glance at Holden as the other man kept scrolling. "Before you saw it online," Constantine finished with a long exhale. "It's a big fire."

"Looks like an inferno," Holden whistled. "That shit is blazing."

Her home? Her stuff? Blazing?

"Could be that he wanted to destroy the place in case evidence was left behind," Holden noted as he kept looking at his phone. "I didn't think the cops were collecting enough from the scene. I know they were supposed to send in another team, but this way, they sure won't be finding much."

Because nothing would be left to find?

"Juliet."

Her lashes fluttered. She focused on Constantine. "My home is gone?"

His jaw locked. "You're safe."

But her home was gone.

Holden cleared his throat. "Yeah, this seems like a real piss-poor time to say this but...you got a bigwig from Lancaden waiting for you. I was sent to hurry the meet-and-greet process along."

Constantine stepped in front of her. "Tell the asshole he can keep waiting." He reached out and jabbed the button on the elevator. The doors began to slide closed. "Juliet is busy right the hell now."

The doors shut on Holden's shocked expression.

*** 

"Cool, cool," Holden said to the elevator doors. "This partnership seems to be flowing really well. I think we're gelling." He turned away. Blew out a breath. And, since someone had to go deliver the news, he began striding down the hallway that would take him to the boss's office.

Eric's assistant was waiting to greet him, but when he saw there was no princess in tow, the man's eyes almost bulged out of his head. "Incoming," Holden assured him. Maybe.

For all he knew, Constantine might decide to run with the woman.

*Wait, surely not.* Uh, maybe not?

"Incoming," he said again, trying to project a whole lot more confidence than he actually felt. Then Holden opened the door and let himself in Eric's office.

His boss sat behind his lush desk, and a less-than-pleased expression was on his face. Eric didn't usually show his emotions when clients were around, so that glower was the first sign that something about this meeting was already going wrong.

Something *other* than the princess not actually being present.

Holden directed his attention to the other person in the room—correction, other people. One man sat in the chair across from Eric, and all Holden could tell about him was that he had light brown hair. As for the two hulking figures who flanked him in their matching black suits...

Bodyguards.

One of the bodyguards appeared to have used a ton of hair gel because he'd slicked his hair back in an incredibly hard and heavy fashion. As for the other guard, his black hair had been buzzed. The style made his boulder-like features appear even starker.

Both men stood at hard attention. The kind of hard attention that you found from the military in certain areas.

The door click closed behind Holden. At that soft sound, the man in the chair rose. He turned with a warm smile on his face and with his hand outstretched.

His smile died a quick death when he saw Holden.

"Where is the princess?" he demanded.

"Holden Blackwell," Eric stood behind his desk. "Allow me to introduce you to Alexandre Aude, the counsellor of Lancaden." He waved with his hand toward the two silent shadows near Alexandre. "And his two guards, Dmitri—"

The man with the slick-backed hair dipped his head forward.

"And Emile."

The other guard didn't move at all. He seemed to have frozen, statue-like.

"*Where is the princess?*" Alexandre demanded again.

"Charmed to meet you," Holden replied. "And she's incoming."

He saw Eric's lips move to silently mouth... "*Fuck.*"

Yep. "Don't worry." He was trying really, really hard not to worry. "Constantine has her. He takes the job of guarding her body very seriously." Oh, yes, he did. "They'll be along shortly."

Alexandre spun toward Eric. His two guards followed suit. "I'm not paying to be kept *waiting,*" Alexandre snapped. There was a noticeable accent in his words. Not French, but close. A whisper that dipped and flowed and thickened with his anger.

"No, you're not," Eric agreed. His voice had iced. "You're paying to make certain that she's safe. Juliet Laurent *is* safe. She's in the building right now, and she'll be joining us very soon. Until then, we'll just continue our pleasant chat."

Holden had the feeling the chat hadn't been pleasant at all.

Alexandre motioned to his guards. "Go find her. Bring her to me, now."

The men immediately strode for the door.

Holden was still in front of the door, so he blocked their path. "That's a terrible idea. Truly terrible." Someone had to tell them.

They glowered.

"She's being guarded. Her guard does not know you. You come at her, you try to take her anywhere she doesn't want to go—even if that is just a short walk down the hallway—and I think that guard will enjoy kicking your asses."

"*I* am paying that bodyguard," Alexandre stated flatly. "He'll do exactly what I say."

Holden had to laugh. The dude was hilarious.

But Alexandre didn't smile back.

"Oh." Holden realized, "You're not joking." A shake of his head. "That's precious."

# CHAPTER SEVEN

*Step Seven: Slay all her dragons. They deserve it.*

"Breathe, Juliet."

"I *am* breathing!" she snapped back.

Okay, yes, she was. Breathing hard and fast and her cheeks had flushed and her eyes glittered with tears and she made him want to drive his fist into the elevator wall. No, he wanted to find the bastard who'd torched her house and drive his fist into that jerk's face. Again and again.

"Then...try taking deeper breaths? Slower ones?" That was supposed to help calm a person, wasn't it? Deep breathing? He put his hand on her back. Stroked her in what he hoped was a soothing manner.

"My house is gone?" She bit her lower lip. "All of it? Everything?"

If it wasn't yet, it would be. Raven had been clear that one hell of a fire was busy engulfing the home at 280 Second Street, and by the time the firefighters put out the blaze, there would barely be any sodden remains. "We'll get you new stuff."

"I don't want new things. I want what I had!"

Yeah, he could certainly understand that, but she wasn't going to have a choice in the matter.

"Why?" Pain. "Why would someone do this to me?"

He had a suspicion, and he damn well didn't like it. But Constantine couldn't voice that suspicion to her, not yet. "We'll find out." A promise. "Trust me?"

"I-I do."

His heart ached. "I won't let you down. Wilde will find out who is behind this, and we'll get him locked away. He will pay for what he did."

She swiped her hand over her cheek. "I never thought I was the vengeful type. I wanted to heal people, not hurt them."

He got that about her.

"But I am so angry right now." Her hand fell and balled into a fist. "I'm angry and scared, and I feel lost. Everything I knew is just gone."

"I'm not gone. I'm right here." Where he intended to stay.

"My bodyguard."

*I'm whatever you want me to be.* He didn't say those words. If he said them, there would be no taking them back. "Right. That's what I am."

"I-I have to go to the meeting."

Screw the meeting. "We don't have to go any-damn-where."

That response made her lips kick into a tremulous half-smile. "Not like we can hide in the elevator forever."

"I can take you back downstairs." An offer that just spit out from him. "We can go for a drive. You can clear your head. You just had a big shock, and if you need some time for yourself, then you take it."

"That's really sweet of you."

Was it? Shit. Maybe he was sick. A cold? Not the flu. He hated the freaking flu.

"But I need to just get this over with before something else happens. At this rate, I'm afraid to discover what might be coming at me next." She straightened her shoulders.

Constantine realized he was still rubbing her back. Hell. He pulled his hand away.

"You can open the elevator doors again. We'll do this, but..." Her long lashes flickered. "You promise to stay with me?"

"Yes."

"Thank you."

He hit the button. The elevator doors opened.

And two dumbass, goon-looking bozos stood in his path. "We want her," one snapped.

*What the fuck?*

And the dick with too much goo in his hair made a fatal mistake. He grabbed for Juliet.

Oh, the hell, no.

Constantine caught that grabbing arm and twisted. As the goon screamed in pain, Constantine distinctly heard Holden announce, "I tried to warn you. Should have listened to me."

The other bastard came at Constantine, swinging, so Constantine let his own fists fly.

\*\*\*

"Well..." Eric Wilde tapped his fingertips on the top of his desk. "This has certainly been an eventful morning so far, yes?"

With her back ramrod straight, Juliet sat in one of the two chairs across from his desk. She was in the chair to the left, while a brown-haired man with bright blue eyes sat in the right chair. Alexandre Aude, the counsellor of Lancaden. Tense introductions had been made moments before.

"You need to fire that bodyguard," Alexandre demanded, voice hot and accent sharp. "He attacked my men."

"Aw, come on," the muttered exclamation came from Holden as he stood near the wall a few feet away. His arms were crossed over his chest. "Constantine barely roughed them up at all. And, honestly, they had it coming. I warned them. I know you heard me warn them because you were right in this very room when I did so."

Constantine's shoulders pressed against the wall, too. He didn't look stressed. Not even mildly concerned. Actually, if anything, he seemed almost bored. "Doing my job," Constantine stated like it was just a simple fact. "Protecting her. Two jerks come rushing at her—two men I'd never seen before—what else could I do but teach them a few manners on how to approach a lady properly?"

Alexandre's cheeks flushed. "You should be—"

"Commended," Eric interrupted. "Because Constantine *was* doing his job. I told your men to stand down." Anger snapped in his words. "This is my building, and I'm the one who gives orders here. They had no business storming to that elevator and trying to physically drag Juliet into this office."

Her head turned toward him. Her stiff posture didn't relax. She couldn't relax. All she could do was fight hard to hold herself together. *My home was torched. Everything I had in that house is probably gone.*

"You have my apologies," Eric told her with an incline of his head. "You should feel safe here. A situation like that will never, ever happen again."

"*You kicked my bodyguards out onto the street!*" Alexandre surged to his feet. "They deserve the apology. They deserve—"

"They deserved to be taught manners," Constantine informed him. "They can lick their wounded pride for a moment. When you leave, they can follow you."

Alexandre whirled to face him. "I thought I was supposed to be getting the best that Wilde had to offer."

"You did." Constantine motioned between him and a glaring Holden. "You're welcome."

Alexandre's nostrils flared as he angled his body away from Constantine and Holden and back toward Juliet. He towered over her as she remained sitting in the lush chair. "Do not worry. You will not have to deal with that bodyguard's uncivilized behavior much longer. I'm sure it has been trying for you."

No, not particularly. "He's helped me. I'm grateful to Constantine."

Did she just hear a gritted curse? From Constantine? Her stare jumped to him, and she saw that his jaw had clenched even more.

"Yes." Alexandre straightened his tie. "We're all very grateful that you were delivered safely."

Delivered? "I'm not a package."

Alexandre sat back down in his chair. Exhaled slowly. "Now that you have—"

He'd better not say that she'd been delivered again.

"Arrived," he nodded, "we can move on to the real business at hand."

Yes, they should do that.

He smiled at her. It was a charming smile. One that made his eyes gleam and flashed a dimple in his right cheek. Not a slant like Constantine had, but a real, dipping dimple. Alexandre looked engaging, warm.

But ice slid down her spine.

"Your grandfather wishes to see you."

A lump rose in her throat.

"The doctors are not certain how much time is left." Alexandre's lips curled down with sadness. "So speed is of the utmost importance."

She could hear the hard drumming of her heartbeat echoing in her ears. "How long has he known about me?"

Alexandre's eyelids flickered.

She took that response to mean...*a very long time.* "Since I was born?" Juliet guessed.

"What matters now is that your grandfather— the king—wishes to end this unnecessary rift with his granddaughter."

So, yes, he had known about her since she was born. And he just hadn't cared. "Did he keep thinking someone else—someone better—would come along to take the crown?"

He leaned toward her and put his well-manicured hand on the armrest of her chair. "Your grandmother tried to kill him. He wasn't even certain your mother was his child when she was born, and by the time he had proof, the king had already remarried and started a new life."

"My grandmother wouldn't have done that. She would *not* have tried to kill him." Yes, the woman had certainly possessed her faults, but her grandmother hadn't been a killer.

A line appeared between his brows. "Yes, she would have. She did, in fact. She hired one of the deadliest assassins known in Europe at the time—a man she was having an affair with, by the way—and she gave him her ring as a down payment. She wanted the king dead before he could replace her with someone younger and prettier and—"

"You have no fucking tact, do you?" Constantine snapped. "How about you take a freaking second and back off?"

Constantine's hand closed around her shoulder. She hadn't even realized that he'd left his position near the wall. He'd moved on silent steps, swiftly, and his touch pushed aside the cold that had spread through her.

Alexandre looked at Constantine's hand on Juliet's shoulder. Then at Juliet's face. His gaze hardened. A quick flash. One that was smoothed away in the next instant. "Thank you for bringing

Juliet to me. I know that you probably had to use some...unfortunate tactics to get the job done."

What in the world was he talking about now? Constantine hadn't used any "unfortunate tactics" during their time together.

Alexandre sighed. "I was warned that you would have no interest in seeing the king. I passed that intel along to Wilde." He reclined back in his chair but kept his head turned toward her. "Perhaps that is why Wilde had no choice but to leak your story to the press? Once you couldn't hide in plain sight any longer, they knew you'd realize you had no choice but to accept your heritage."

She nearly bolted right out of her seat. "No." No, he was wrong.

Constantine's hold tightened on her. "You will want to tread very, very carefully," he said to Alexandre, the words a lethal warning that was clear to everyone.

But Alexandre shrugged. "I applaud your cold-blooded work ethic. Truly, I do. As a person in a position of power, I understand that sometimes we must make difficult decisions in order to meet the end goal. If you hadn't told the press about her, then Juliet could have kept right on living her small life in Baton Rouge."

Okay. The guy was a dick. And the drumming of her heartbeat had doubled. She rose, aware that her knees shook. "Constantine is right. You desperately need to work on your tact." *Boom. Boom. Boom.* Her heartbeat seemed to shake her body, but her voice came out surprisingly steady. She'd been trained by the best, after all. Her grandmother had told her to always keep her emotions in check.

*The same grandmother who hired an assassin?*

Alexandre looked up at her with mild surprise on his face.

"Just so you know, there is no small life in this world. Just some people who happen to think small because they don't bother to understand others out there. I believe I may be looking at one of those individuals." She let her stare linger on him. "Our meeting has been interesting, but as Eric pointed out, it has been an eventful morning. I find myself feeling very tired, so I am going back to my hotel. I do hope that you know it's been a rare pleasure having the chance to speak with you."

Behind her, she heard Constantine choke out a laugh. She knew he'd picked up on her deliberate use of "rare pleasure" to describe her feelings for Alexandre.

She turned toward Constantine. "And if what he said is true..." *No, no, it can't be true. Constantine, tell me it's not true.* "I hope you know our time together will be remembered as the rarest possible pl—"

He lost his laughter. "It's not true. I would not sell you out. I was there to protect you, not to feed you to the frenzy of reporters."

Juliet searched his eyes. She wanted his words to be true. She desperately needed them to be.

"I no longer require Wilde's services," Alexandre said. "Please tally up my bill, and I will settle the account. As of now, Wilde is no longer engaged in the protection of Princess Juliet Laurent."

Because she was still staring at Constantine, she saw the fury flash on his face. It was a fury she didn't understand.

"You sonofabitch," he breathed. She was pretty sure that he was about to leap right at Alexandre.

Alexandre must have feared the same thing because he shot out of his chair and scurried away. "When you walk out of the building, Juliet," Alexandre spoke quickly, as if he feared he didn't have much time, "you will be on your own. No Wilde guard shielding you from the press and none of my guards either—unless, of course, you decide that you wish to accompany me to Lancaden. Then you will have the full protection given to the royal family. You will be guarded twenty-four, seven, and you won't have to worry about any unfortunate attacks from—"

"*You know,*" Constantine charged. "You know everything that went down in Louisiana. You had someone in Baton Rouge, didn't you? Someone reporting to you on what happened."

Her head was spinning.

"Do you mean...do I know about the break-in at her house? It's all over social media, so, of course, I am aware." A smooth reply from Alexandre. "As for the fire, I learned about that terrible incident while you were pummeling my guards."

"He was teaching them manners," Holden corrected. He'd moved away from the wall and come up on Alexandre's side. "Thought we went over that part."

Alexandre jerked, as if he'd forgotten about Holden. Considering that Holden had been quiet and still for the last few moments, maybe he had.

"I don't think you're doing a very good job of handling this situation," Eric informed Alexandre. His voice was tinted with definite censure. "You told me that you wanted to meet Juliet. That you wanted to present your case to her."

"The case is simple." Alexandre thrust back his shoulders. "It's time for you to come home, princess. Whatever happened in the past is over. Your life in Baton Rouge is over. Your future is in Lancaden."

"That's her decision," Holden pointed out. "Her choice. Not yours."

"There is no choice." Alexandre's eyes remained on her. "You go back to Baton Rouge, and apparently, you'll be walking straight back to some insane person who has a sick obsession with you. You will be without the benefit of guards—"

"You're right, Con," Holden drawled. "Definite sonofabitch."

"And you will be swarmed by the media. I think you've already gotten a taste of how determined they can be." A low exhale from Alexandre as he seemingly ignored Holden's taunt. "Princess, you looked quite panicked in that video—the video that I believe was taken behind a bar? You were on the ground, on your hands and knees, and there was no escape."

The moisture dried from her mouth.

What *could* have been sympathy flashed for just an instant on Alexandre's face. "I am what I have to be," he said suddenly.

She shook her head.

"The country comes first. It always must. You'll understand that soon enough. I have to get you there. Your grandfather needs you. So I have to do whatever is necessary in order to see the king's wishes carried out." He took three quick steps toward her. "You will love it in Lancaden." His voice dropped. "You will live in luxury. You will have everything you could ever desire, and you will be protected at all times. There will be no dangerous threats that are allowed near you. You will be home, where you belong."

She didn't trust him. But did she think he would do "whatever was necessary" for Lancaden? Absolutely. And that was chilling, not reassuring. "If my grandfather knew about me when I was born, then he always knew where I was." Because she'd been born in Baton Rouge. Grew up there. "If he knew, why did you have to hire Wilde to find me—"

The shaking of his head interrupted her words. "Your grandmother sent him a picture of you when you were born. The same way she sent a picture of your mother. He knew you existed, but he had no idea *where* you were. Over the years, he hired dozens of investigative firms to track you. They failed in their efforts."

"Maybe he should have started with Wilde," Eric suggested. "Could have moved the whole process along faster if he'd come to us sooner."

Alexandre's head swung toward him. "We thought she was in Europe. Most likely in France. That was where the letters he received were postmarked. The queen had so many resources, so many contacts all over the world. They hid her when she first escaped. Gave her new identities over the years. His search for his daughter and granddaughter proved fruitless, until word of the discovered ring reached us." His head turned back to Juliet. "I'm not sure if you heard the story, but Wilde recovered a ring that belonged to your grandmother. The jewel that an exiled queen tried to use in order to murder her king."

Goosebumps rose on her arms.

"That ring led me to Wilde. And then they led me to you." He reached for her hand. Clasped it between both of his. "You are needed in Lancaden. It is the only path forward for you. Come with me, and you'll be safe." He squeezed her hand and then let her go.

His touch hadn't warmed her. It had just chilled her even more.

"But refuse me," Alexandre stared almost mournfully at her, "and you will be on your own. Are you truly ready to face the pack of wolves that will come for you without my protection, princess?" He glanced down at his watch. "Why don't you take a few minutes to think about my offer? I'll just step outside and make sure Eric's assistant has my bill ready to go."

No one spoke until he exited. And then...

"Yes," Eric noted with certainty. "You gentleman are right. That guy is a complete sonofabitch."

# CHAPTER EIGHT

*Step Eight: Be prepared to lie. To steal. To betray. All part of the job. And the job...it's her.*

"Holden, why don't you escort Ms. Laurent to our private break area for clients? I think she deserves some time to relax and think for a bit." Eric's tone was polite, almost warm, but Constantine noticed the faint tightness near his mouth.

*Yep, Eric's pissed. We both are.* Understatement. That sonofabitch Alexandre thought he was going to just take Juliet away?

*Not happening.* But Constantine wasn't tossing out all his suspicions about the guy, not yet. Not until it was just him talking one-on-one with the boss.

Juliet exhaled slowly. "That sounds like a very good idea, but first, may I ask..." She licked her lips as she straightened her shoulders. "Just how much is the going rate for daily Wilde bodyguard protection?"

Eric's gaze slid to Constantine.

Constantine shook his head.

And, dammit, Juliet turned in time to catch that movement. Pain flashed on her face. "Oh, I see." A brisk nod. "You don't wish to work with me any longer? I, ah, fine." Her cheeks flushed but she still managed to look so incredibly dignified as she gave him a fucking *understanding* smile. "I'm sure this whole case was more than you bargained for, and I certainly can understand you wanting to take a step back." She directed her gaze at Holden. "I would very much like a few moments in that break room now, please."

"Right this way." Holden glared at Constantine. One of those what-the-hell-are-you-thinking glares.

Ignoring his partner, Constantine stepped into Juliet's path before she could flee. And fleeing—*from me*—was exactly what she was doing. "It's not you I don't want to work with." Blunt. "I don't want to be taking orders from that Alexandre asshole. I don't trust him."

Eric coughed. "Uh, Constantine? Remember our talk about what to say and not say in front of clients?"

Yeah. He remembered. And he'd planned to hold back—for a while—but then he'd made pain appear on Juliet's face.

"I don't trust him, either," she whispered. "But what choice do I have?" Her long lashes swept up. Her eyes were dark pools of worry. "Everything I had before is gone. Within such a short time—*gone*. And if I don't go with him to Lancaden, what's going to happen to me?"

"I will protect you." A vow.

"Not anymore, you can't. Because you're not my bodyguard any longer." She sucked in a breath. "I'd really like some time alone."

Hell. He moved to the side, but tossed a pointed stare at Holden. "Stand guard outside the break room. No one enters, understand? Definitely not—"

"Oh, you don't even have to say his name." Holden saluted. "I've got this." He bent at the waist, making a fairly decent bow to Juliet before straightening. "This way, princess. Bet there's even some crazy-expensive, deluxe coffee waiting for you."

Constantine's gaze remained on Juliet until the office door closed behind her. As soon as it did, he spun to confront Eric. "What the hell? Since when does Wilde work with such absolute pricks?"

"Do you have any idea how much money that prick paid us?"

"Like I give a shit?" He stalked toward Eric's desk and slapped his hands down on the surface. "And the man I *thought* you were—he wouldn't give a shit, either."

Eric lifted a brow. "I'm sorry. Are *you* the same guy who is the best friend of an international criminal? Who participated in more shady deals with the FBI and the CIA than I can even imagine?"

"Oh, really? Gonna bring all of that up now?" Typical. "When I interviewed for the job at Wilde, you said that my contacts would be beneficial. That my past could be an asset."

"*In certain situations,*" Eric clarified. "I told you that your past could be an asset *in certain situations.*" A pause. His head inclined toward

Constantine. "This would probably be one of those situations."

His shoulders stiffened. "You have my attention."

"Did I not always have it?"

No, he'd been focused on Juliet. Still was. "We aren't letting her walk out of here without protection. Not after some bastard left a knife in her bed and then torched her place."

Eric tapped his chin. "What makes you think it was the same person doing those acts?"

Now that question gave him pause. "The fact that they were both committed within such a close span of time? Do we really think she has two freaks on her tail?" He hoped to hell not. "One is bad enough." But then when you added in Alexandre to the mix... "Unless someone was *paying* for her to be targeted." His suspicion. One he could voice to Eric now that they were alone. "Because it certainly seems possible to me that if you wanted to force Juliet to visit her dying grandfather, then you'd eliminate everything that kept her tied to Baton Rouge."

"Her house is gone," Eric noted. He winced. "I got the news right before you walked in."

"She can't go back to her job." The bar wouldn't be safe for her. "At least she can finish up her degree work." One thing Juliet wouldn't lose. But as for the easy, carefree life she'd had in Louisiana...*over*. "Her image has been splashed everywhere. She has no anonymity. She'll be mobbed wherever she goes."

Eric nodded in agreement. "It takes people a while to forget. And when you're dealing with a missing princess who just happened to be found in the US..." His lips tightened. "Forgetting will take even longer."

And in the meantime... "Alexandre isn't going to give up."

"Nope. I don't think he understands the concept," Eric agreed.

"His freaking goons tried to physically *take* her from the elevator." What if they tried that crap again? What if—without Wilde protection—they found Juliet and they forced her onto a plane to Lancaden? "You don't actually think they'd pull some kidnapping shit with her, do you?"

"I think the laws in Lancaden are different from those in the US, and that's a big part of the problem we face."

An ache built behind his right eye. "You can't tell me they allow kidnapping. Not happening."

"No, but...if she gets back to that country—if she goes there of her own free will—then once she gets to Lancaden, she *will* have to follow the laws."

"She's the princess. She should be able to do whatever the hell she wants."

"Not quite how Lancaden is set up. There are lots of checks on royal power. In fact, many say that since his illness took over, the king is nothing more than a figurehead. The real power—that would rest with the gentleman that we both think is a sonofabitch."

What a clusterfuck.

"Alexandre would be in charge of her guards once she reached that country. And he could tell those guards what to do and what not to do. If he didn't want her getting access to leave the country, if he wanted to force her to stay there, that could very well happen."

There was nothing about this conversation that Constantine enjoyed. "You're saying she could become his prisoner?"

"Until *she* gets the throne. Yes, that would be a possibility."

"Then we can't let her go there!" Obviously. "We will set her up with a safe house." He considered possibilities as he shoved away from the desk and began to pace. "I can get her a new identity with a snap." He snapped his fingers. Kept pacing. "She can have a new life away from the press and the drama of the crown. She can set up a counseling practice and live below the radar. She can—"

"Make her own choice?" Eric cleared his throat. "Because the king is her only living relative. And he's dying. Seems to me that someone like Juliet might want to see him."

*Someone like Juliet.* Constantine stopped his pacing. Whirled back toward Eric. "What's that supposed to mean?"

"I read the dossier on her, too. She's spent the last two years volunteering at a shelter for abused women and children. Before that, she worked at a homeless shelter in Baton Rouge. She mentors kids in the afternoons when she doesn't have classes. She hasn't even gotten so much as a speeding ticket." Eric's lips curled down. "A nice person. Good. Someone who probably doesn't have it in her to deny a dying grandfather his last wish."

"Even if that grandfather denied *her* for Juliet's entire life?" Another thing that pissed him off.

"You tell me." Eric walked around the desk, but only so he could prop a hip on the front as he studied Constantine. "You think she'll tell the king to fuck off or will she get on a plane to try and give him some closure even as she attempts to find out the truth about her past? Because I don't think Juliet bought that her grandmother was the villain in this story. I saw her eyes."

Constantine had, too.

"I think she's gonna want to find out the truth for herself."

Dammit, Constantine did, too. "So we send Wilde guards with her." *We send me with her.* No way could she fly off alone.

"And who will pay for those guards?"

*"I will,"* he returned instantly. "I will pay for all manpower and any expenses that arise from the case." He wasn't working at Wilde for the cash. Over the years, Constantine had acquired plenty of wealth on his own. Why *was* he working Wilde? To settle the old justice scales. To do something *not* illegal.

"Thought you might say something like that. But that would just be solving part one of the problem. Part two? That would occur the minute the plane touched down on foreign soil. If Alexandre didn't want you close to Juliet, then he could make sure you were not allowed near her once you arrived at Lancaden. He could deem you a threat to her. Could say that his guards were taking over. Basically, the same shit he tried to pull here, he will do there. Only he'll be back in his territory, so he'd have the power to get it done."

This situation *sucked*. And it sure looked like Constantine had to find a way to keep Juliet off the plane—

"Unless..." Eric said. Then he stopped. "Forget it."

Constantine's eyes narrowed as he stalked toward his boss. "Seriously? Do you think I'm in the mood for games?"

Eric regarded him with a questioning gaze.

"A knife in her bed," he rasped. "A fire at her house. She is not going *anywhere* without me. No way she leaves this building without me by her side."

"Sounds almost...personal to you."

Maybe it was. Did it matter?

"Which would be good," Eric surprised him by saying. "Because I had my legal department dig into Lancaden's laws a bit and, sure, some of them are freaking archaic as hell, but one in particular stood out to me as being something that we might be able to use, should the situation arise."

Was Eric trying to draw this big reveal out as slowly as possible? "Christmas is gonna be here again before you tell me this shit."

Eric almost smiled. But the flicker of a smile died away. "The princess can take a consort."

Constantine rocked back on his heels.

"The consort would be the person she *intends* to marry. If she publicly declares the person as her consort, then, by an outdated Lancaden law, well...they're joined. Juliet and her consort. He will have as much power as she does. No one would be able to keep them apart because the consort must always have full access to his partner."

He'd gotten stuck on one big part. *The person she intends to marry.*

"A consort is only allowed in special cases, like when a princess or prince is about to assume the throne, so the timing in this instance would work very well for us since the assumption is that Juliet will be getting that crown."

"You want me to marry her?"

Eric slid off the edge of the desk so that he stood in front of Constantine. "Slow down. No one is asking you to put a ring on her finger."

*But I could.* Fuck. Okay, yes, he needed to slow the hell down. "I'm hardly consort material."

"That's why it would be *pretend*. Keyword there. *Pretend*. It's a cover, like any other cover that the bodyguards at Wilde take in order to stay close to their clients. We're done working with Alexandre, so she would be the client. She would have to agree to the charade, have to go public with you and your pretend relationship, but then, once she does, no one would be able to part you from her."

"What about my past?" he asked, voice grim.

Eric's eyes widened in mock surprise. "What about it?"

"You know what I am."

"I know you can speak seven languages."

More like nine.

"*You* know Europe like the back of your hand, Constantine. If necessary, I think you could probably slip past Alexandre's guards with Juliet and disappear into one of the many safe houses that you've set up over the years."

His safe houses. Not Wilde's. Constantine noted the distinction and filed it away for later. *Eric is saying I may need to go way off grid.* Not like it would be the first time.

Expression considering, Eric continued, "And unlike someone who doesn't have your distinct and intriguing past, I think you know how to blend in very easily with different groups of people. If you want to be noble, you can bullshit all day with the wealthy. If you want to be dangerous, the crime lords in the area would think you were one of them in a blink."

Because he had been both, depending on the situation. Noble and dangerous.

"Your particular skills are the reason I first paired you with Juliet."

Now they were getting to the real point. "You suspect Alexandre is dirty."

"I suspect he's had a real taste of power since the king has been ill. In my experience, people don't willingly give up power. In fact, they do whatever is necessary to maintain that power."

He took the warning for exactly what it was. "You only took him on as a client so that I would bring Juliet to Wilde." The puzzle pieces had clicked. Sometimes, Eric was downright diabolical.

"I thought Juliet might need a Wilde agent on her side. I was right." A roll of one shoulder. "This isn't my first time to play a long game. My name is on the building for a reason, and it's not just because of my dashing good looks."

Constantine shook his head. "I swear, the way you talked just then, you almost reminded me of—"

"Remy?"

Constantine clamped his lips together. But, yeah, he'd been about to say that Eric bore a similarity to Remy. *Rembrandt.*

"Is your best friend still attempting to walk the straight and narrow?" Eric inquired.

"He's married now. Settled down. And he's gone one hundred percent legit." That was his story, and Constantine was sticking to it. He turned away from his boss. Time to present this idea to Juliet. The big presentation would probably go something like...

*Eric and I came up with a great plan. To set the plan in motion, all you have to do is go in front of the press and tell the world that you are madly in love with me. Super easy.*

Uh, huh.

"You might need him on this one."

Constantine stopped before the door. "Excuse me?" He turned toward Eric, sure he must have misheard.

"Remy is someone that will be unexpected. Only you are fully aware of his reach."

"Are you seriously telling me to call in *Remy?*" In what universe would Eric want his help?

"I'm saying it wouldn't be too bad to have a few friends in the pocket. I can and will send Holden with you, but Alexandre will try to keep him away from you and Juliet once you reach Lancaden. Not like we can claim he's her consort, too."

Constantine's hands clenched. "No, we can't," he snapped back.

A nod of Eric's head. "You'll have as much support as Wilde can give you, but I will trust that you will pull in your own resources as necessary."

Eric was telling him to go off book. One of Constantine's favorite things to do. "Message received." Now, he just had to convince Juliet to go along with the plan. Once more, he turned and reached for the doorknob.

"You're willing to risk a lot for someone you've known for such a short amount of time."

He didn't look back. "Like you said, she's a good person."

"Right. I'm certain that's the reason."

Constantine yanked open the door and stalked after his princess. It didn't take long to reach the break room. Or technically, he thought it might be called the "Client Calming Room" or some kind of BS like that. A place for nervous clients to take a breather while they were surrounded with luxury and security.

Holden stood at attention in front of the door leading to that room. When he saw Constantine approaching, Holden stepped forward. "No sign of Alexandre or his crew."

"I doubt that Alex the Asshole has left the building." Not without Juliet.

"You and Eric come up with a plan?"

"Sure, in a manner of speaking." He just needed a tactful way to present it to Juliet.

"Wanna share the plan with your partner?"

No sense using tact with Holden. "She's gonna be my fiancée." He swiped his keycard over the lock on the door and stepped inside.

Before the door shut behind him, he heard Holden mutter, "Oh, yeah, sure, great plan. I bet she'll love it."

Constantine knew sarcasm when he heard it. But the moment he got a look at Juliet, sitting on the couch with her back stiffly straight again, with her hands locked together and her face carefully expressionless, all his plans for tact went straight to hell.

He hurried toward her.

Her head tilted back as she stared up at him. "Perhaps you can refer me to a different bodyguard who would be willing to take my case? Another agency? One with reasonable fees."

"You have a fucking kingdom waiting for you. You don't have to worry about reasonable."

"Yes, I do." Her voice seemed to chill. "It's not my money. I have to pay for my own way." Her hands remained entwined. Her body carefully still as if she was almost afraid to move. "If you could just refer me—"

"No."

"No?" Her lashes fluttered.

"No, no other bodyguard."

"But, but you—" She stopped. Blew out a breath. The ripple of emotion—confusion, anger— left her face. "I see. Well, I don't—"

"You don't see." He needed to cut to the chase. "Any bodyguard you bring in from the US will get sidelined the minute you set foot in Lancaden.

Alexandre will separate you and you'll be surrounded by *his* team."

"I had started to worry about that very thing," she confessed.

"That's why just any bodyguard won't do."

"Then what do I need?"

"Me, sweetheart, you need me." A brief pause. "And you need to marry me."

# CHAPTER NINE

*Step Nine: Go the extra mile. You need to travel
to a foreign country with her? Done. You need
to bring in some shady characters for backup?
Easy. You need to fake an engagement? Why the
hell not? Just remember...it's all for the case.*

"I think I misunderstood you," Juliet stated
with precise care. Probably because her
drumming heartbeat had drowned out part of his
words. "Could you repeat what it is that you
believe I need?"

"Me."

"Yes, I got that part." After watching him
easily take out those two men at the elevator, she
certainly knew he had fighting skills. Constantine
had put those two hulking men down with barely
any effort at all. An impressive feat to watch.

"You need to marry me," he said.

Ah, yes, that was the part Juliet thought she'd
misunderstood before. The words were so wild
that she'd been sure they had to be a mistake, but,
no, Constantine had just stated them very clearly,
and he stared down at her face with stark
determination plain to see in his expression.

It was a good thing she was sitting, because
Juliet was pretty sure the shock of his

pronouncement might have made her knees buckle. "You want to marry me?"

"It's only pretend. Not the real deal."

*Do not change your expression.*

"You know about the consort rule at Lancaden?" Constantine asked.

A little. After finding out who she was, Juliet had done some digging. Fine. She'd done a lot of digging on Lancaden. "The consort is the person that..." In her case... "The person who is the princess's personal companion."

"Intimate companion," he corrected.

She shifted a bit on the incredibly comfortable couch.

"The person you plan to marry," Constantine continued in his low, rumbly voice. "That individual is provided with unlimited royal access, as determined by some old Lancaden law. We don't have to be married, we just have to say that we are planning to wed. As soon as we do that, I can accompany you anywhere in Lancaden, and Alexandre won't be able to do a damn thing to separate us."

*Not real. Not real.*

"It will just be pretend. I'm not trying to get my hands on your title or your fortune. It's just for your protection."

Her protection. Check. Not like he was going to pretend to be her lover just because he wanted to get close to her or because he wanted to put his hands on her body.

"Juliet? What are you thinking?"

Dammit. Had her cheeks flushed? "I never thought you wanted my money."

"And I'm definitely not after the title. I'm the last person anyone would ever want being king of some country."

"It's not my title. My grandfather is still alive."

"And you want to see him." His lips thinned. "You want to talk to the man before he dies, and you think that you'll be able to find out the truth about what your grandmother did or didn't do all those years ago."

"Yes." Though she was a bit surprised that Constantine knew her so well.

"I get it, I do. I'd want the truth, too." His hand lifted. His fingers brushed over her cheek. "But it's not safe there for you alone."

Maybe. And her mother's old warning about Lancaden did give her more than a little pause. *They want to kill us. Never step foot in that country. Never.* But her mother had just been repeating what she'd been told over the years. What if her mother had been wrong? *What if my grandmother was the villain in the story?* The uncertainty had her head spinning. "The attacks have been here in the US. It's highly unlikely that the person who did that stuff in Baton Rouge will follow me across the Atlantic Ocean." What she'd been telling herself, over and over again. But as far as any potential threats *in* Lancaden...

*Having Constantine at my side would make me feel so much safer.*

"There's a country at stake, sweetheart." His strong, warm fingers lingered against her cheek. "For all we know, Alexandre is behind the attacks in Baton Rouge. I told Eric I didn't trust him, and I fucking don't. Alexandre could be manipulating things so that you have to go back with him, and once there..." He stopped.

"Once there, what?" He couldn't just leave her hanging.

Constantine's hand fell away from her. "Maybe he wants to rule. Maybe you're his ticket to doing just that."

Despite everything, a surprised laugh sputtered from her, and Juliet found herself surging to her feet. "What are you suggesting? That he's going to try and marry me? That he will seduce me in order to get the crown?"

*"Not fucking happening."*

"Well, yes, that's what I'm saying. It's preposterous." Laughable. That was why she was laughing. "I'm sure he has no interest in—"

"In what?" Constantine pushed when she broke off and floundered. "Ruling a country? Having a crown? Having sex with the most beautiful woman he's ever seen? A woman he can't get out of his head?"

Silence.

"Oh, wait." Constantine's lips twisted. "I might have been talking about myself there at the end." He spun away from her and took several determined steps toward the door.

"Don't mock me." Brittle. Her spine straightened as she stared after him.

His broad back stiffened.

"I get that you're in a bad situation and now you feel duty bound to keep staying with me and even possibly taking up this crazy charade..."

"Duty bound?" He turned slowly toward her. "That's what we're saying I feel?"

It was what she'd just said, yes. "But you don't have to make fun of me. You told me the kiss was a mistake. If we go through with this..." *Crazy, impossible plan that might be the only option I have.* "I promise to keep my hands off you. Does that make you feel better?" Wow. She'd just taunted him. She didn't normally taunt anyone.

With his gaze never leaving her, Constantine strode back to her side. He reached out and caught her hand.

Her breath whispered out.

He put her hand on his chest. Kept it there with his warm and strong grip. "Won't work."

That stupid heat surged through her. The man was just some kind of human furnace, and his heat swept over her whenever they touched.

"In order for the world to believe we're a couple, you'll have to put your hands on me, princess. I'll have to put my hands on you. We'll need to act like we're in love or I'll find my ass booted away from you, and that can't happen. Not until we can figure out what's really happening with these attacks on you. Or not until *you're* the one in charge of Lancaden, and everyone has to follow your orders."

"I don't want the crown."

"Too bad, because I think it's yours for the taking."

She should pull her hand free. So why wasn't she?

"Will you be able to handle my touch? My hands on you?" Constantine demanded.

"Yes." Why did her voice sound so husky? "It's just pretend, right? Putting on a show for the people who like to watch?"

"Then you agree to the game?"

*Game.* "I didn't say that."

His fingers slid down, caressing along the inside of her wrist. "Why not?"

Oh, just about a hundred different reasons. She grabbed the first one that flew through her head. "Because I don't think I can afford you. You wouldn't even tell me Wilde rates, and what you're talking about—going to Lancaden, staying there for an indefinite amount of time—the price must be astronomical." She shuddered to think about it. A hard, physical shudder.

"You have a kingdom waiting."

How many times did she have to tell him? *"And it's not my money."*

"Fine." A muscle jerked along his jaw even as his touch remained feather light on her. "Then how does this work for you? An anonymous donor has stepped in to provide for your protection."

"Lie," Juliet called.

"No, I assure you, it's quite truthful. Someone volunteered to foot the bill for your protection, so you do not need to worry about that aspect of the situation. The money isn't coming from your kingdom—sorry, your grandfather's kingdom. It's coming from some too rich asshole who should be parted with his wealth. Probably ill-gotten gains, knowing him."

Her breath rushed out. "Are you serious right now?"

His fierce gaze never left her face. "One hundred percent. Your bill is covered. Eric green-lit the trip to Lancaden. You want to go visit your dying grandfather, then I'll be at your side. If you agree to the cover, no one will be able to separate us. You can go to Lancaden, meet with him, and if you decide to stay, if you decide to rule, then soon you'll be making the decisions there and you can control all the royal guards. When we reach that point and it's safe, I'll step away. We'll feed the press some breakup story, and you'll never see me again."

"What if I don't decide to rule?"

His lashes flickered. "Then I'll spirit you away from there. I can make you disappear. Give you a new life, if that's what you want. And the world will just move on without their new Princess Juliet."

Did he mean those words? She bit her lower lip even as she tried to ignore the fact that, apparently, her inner wrist was now the most sensitive part of her body. "Why would you do all of this for me?" Quiet. Husky.

"Wilde service. We go the extra mile, and we fucking love undercover operations. I'm pretty sure that's the company motto or something."

She wouldn't let his attempt at humor distract her. "It's more than the extra mile. You'd be putting yourself in front of the world for me."

"Damn straight I would. That's my job as your bodyguard. To stand between you and the world."

"No, no, that's not what I mean." Juliet tugged her hand free. "I mean—the world will see you. Your face will be splashed everywhere." At the moment, she was still trying to get used to the idea of her face being everywhere. And he was willing to be thrown into that nightmare maelstrom with her? "Having your personal life destroyed isn't something you want. I've read tabloid stories before. They love to rip into people's lives. They'll pull up all your secrets and smear them across the internet."

His hand fell to his side. He stared at her with a gaze that seemed to glimpse right into her soul, and then Constantine laughed.

Her brows rose. "I don't think I made a joke." On the contrary, she'd been quite serious. "I'm trying to look out for you. It's your life, and I don't want you throwing it away for me."

His laughter—warm and rich though it had been—faded. "I know. It's new. Kinda fun."

She wasn't seeing the fun in this conversation. "I don't understand you."

"The press will find the secrets that I let them find. I've got a cover story in place. They'll discover what I want, nothing more. They'll be told what I let them know. You don't have to worry about me."

"I—"

"And we won't stray too far from our actual relationship."

"We have a relationship?"

"Um. Yes. I'm your bodyguard, remember? The reporters have no idea just how long I've been guarding that body of yours. For all they know, we've been together for weeks. Maybe months."

It *felt* as if they had been together for a long time, and not just the whirlwind that had occurred since he walked into the bar and said, *"I'm Constantine Leos, and I'm your bodyguard."*

"We'll say I fell in love with you while I was protecting you. We crossed lines. Desire got too intense. I couldn't keep my hands off you and you...you fell for my charming, good looks."

She swallowed.

"My incredible bravery," he continued without missing a beat. "My willingness to put you before everyone else in the world because you are the priority for me." His voice thickened. "You are the one who matters, and the longer we were together, we knew that we couldn't hold back our feelings. You wanted to be with me, and damn the consequences."

She did want to be with him. She did want to damn the consequences. The cover story wasn't so far from the truth, at least not for her, but... "I just don't understand why you would do this for me." Why would he give up so much?

"It's my job."

Hardly the undying declaration of passion that she'd hoped to get from him. But that was foolish, wasn't it? To secretly hope for something so dramatic. Of course, he wasn't helping her because Constantine actually wanted to be with her. He was helping her because he was probably going to get some insanely fat check from the anonymous donor who'd offered to foot the bodyguard bill. About that donor... "What does he want?" Juliet blurted.

Constantine backed up. Took a few steps away from her. She saw his fingers stretch and flex at his sides. "He?"

"Whoever is footing my bill. This stranger I don't know."

Constantine turned away. "He wants to do a good deed. What's so bad about that?"

"It depends. Is this one of those good deeds that will come back to bite me in the ass?" A blunt question when she usually exercised more tact.

More laughter spilled from him. Constantine shook his dark head. "You surprise me. You seem so elegant and poised, and then you say fun things like 'bite me in the ass.'"

Poised? Since when? Had he *looked* at her? She was about to fall into a thousand jagged pieces. "You didn't answer my question."

Constantine's eyes glittered as he glanced over his shoulder. "You want to know if the guy intends to bite that sweet ass of yours?"

"I—" Dammit. "What does he want?"

He turned fully toward her. "Maybe he wants to finally do one good thing in his life. Sometimes, that happens."

"How did he even know about me?"

Constantine tilted his head to the right. "Really?"

Ah. Yes. Her social media storm. "I will have to pay him back."

"Why the hell would you want to do that?"

"Because I can't owe some stranger that I don't know! I'll come up with a payment plan. I'll get us squared away."

"You can take the man on a tour of your castle."

When she opened her mouth to tell him a tour would hardly square things away with the mystery donor, Constantine sighed and said, "I'm sure he'll come up with some future request that will make you equal. Just forget about the payment for now, would you?"

"It's the 'future request' thing that worries me. How do I know he's not going to come demanding some—some—" But Juliet broke off because she didn't even know what to say.

Constantine lifted his eyebrows. "The guy isn't going to demand that you sleep with him to pay off the debt. The price isn't gonna be a night with a princess."

Her arms wrapped around her stomach. "Good to know because that wasn't an option that I had on the table."

That muscle jerked along his jaw once more. "Then we're clear. You're agreeing to have me continue as your bodyguard?"

"I want you."

At her stark confession, the gray in his eyes grew stormy. "You have me."

As her bodyguard. "I want you..." Juliet rushed to add, "because I trust you. You've helped me. You've been someone I can count on. Someone who is honest with me."

Constantine winced. "Slow down with that, would you? Let's not give me too much credit. I can assure you, I am a cold-blooded bastard most days."

She was the one to close the distance between them. She was the one who reached out and touched him this time. "And some days, you can be a knight in shining armor."

"Hardly my style." He looked down at her hand as it curled around his arm. "I think you should probably see me more as the royal executioner."

"I don't think Lancaden has one of those." Not anymore, anyway.

His head lifted. His eyes met hers. "You have one now. I'll eliminate any problem in your path. I will do whatever it takes to keep you safe. You have my absolute vow on that."

She believed him. "You make me feel safe." Her wicked feet crept a little closer to him. So close that their bodies brushed. The truth of the matter was that he made her feel a million different things. So many emotions that they blasted past her normal control.

She was the careful one. The one who didn't take risks. The one who didn't attract attention because that was how she'd been raised to be. To stay in the background. To never seek the limelight. When the truth about her family came out at the hospital, Juliet had realized why she'd been brought up that way. Secrecy had been a matter of survival.

Now, the time for secrecy had ended. Survival meant Constantine. "I want you to stay with me. Please."

"Done."

Her lips curled.

His gaze shifted to her mouth. "You in for everything?" Deeper. Rumbling. "You in for the show we'll have to present to the world?"

Acting like lovers, being close to him, touching him, pretending to be *in* love with him? "I can handle it, if you can."

"In my sleep." His head lowered toward her.

Constantine was going to kiss her. She wanted him to kiss her. But this wasn't for show. No gawking reporters were close by. If he kissed her now, then he was doing it just for them.

She wanted that. *Just for us. Just passion. Just need.* Juliet pressed up onto her toes so that she could reach his mouth—

A fist banged on the door. "Yo!" Holden called. "I got a pissed off counsellor out here who is demanding to see the princess. Says this is her last chance. Either she gets protection from the royal guards or she is on her own."

Juliet's and Constantine's mouths were separated by an inch. Maybe two. She wanted his mouth on hers.

"Do we have a deal?" Constantine whispered.

"Yes." A breath.

He pulled away. Turned away.

Startled, Juliet shook her head and stumbled back a step.

"Let him in!" Constantine shouted.

They weren't kissing. They weren't getting romantic or personal. They had to talk to that jerk Alexandre and the door was already flying open. Frantic, she schooled her expression even as she locked eyes with Alexandre. He filled the doorway, with Holden waiting at his back.

Alexandre opened his mouth.

Constantine pulled Juliet into his arms. Her body pressed tightly against him.

"I love you, too, sweetheart," Constantine declared clearly, distinctly, and then his mouth took hers.

# CHAPTER TEN

*Step Ten: Fight dirty. Fight hard. Be the bastard that everyone fears.*
*Everyone, but her.*

Fuck but she tasted *good*. She felt good. Better than good. Amazing. The kind of amazing that would haunt his dreams and fantasies for a long time to come. *More like forever.* He had his hands on her. Had his mouth on her. Was tasting and savoring and wanting to explore every single inch of her delectable body—

"What is the meaning of this? How *dare* you put your hands on her in this manner?"

Ah, yes. The reason he couldn't do all that fantastic exploring. Their audience. But, then again, the audience was also the reason for the kiss.

*I am such a freaking liar. I just wanted to kiss her. I didn't have to do it for the dick who sounds like he's strangling on his own words.*

Juliet gave a little jolt at Alexandre's snarl, but Constantine just kept right on kissing her.

Then he felt fingers close around his shoulder. A surprisingly strong grip for a jerk who spent his time giving orders on someone else's throne. Alexandre tried to use that grip to pull Constantine away from Juliet.

Laughable. He didn't get *pulled* from her.

So Constantine kissed her a little longer.

"*Stop!*" Alexandre thundered. "You are her bodyguard! How dare you—"

Now he lifted his head. Juliet's lashes had also lifted, and for just a moment, he got caught by her gaze. In that instant, he didn't hear the rest of Alexandre's rumbling words. Mostly because he didn't care about them. What did matter? The desire in Juliet's dark eyes. The soft need even as her cheeks pinkened with her embarrassment.

The desire—he could work with that. *She wants me as much as I want her.*

The embarrassment? That pissed him off. No one should make her feel embarrassed. *Not me and not him.* "Give me just a second, sweetheart." Ignoring the grip on his shoulder and the angry demands that still spewed from Alexandre, Constantine took her hand and raised it to his lips. He pressed a kiss to her knuckles. "I need to set an idiot straight."

"How *dare* you—" Alexandre sputtered.

Constantine let go of Juliet's hand and turned to face his new nemesis, breaking out of that stupid grip. He'd gone too long without a nemesis, so it was nice to have a new target. "You asked 'how dare' twice now. At least, I think it was twice. Maybe you asked it a third time, and I was too busy kissing her to notice."

Alexandre's mouth dropped open.

Constantine rolled his right shoulder. "Don't ever put your hands on me again." To be clear, as crystal as possible, he warned, "You do, and I'll break those fingers of yours."

"I am the *counsellor*—"

"And I am the consort," Constantine threw out with a shrug of that same shoulder. "A consort who doesn't give a shit about who you are. I've warned you, so what happens next will be on you. Grab me again, and those grabby fingers will be broken."

Shock washed across Alexandre's face. "What did you say?" His accent thickened.

"I said, 'Grab me again, and those grabby fingers will be broken.'" Constantine had certainly thought his words had been clear enough the first time, but he was more than happy to repeat himself.

A hard, negative shake of Alexandre's head. Alexandre took a lurching step to the side—so that he could lock his gaze on Juliet. "He's lying."

"No." Constantine rubbed his chin. "I am telling the truth. I will take extreme joy out of breaking—"

"You're not her consort! You're her bodyguard!" Spittle flew from his mouth.

A wide grin slowly curled Constantine's grin. "Ah, yes, I see the confusion." A nod. "I *was* her bodyguard. Then you fired me about...twenty minutes ago? Thirty? Well, when you did that, I realized that I no longer needed to hold my feelings in check for Juliet." He reached back to take her hand once again. His fingers threaded with hers. "But before I could even begin to tell her how much she has changed me, Juliet confessed her love."

Alexandre's face turned purple. "You *just* met her."

"And I, of course, had to immediately tell my sweet, wonderful Juliet that I love her, too," Constantine continued as if Alexandre hadn't so rudely interrupted. Constantine pursed his lips. "But perhaps you caught that part?" *Because I know that you did. I said it just so your prick self would overhear.*

Alexandre erupted into a spate of furious French. Like its nearby neighbor Monaco, Lancaden's official language was French, though many of the residents also spoke Greek, Italian, and English.

"Uh, no," Constantine retorted in English when Alexandre's eruption finally subsided. "I have no interest in fucking myself. But I certainly do appreciate you making the suggestion. *Merci beaucoup.*"

Alexandre's lips snapped together.

The man clearly needed to do some deep breathing exercises because that shade of purple looked alarming.

"Want to sit down?" Constantine offered, attempting to be helpful. "You seem rather flushed."

Alexandre glared at him, then at Juliet. "Tell me this is a lie."

Juliet raised her chin. "I love him."

His fingers squeezed hers even as an ache lodged in his chest. She didn't mean the words. Just as Constantine hadn't meant them when he'd said those words to her. Simply a ruse. Another cover. He'd had a million covers over the years.

So why did this feel different?

"When I go to Lancaden," Juliet continued in a voice that was clear and firm, "Constantine will be going with me, as my consort."

Alexandre took a step that brought him closer to Constantine. "You speak French."

Wasn't it obvious? *"Oui."*

"I'm sure she does, too." Alexandre's gaze flickered to Juliet, only to slit as his stare returned almost instantly to Constantine. *"Leos.* Your last name is Greek."

It was.

"I happen to speak Greek, too." Alexandre gave him a cold smile. And then, in perfect Greek, he said, *"You're nothing. You think you'll fuck a princess and get a crown? Think again. I will destroy you."*

Constantine smiled back at him even as his gut clenched. "I took some French back in school, but they didn't offer Greek classes." Absolute truth. But he'd learned Greek later when he spent seven months living in Athens. "Don't let the last name fool you. I was born and raised in the United States."

Alexandre's lashes flickered. "Oh, my mistake." A dip of his head. "I was just saying that I think you will find my country to be very beautiful on your trip. We will need to fly out immediately because time is, of course, of vital importance."

*You are such a jackass.* "Right away, check."

"I have a flight booked," Alexandre informed them. The rage still cracked through his words. "You and Juliet will be my guests—"

"No, I think Wilde will take care of our trip, but I do look forward to seeing you in Lancaden." A dismissal. Time for the guy to go so Constantine could get on with his plans.

The next step? A very public declaration between him and Juliet. Before they touched down in Lancaden, he needed the world to know they were together.

Alexandre didn't take the hint to leave.

Sighing, Constantine asked, "Is there something else I can do for you?"

"You? No." Alexandre took note of Constantine's hand as it curled around Juliet's, before he shifted his focus to her face. "But you, Juliet, you are very important. I am glad that you will be coming home."

*Home.*

"You will see that your grandfather isn't the man you've been told he was."

Constantine wasn't sure she'd been told anything about her grandfather's personal life. She'd seemed shocked over the realization that her grandmother had once tried to kill the man.

"You will need someone to guide you in Lancaden politics. Someone to tell you everything you need to know about the country. I will be happy to be your guide."

Right. Like Constantine hadn't seen that one coming.

"You and I will be a great team," Alexandre continued. The purple had finally lightened in his skin. "And I look forward to having you in the castle with me."

*Okay, this is where I want to tell you...go fuck yourself.*

Alexandre dipped low into an elegant bow. "Until next time, my princess."

Oh, the fuck, no. Had he really put a possessive emphasis on the *my* right then?

Smiling a bit smugly, Alexandre straightened, turned on his heel, and marched for the door.

Nope, not the way the scene would end.

Constantine brought Juliet's hand to his lips. Kissed her knuckles. Then realized what he'd just done. Hell, that caress hadn't been for show. It had just...*been*. He let her go. "Be right back."

Whistling, because he didn't want her to know quite what he had planned, and he did need to appear cool—for the moment—Constantine followed the counsellor into the hall. Outside that break room, he saw Holden lounging against a nearby wall.

"All good?" Holden asked, not moving from his relaxed pose.

No, it wasn't. But it would be. Alexandre had reached the elevator. He reached out to press the button on the outside control panel.

"Make sure Juliet doesn't leave that room," Constantine ordered Holden even as he closed in on his prey.

At his words, Alexandre jerked to attention. He spun around and came almost face to face with Constantine.

"Hi, there." Constantine didn't smile. What was the point? Juliet wasn't around to witness this scene. "I think you and I need to have a chitchat."

"Excuse me?"

"She's not your anything. She's mine."

"The princess belongs to the entire country, hardly to just one man."

Cute. "She's mine," Constantine said again. "You've been told, and you need to take that message and let it sink into your soul. You will not be taking her from me."

The sonofabitch shrugged. "We shall see."

The elevator doors dinged. When they slid open, it was so easy to imagine putting his hands on Alexandre, shoving the bastard back into that elevator, and going in after the prick and teaching him—

"Uh, Con?" Holden called.

*But that would create a bit of an international incident if I kicked the shit out of the guy in the Wilde building.* And Con always believed you didn't hit first. *I don't start the fight. I just end it.* "See you in Lancaden."

Alexandre's eyes gleamed with his fury. "You are not worthy of her."

Like he didn't know that shit.

"She will cast you aside when she sees what she can have. She's lived with nothing, and I am about to give her a kingdom."

"Not your kingdom to give, buddy. It's already hers. And you know, you really should watch what you say to me. When I marry Juliet and I'm sitting next to her, well, I might just decide you are of utterly zero use to me." A slow exhale. "Have a safe trip home now, would you?"

Jaw clenching, Alexandre stepped onto the elevator.

Constantine didn't move. They locked eyes until the doors slid closed. When they did...

"He hates you," Holden announced, all cheery. "I'd say that was a job well done."

Nodding, Constantine strode back toward him. "I'd say so, too." Because that had been his goal. To get Alexandre's focus shifted to him.

"Just so we're clear, though," Holden straightened away from the wall. "Want to brief me on the full game plan?"

"Sure." He took a breath. "I think I need to propose to a princess. Do you know where I can get one big-ass ring? One that will be large enough to easily be spotted by reporters in a crowd?"

# CHAPTER ELEVEN

*Step Eleven: Get as close to the target as possible. She has to trust me completely. When it's life or death, she has to do what I say without question. No hesitation.*

"Don't get me wrong." Juliet paused to take a sip of water. She could feel the eyes of the other patrons on her as she sat with Constantine in the middle of the elegant Atlanta restaurant, one that perched on top of a downtown skyscraper. "I'm not complaining about the food or the service. Both have been impeccable. But I'm just not sure I understand why we're here." None of the other diners had approached them, but she'd been acutely conscious of the whispers around her.

Across the table, Constantine smiled. The light of a candle danced between them, and by candlelight, that mix of gorgeousness and danger that he carried off was even more apparent.

The restaurant was high-end and romantic. The perfect escape for two lovers who wanted to dine as they looked out at the city below.

Except, they weren't lovers. Not really.

"I thought you'd enjoy the view."

She did.

"And it will go well with the proposal."

Her hand dropped to her lap. Fisted around her napkin. "This isn't necessary."

Constantine reached into his suit pocket and pulled out a small box. "There's a reporter sitting three tables away. But I bet you recognized him, didn't you?"

Hard to miss Jeremy Knight. "*Insider Confidential,*" she whispered. The man's image had been branded into her mind. "How did he get to Atlanta so fast?"

"*Insider Confidential* is actually based here, so when he found out that we'd headed this way, I bet the man was thrilled to return home."

Deliberately, she didn't look Jeremy's way.

"He bribed the hostess so he could get that table. I suspect he even snapped a few pics of us during the meal."

She forced herself to release the poor, balled-up napkin. "You want him watching us."

"I want him seeing the show, so maybe I had the office tip off his people about our plans for tonight."

A shiver skirted over her. *He just tipped them off for tonight. Because of the cover he's creating. Constantine didn't tip anyone off about me in Baton Rouge.* He hadn't.

Right?

She looked down at her lap.

"Juliet?"

"I can trust you, can't I, Constantine?"

"Thought we covered this."

*Breathe.* She took a few slow, deep breaths. "You didn't sell me out in Baton Rouge."

"No, baby, I didn't." Soft. Tender.

It was the tenderness that got her. Her head snapped up. *I want that tenderness to be real.* Only, it wasn't. None of this was real. He was crafting an elaborate setup so he could protect her. Just doing his job.

When she looked across the table, she saw that he'd opened the box that he'd taken from his coat. As usual, Constantine was dressed like some model from *GQ* magazine. Effortless style and grace that barely cloaked his masculine strength and power.

Meanwhile, she kept shifting uncomfortably in her black dress. A dress that had been purchased by someone at Wilde. Someone who clearly liked dresses that were a lot shorter and lower cut than the ones Juliet normally wore. Her shoes were a vivid, distinct red. Louboutin with a pointed toe and a four-inch heel. Another purchase from Wilde. The place must come equipped with its own stylist or something. All she knew was that *someone* had bought her an entire new wardrobe for her trip to Lancaden. Who had footed the bill for that? The anonymous donor?

*Who is paying for all of this?* Who...and why?

"I didn't set you up in Baton Rouge. You think I really would have turned all those reporters loose on you and let the pack swarm you in that back parking lot?" A shake of his head. "I wouldn't do that. Not to you."

"But you didn't know me then." And they still had so many secrets from each other even now. Now—while he held a ring box in his hand and while she was pretty sure he was about to fake propose to her.

Not that she could pretend to be shocked by the proposal. He'd told her that someone would pick up a ring. She'd known it would appear at some point before the plane departed. She'd just kind of thought he'd slide it onto her finger casually. No big deal.

Then they'd gone to the fancy dinner…

Juliet wet her lips. She leaned forward. Curled her hand over his as he held the ring box. "Tell me your darkest secret."

His expression hardened. "Excuse me?"

"We still don't know a lot about each other." The candle's light danced and flickered.

"You know that I'd kill to protect you."

She sucked in a breath. "Well, actually, I don't think I quite realized that."

"I would. Without hesitation. Just like I'd jump between you and any threat."

Because it was his job. "Why?"

"It's what a bodyguard does."

"I don't think bodyguards are supposed to kill."

"I'll try to use less lethal means first, promise."

Was he teasing her? How did you even tease when you were talking about potentially killing someone? She released his hand and slumped back in her chair. "Who are you?"

"Constantine Leos. Consort, bodyguard, former FBI. There. You know lots about me."

"Your darkest secret." She wanted to know everything about him, but they could start with the secret he'd buried deep.

He put the box on the table, but kept his fingers curled over it. "Is this one of those you-tell-me-yours-and-I'll-tell-you-mine situations?"

"If you want, yes."

His voice dropped. "If I'm telling you my deepest, darkest secret, I'm doing it when we're alone. When we are far away from prying eyes and neither of us is pretending about anything."

The waiter walked toward their table. "Check!" Okay, way too breathless. But she wanted to be out of there and alone with Constantine because she did want to know his secrets.

A soft laugh rumbled from Constantine as the waiter scurried away. "Not quite so fast, Juliet," Constantine murmured as he flashed her a smile. "One thing we need to finish here first."

He'd scooped up the box.

And before she could stop him, he dropped to one knee before her.

From the corner of her eye, she saw that Jeremy Knight had his phone up. *Filming this whole scene.*

"Marry me, Juliet," Constantine said. Not a murmur. Not a rumble. Loud and clear and gasps were heard from nearby tables.

And she knew what she was supposed to do.

She looked at the box as he opened it. The pear-shaped diamond caught the light and sparkled brightly enough to have her blinking.

"I want to spend my life with you. I want to be with you, all the time."

Certainly, that was the point, wasn't it? Close access. She let the smile slide over her face. "Yes.

Yes, I'll marry you." Why did saying those words make her feel so hollow on the inside? This was what they needed to do.

He slid the ring onto her finger. Distantly, she was aware of the other patrons clapping, but she didn't look their way. The ring felt cold around her finger.

A shiver slid over her.

Constantine's fingers curled under her chin. He tipped her head up because she'd been staring down at the ring. "Now you're mine."

Was that part of the script?

His lips took hers. Softly. Tenderly. He kissed her just like a man in love would kiss. And she closed her eyes and pretended that was exactly what he was. A man in love.

*If only.*

***

The kiss had been too damn chaste. When they left the building, heading for the limo that waited for them, Constantine mentally cursed the desire that raged in his blood. He'd been trying to act like a gentleman. The goal had been to press a careful, tender kiss to Juliet's lips. He'd needed to get the kiss just right, after all. Appearances and all that shit. He'd even angled his body so that Jeremy Knight could see both the ring and the kiss at the same time for his photos.

But that little taste had not been nearly enough for Constantine. He'd wanted to kiss her harder. Deeper. To make her moan. To claim her with his mouth and let the passion roar free. Fuck chaste and tender. He wanted passionate and wild.

*"Princess Juliet!"* The reporters swarmed.

He tucked her beneath his arm. Holden had appeared the moment they exited, and he was at Juliet's right.

*"Are you heading to Lancaden?"*

*"Are you eager to see the kingdom?"*

*"Will you take the crown?"*

They kept walking.

*"Princess Juliet! Is that an engagement ring on your finger?"*

Well, freaking finally. Someone had asked the question they'd been waiting for. And, as he'd instructed her on the elevator ride down, Juliet stumbled just a bit, as if the question had caught her off guard. He had to give her props. She had some pretty good acting skills.

Her head turned toward the reporter who'd just asked the question. "Yes." Soft. So soft that he knew that to the cameras, it might even look as if she'd just mouthed the word. But her shoulders squared, and she said again, louder, *"Yes."*

The crowd seemed to shriek in unison.

"Feeding frenzy," Holden muttered.

Damn straight it was. Now to get Juliet in the car because the crowd was not going to touch her. He pulled her even closer and in seconds, he had her settled in the back of the limo. But right before he joined her inside, Constantine turned back to the reporters. "My fiancée has no additional comment at this time."

Oh, yeah, that was what they needed to hear. *My fiancée.*

Cameras focused hard on him.

He let them linger a moment, then he ducked inside. Holden followed behind him, and the door slammed shut.

"You good?" Constantine asked Juliet.

A faint glow lit the back of the limo. The glow of lights came from the bar and along the floor. The illumination wouldn't be seen by anyone outside because the tinted windows provided plenty of privacy and protection.

The whole vehicle was about protection. Special glass. Bulletproof.

"Good isn't quite the word." She slipped off the ring and held it out to him.

"You're gonna need to keep that on." He wanted it back on her finger. "It comes off too soon, and we'll have a whole world of trouble on our hands."

"Oh. Right." She slid it back on. "How is it a perfect fit? You didn't even ask my ring size." She swung one heel. "Just like the shoes and the dress."

"Wilde knows everything about you," Holden answered before Constantine could. "Your sizes were like, day one info."

She stopped swinging her heel. "Of course." Her head turned toward Constantine. "I guess you already know all my deep, dark secrets. Silly of me to ask for yours."

No, it hadn't been. But she didn't need to know his secrets. Not when they might make her go running. Something that could not happen.

"Well, you have the target now thoroughly painted on your back, buddy." Stretching out his legs, Holden settled comfortably onto the seat. "Congratulations on a job well done."

"A target?" Juliet shifted position. The skirt of her dress decided to shift *up* at least an inch.

Who the hell had picked out her dress? And the shoes that were too freaking sexy—who'd chosen them?

"He's just setting up cover," she added as a little furrow appeared between her brows. "He has to be seen as my consort. Why would you say he had a target on him?"

The skirt had just slipped up a little more.

"Uh, because he does." Holden cleared his throat. "He made certain to piss off Alexandre so the guy would come after him, and he just waved a giant red flag—in the form of that mega rock on your hand—in front of any enemies that you might have."

"You...you never said anything about being a target!" She grabbed Constantine's hand. The hand that had been reaching out to tug down the hem of her dress because if it hiked up much more, he was sure Holden would see her underwear.

*Dammit, she'd better be wearing underwear.*

But first, the matter of being a target. "I'm sure I mentioned it." Of this, he was pretty certain. They'd gone over this point before. But her wearing underwear? On that, he was not so certain. He'd love to find out, though. "I told you that I'd stand between you and any threat."

"You didn't say you'd be a target!"

About that... "Getting the attention of anyone who wants to hurt you would be part of my whole standing-in-front-of-threats strategy."

She let him go. "I don't like it."

He tugged down her dress. "Neither do I. The damn thing is way too short."

A quick, startled silence. Then, with excruciating politeness, Juliet asked, "Did you just pull down my dress?"

Fuck.

"Ahem." Holden again. "This feels a bit personal. Should I go sit up front?"

They both jerked their heads toward him.

"Hi," he said with a wave. "I'm here."

Of course, the guy was there. Why else had Constantine tugged on her dress? And, shit, his hand had lingered on her thigh. His fingers were touching her silken skin, and the hard-on he'd had ever since that ridiculously chaste kiss in the restaurant was even stronger. With a supreme effort of will, he pulled his hand away. After all, no reporters were watching. "Sorry. Shouldn't have touched you."

"Why did you?" Juliet watched him with her dark, intense gaze.

He swallowed. "Because Holden doesn't get a fucking show."

"Okay." Holden clapped his hands together. "There is a lot to unpack here. First, I wasn't looking for a show. Juliet, consider me showless. Because, clearly, if I look at you even briefly in any kind of sexual way, Constantine is gonna kick my ass. Or try, because, you know, one of us is former MMA and one of us is some former spook who may or may not have been a government assassin at some time."

More silence. The stark and dangerous kind.

"Uh, that was a joke?" Holden laughed. Uncomfortably. "No way is the super model here an assassin. I was just trying to lighten the weird sexual tension that you two have going on."

*He was making a joke.* Right. Holden didn't have access to Constantine's files. Those were sealed by Uncle Sam. They'd better be. If anyone actually did get access to his true past, the whole stack-of-cards cover he was building to protect Juliet would crumble. Or, not so much crumble as implode.

"And, apparently, my effort was a failure because things seem even weirder. Noted." Holden tapped his fingertips along the seat near him. "So, let's just focus on business, shall we? Plan recap. Let's talk about our agenda. We go back to the safe house. You two stay in and get beauty sleep tonight. We head out early on our eagerly anticipated trip to Lancaden. And once there, she meets the king. Does her thing. We make sure she's safe and we see if she's gonna rule a kingdom." A deliberate pause. "Did I miss anything?"

"You missed the bastard who torched her house in Baton Rouge." A person Constantine did not intend to miss. After all, he'd had the target painted so boldly to catch that bastard's attention. *You want to get her? I'm in the way. Come get me.*

"You...you don't think that he'll come to Atlanta?" Juliet seemed surprised.

"That's exactly what I think. A man who breaks into your home, leaves a knife in your bed, then torches the place isn't a guy who is just gonna move on." He'd had enough classes in behavioral eval to know that. He hadn't been part of the BAU at the FBI, but that didn't mean he hadn't picked up plenty over the years. *And most of that came when I was working with a certain thief, not with the Feds.* "If he's got an obsession with you, he will follow you wherever you go." His lips pressed together, then he revealed his deeper suspicion as Constantine noted, "But it might not be an obsession. Could be that Alexandre just hired the bastard to terrify you. Either way, we will be ready for him."

Ready and eagerly waiting.

*Bring it, bastard. Because I will wreck you.*

# CHAPTER TWELVE

*Step Twelve: Proximity is key. You can't protect the client if you're not close to her. Sometimes, you must be intimately close. Not because you want to be, but because you have to be. It's the job.*
*Yeah, right. Tell yourself that shit often enough, and maybe you'll believe it.*

"How do you know we weren't followed?" The worry that kept nagging at Juliet. There had been so many reporters near the limo. What if one of them had tailed the vehicle?

"The driver is paid not to be followed. He's a trained Wilde agent."

"Even trained agents don't make mistakes?" She eased onto the couch. Across from her, the flames flared in the fireplace.

"He'd better not." Constantine dropped his suit coat onto the back of a chair and jerked at the knot of his tie. He didn't toss the tie aside, though, but instead let the ends hang loosely. With a jerk of his fingers, he unhooked the top few buttons of his shirt.

Then his gaze returned to her. Had to be her imagination, but she could have sworn there was a dark desire in his gray eyes.

*I see desire because that's probably how I'm looking at him.* Projecting, that was what she was doing. Her gaze immediately flew toward the fire. "You lied to me."

Silence. Then, careful, "When?"

"When you said you'd tell me your deepest, darkest secrets in exchange for mine." She kicked off her heels. Tucked her feet under her body as she cuddled into the sofa. "You already know my secrets so there was never any point in an exchange."

"No, I don't." He moved to stand in front of her, blocking her view of the blaze. "I kinda think I could know you forever, and you'd still have secrets."

Her nervous laugh danced in the air. "I'm an open book."

"Really, *secret* princess? Are you?"

Okay, fine. He had a point on that one aspect of her world. "Ask me a question about my life. About me. Any question. One you *don't* already know the answer to, and I'll tell you the truth." Because she wanted her chance to ask him questions.

"Do you want me?"

Her heart thundered. "I said you had to ask a question that you didn't already know the answer to." She wet her lips and tipped back her head a bit more to better look up at him.

"I don't know the answer." Rasping. Hard. "And it's making me crazy."

Her breath heaved in and out. "I kissed you on the plane. Didn't you get a clue then?"

"You felt sorry for me on the plane."

Her jaw nearly hit the floor. She hurriedly snapped it closed then said, "No. I mean, yes, I felt bad for what you'd been through, but that's a normal reaction. A human reaction. We feel sympathy for each other, and we want to help. A desire to heal old wounds is absolutely something that is a normal, empathetic response."

"Are you being a psychologist on me right now?"

"I don't know what I'm being." Truth. "But I can tell you that I have felt badly for plenty of people." She'd worked to counsel and try to help so many over the last few years. "And I never kissed any of them." Trying to lighten the tension that made the air thick and hot, Juliet sent him a faint smile. "That sort of thing will get your license suspended if you're working with a client."

"I'm not a client."

"No, you're the bodyguard, so I guess that makes me the client." She was oddly conscious of the ring's weight on her finger. They were alone, so no point in pretending anything and yet...He'd asked if she wanted him. The fire was the only light in the room, so maybe he couldn't see that her cheeks were turning red as she decided to screw the consequences and go all in. "Yes."

"Yes—what?"

He seriously wanted her to spell things out for him? Fine. "I want you. I felt an attraction to you from the first moment we met. Granted, I thought you might be some reporter who was there to rip my world apart—"

"I literally began our association by saying I was your bodyguard."

She plowed right on, saying, "But you have this dangerous, sexy vibe that I'm sure you are very aware of. It's just..." Her words tangled and halted as she tried to figure out how to explain what she felt. "A physical attraction. Instant. Happens sometimes with certain people. Don't worry. I'll ignore it. I won't be jumping up and kissing you again. Your virtue is safe."

His hand reached out. His fingers curled under her chin. "That's a fucking shame."

She leaned toward him. "It's my turn."

"Your turn to ask if I want you? Easy. With every breath I take, I want you more. I wanted you from the first moment I saw you—sure, we'll call it that instant attraction you mentioned. But it didn't happen when I walked into the bar and you were looking sexy as hell as you stood there in that little black apron."

She'd never particularly thought that black apron was sexy. Functional, yes. Sexy, no.

"It happened the first time I saw your picture. When I first took your case. I looked at you..." His words trailed away. His thumb moved to brush lightly over her lower lip. "How will she taste?"

Her lips parted. "Excuse me?" Her breath blew lightly over his thumb.

"I wondered how you'd taste. I wondered where the hell you'd been for so long and why I hadn't met you sooner."

Her tongue darted out and *may* have lightly licked his thumb.

His breath hissed out. His hand jerked back as if he'd been burned. "Then I reminded myself you were a princess, and I was the last guy you should want in return." He spun away, giving her his back as he put some distance between them. "Get some sleep, Juliet. I'll be standing guard, so you don't have to worry about anything. We'll head to Lancaden tomorrow, and you can see your long-lost grandfather."

She remained on the couch, feeling oddly bereft without his touch. Her shoulders hunched. He'd moved away and was clearly dismissing her. Too bad she didn't feel like being dismissed. "I didn't ask my question. You just assumed I'd have the same one you did. You know what they say about assuming."

He whirled toward her. "Juliet—"

"Why are you 'the last guy' that I should be wanting? Why are you so wrong for me? I'm not talking about forever. I'm talking about right now. Me and you." She couldn't think far enough ahead for any kind of forever business. "This kind of attraction doesn't happen a lot. You don't see someone and instantly want to rip off his clothes." She rose from the couch. The skirt of her dress slid down. She remembered him tugging down the dress in the limo. The way his hand had lingered against her thigh. The way she'd wanted him to move his fingers a little higher. "If you want the truth, then here's another deep, dark secret for you." She was spilling them left and right. "I've never felt this kind of attraction for anyone else. I didn't even think this crazy need was real until I met you. Thought it was just the kind of thing that you saw in movies or read about in books. Or maybe..." She was putting herself bare before him. "Maybe there was just something wrong with me.

Because I didn't feel that connection, that intensity with anyone. My last boyfriend, Christian, he said he loved me. That he knew it from the start—"

"The guy was a dick."

"He never felt right to me." The truth of the matter. The thick carpeting swallowed her steps as she closed in on him. The flames kept dancing and casting shadows around the room. Around them. Juliet stopped right in front of Constantine. "You do. You feel right, but you keep saying you're wrong."

His jaw hardened. "You should go to bed."

"And you should kiss me like you mean it." She sucked in a breath. *Oh, no.*

"Fuck, yes," he rumbled, and his hands were on her. Pulling her against him. Holding her tight and possessively, and he kissed her. Absolutely like he meant it. His mouth crashed onto hers. Not the careful, delicate kiss he'd given her when they were in the restaurant. The kiss that had been meant more for others. No, this kiss was so different.

Hot.

Consuming.

Passionate.

Lust burned in her blood and had a moaning cry rising in her throat. Her hands grabbed for his shoulders. Her nails bit into the fabric of his shirt. Her mouth opened even more for him as he tasted her. His tongue was wicked and wonderful, and desire quaked through every cell of her body.

*This* was what his kiss should have been like before. Only, if it had been, they might have just wound up making love right on the table in front of the crowd at that swanky restaurant. Hardly appropriate behavior but...screw appropriate. Maybe she was tired of doing everything right. Tired of being so excruciatingly careful all the time. He was her bodyguard. There to keep her safe. She didn't have to worry about him hurting her. Constantine wanted her safe. More, he *wanted* her. There was no missing the hard, long, and thick length of his arousal. She rubbed her body against his.

"Sweetheart..." A sexy growl. "You play with fire, and you'll get burned."

Her lashes lifted. His mouth hovered over hers, and she wanted it back. "Who says I am playing?"

She saw his need, his desire for her, take over. She wouldn't have even thought it was possible to see something like that, but she did. His features hardened even more. His gray eyes glittered, and then a wild, reckless smile curved his lips right before he kissed her again.

His tongue drove past her lips. She sucked on his tongue, and he lifted her up. The move caught her by surprise, and Juliet gasped, but he just swallowed the sound. He held her easily, with that casual strength of his, and Constantine carried her back to the couch. He lowered her, spreading her out, and still kissing her. But his hands slid down her body. Moved to her thighs. When his slightly callused fingertips skimmed over her sensitive skin, she jerked.

"I'm not going to hurt you." A deep promise. "Just have to satisfy my curiosity."

She had something that needed satisfying, too, but it wasn't exactly her curiosity. Fire heated her blood, blazing even more than the flames in the fireplace. This lust, this need was almost dizzying. It filled every cell and spurred her on with a fast, aching intensity. This was the passionate, intoxicating rush of need that was supposed to sweep lovers away.

In the past, she'd been hesitant. Careful. Controlled. She didn't have to be any of that, not with him.

Her legs parted for him as he sat on the edge of the couch, his body near her hip, and she was spread out for him. Her breath panted as those wicked fingers of his slid up, up...

"This is like going from first base straight to home plate," she said, voice soft.

His fingers stilled. "You want me to stop?"

What she wanted was for his fingers to go higher and touch her in the spot where she ached the most. "Do not *dare.*"

"That a royal command?"

"Constantine—"

"I'm not fucking stopping." An inch higher. Her whole body tensed. "Been going crazy all night wondering...are you wearing panties?"

Then he was touching her between her legs and discovering that, yes, indeed, she was wearing panties. Those extremely thin, barely-there panties that you couldn't see beneath clothing. Panties that were so thin they didn't offer much protection from his touch, and that was a great thing. An incredible thing. Because it seemed as if he was stroking her sex right then. Her hips surged up against him.

"Nice," he murmured. "Feels like silk. Wet silk."

Because she was wet. Wet and hot and speeding toward a climax when all he'd done was stroke her a few times with his fingers. Was she this hard up? How long had it been since she'd been with someone?

She couldn't remember other lovers. Not like it was a long list, anyway. All she could do was arch up against his touch and wish that he would give her more because she couldn't quite get *there*. "Constantine!"

His fingers dipped under her panties. Okay, no, it had *not* been like he was stroking her sex when he'd been caressing her through the fabric. This was entirely different. This was a million times different. Hotter. More intense and he was making her crazy.

He thrust a finger into her. "You are so tight. Hot."

Her eyes squeezed shut. She bit her lower lip because she was afraid she was getting too loud.

His finger withdrew. Thrust again, even as his thumb began to press over her clit. Press, rub, circle.

Her body shuddered. So close. Her release was *so* close, and she'd never been able to come just from a man touching her like this. Maybe she wouldn't be able to come now, either. Maybe she'd just stay on this sensual precipice when all she wanted to do was tumble over the edge and get lost with Constantine. Maybe she wouldn't be able to— "Help me," she pleaded.

His fingers stilled. "Anything."

"Make me come. I want to come with you." Forced out. Husky. So low.

"Oh, you'll come. And it will be so good that I will wreck you for anyone else."

That was a rather arrogant promise. She started to tell him just that. Like, maybe they should start with the basics. Her actually reaching climax before the being-wrecked-for-anyone-else bit but...

He moved.

Moved fast and spread her legs apart even more. More so that he could get between them. So that he could shove the skirt of her dress all the way to her waist. So that he could rip away her panties and put his mouth between her thighs and work her with his lips and tongue and mouth, and she couldn't hold back the cries that broke from her because suddenly, she wasn't just on the precipice any longer. She was falling. Careening headfirst into the best orgasm of her life. One that hit her while his tongue licked her clit over and over and all she could do was come for him on an endless wave of release.

Distantly, she became aware of the crackle of the fire. The drumming of her heartbeat. The drumming that seemed to get louder and faster as...

*That's not my heartbeat.*

Her breath choked out.

"Easy." Constantine lifted his head. He licked his lower lip. "The bastard can wait a bit longer."

He *knew* someone was at the door? Just how long had he known? How long had that pounding been happening?

Oh, God. Oh, God. She'd been loud. "Holden?" she squeaked. It had to be him at the door, right?

"He can wait." Constantine rose to stand beside the couch. He caught her dress. Lowered it slowly until it covered her thighs. "You're beautiful."

She was still having aftershocks of release quake through her sex. "Did he hear us?"

"No."

That answer had been quick, and, she sure hoped it was truthful.

"He's just checking in. Don't worry about him. I'll deal with Holden." His eyes glittered as he stared down at her.

He stood beside the couch, and because he stood in that exact position—so close to her—when she turned her head toward him, she was pretty much face to face with a certain very large portion of his anatomy. A portion that told her that while she'd had a fabulous time, he hadn't.

Or, he hadn't...yet.

"Juliet." Rough. Demanding. "You keep looking at my dick that way, and I'll be inside you in the next three seconds. I won't care that Holden is at the damn door."

Juliet sucked in a sharp breath as her gaze flew up to find his laser-sharp gaze locked on her.

"You need to go in the bedroom," he told her flatly. "You should go now."

She should because if Holden saw her, she was afraid she'd just blush furiously and stammer, and he'd know exactly what they had been doing. *If he doesn't already know.*

"By a thread," Constantine grimly told her. "That's what is holding my control right now. A freaking thread. Stay here much longer..."

More pounding at the door.

"And the thread will snap."

She slid off the couch. Managed to get to her feet. Not the most graceful movements ever. Mostly because she felt incredibly awkward. Her body seemed too sensitive. Her fingers were shaking. Her heart racing. "You didn't come."

He tipped back her head and kissed her.

Need thundered through her again. Just that fast. So much for being satisfied.

"You are fantastic," he whispered against her mouth. "And I will want more."

So did she.

But his partner was at the door, and she needed to get away before she did something horrible like collapse into a puddle of need right in front of Constantine. How, *how* had she gotten this responsive? She'd gone from thinking that she didn't respond passionately enough to—to coming against his mouth in record time.

With an effort, she pulled her arms from him. They'd moved of their own accord to hold him tight. She straightened her spine. Squared her shoulders. "I enjoyed that very much." Oh, no. That sounded way too prim. But when she felt anxious, she tended to revert back to politeness. All those lessons ingrained by her grandmother.

*The would-be killer?*

"So the hell did I, baby. Can't wait to do it again and again."

It was so hot in there. They should probably put out the fire.

"Bedroom, princess."

Right. She put one foot in front of the other and headed for the bedroom. But at the door, she stopped. Her hand rose and curled around the doorframe. "Join me when he's gone?"

"Like I have to be asked twice."

Smiling, she crept into the bedroom and shut the door.

\*\*\*

"You are not supposed to be here," Constantine snapped as he hauled open the door and glowered at his partner. "Unless this is some major emergency—"

"What the hell took you so long?"

*Juliet was coming against my mouth and nothing in the world would have interrupted that sweet, insane pleasure.* "I was getting Juliet ready for bed."

"What?' Holden gaped. "Like, tucking her in and some shit?"

*Like tasting heaven and having the jerk in front of me ruin the night.* "Why are you here?"

"Because we have a problem. I tried texting you, but you didn't respond." He crossed his arms over his chest and wiggled his brows. "Probably because the tucking in process was so loud that you didn't hear the ding of my text."

Constantine stared stonily back at him. "You really want to go there?"

Holden tried to glance over Constantine's shoulder. "Where is the princess?"

"In bed." Alone. "What's the problem?" He knew it had to be bad because Holden would not have made an appearance at his door otherwise. Fuck, what was the fire now?

*No, no, it had better not actually be another fire—*

"Someone else is claiming your princess."

The last thing he'd expected to hear. "Say that again."

"That Christian asshole she dated a while back? A news story just aired with him as the star. He's saying that he and Juliet are still involved. That they have been all this time." A long exhale. "He's saying they're madly in love."

# CHAPTER THIRTEEN

*Step Thirteen: Be the bad guy. Someone has to take the role.*
*Be as bad as you need to be in order to keep the target safe.*

Constantine laughed. *This* was the problem? "The dude is trying to get his five minutes of fame. Not a deal." Now, if he could get back to Juliet and properly finish what he'd started, he could be a happy man.

"It's a deal if people—people like Alexandre—believe it. It's a deal if Alexandre starts saying you're not her real consort, and he tries to separate you from Juliet. This Christian Hale jerk could mess up our plans. We have to get ahead of the situation. Right now, we've got the news that you and Juliet are a couple airing at the same time that Christian is telling everyone he's madly in love with her and that she is crazy for him."

"Juliet doesn't care about him." A low snarl.

Holden grimaced. "I know that. You know that. We need the world to know that. A public declaration from Juliet saying he's wrong and that she is fully committed to you will cement things before you depart for Lancaden. We need *her* to do it, not you. Because if it's just you saying stuff, you'll look like a jealous boyfriend. Which, um, not to tell you your business or anything, but the way you instantly made fists when I mentioned Christian's name..."

Constantine looked down. *Whoops.* He had done that.

"You *do* seem like a jealous boyfriend. So props on the acting." Holden cleared his throat. "I do have to wonder, are you, by chance, a *method* actor? Because I think I see a little lipstick on your—"

"Fuck off."

"And good night to you, too." Holden saluted as he stepped back. "So shall I arrange to have the reporters at the airport? I can make another tip to our pal Jeremy or..." He snapped his fingers together. "Better idea. Maybe we should just plan on an exclusive sit-down with him? Not an overly long thing. Maybe fifteen minutes, tops. Just need to get everything lined up so the cover story doesn't explode in our faces before we can even really get the plan going."

"She hates that jerk."

"Christian? Good to know, we can go with that in the interview—"

"Jeremy," he snapped. Fuck, he could still feel her body trembling against him. He could feel her. Taste her. He shouldn't have let his control slip. He had, and he'd given in to the fierce desire he felt for her, and if Holden hadn't come banging his big-ass fist against the door, Constantine knew he wouldn't have stopped with Juliet. Tasting her wouldn't have been enough for him. He would have taken her.

*And never wanted to let go.*

"Well, I can't say I know anyone who is overly fond of the reporter, but it's a devil-you-know situation, isn't it? We need to discredit Christian before people start to think that you're lying and—"

"Juliet doesn't like the press. She was about to jump out of her skin tonight." No way would he force her to talk with Jeremy Knight. "I'm not worried about the history professor. Christian will just look like the ex who is trying to cause trouble." *I won't put her through more stress right now.* "We continue with our current plan."

Holden rocked back on his heels. "I think that's a bad idea. We need to eliminate this guy from the equation."

"He gets in my way, he comes near Juliet, Hale will be eliminated. Count on it."

Holden's head tilted as he squinted at Constantine. "I just meant that we need to make clear that he's not involved with Juliet. I didn't mean like—like, kill him or anything." A grimace. "That's what you meant, too, right? Right?"

Constantine stared back at him. *He comes at Juliet with the intent of causing her trouble, and I'll take him out of the picture.*

"Right?" Holden pressed.

"Night, Holden." He stepped back and slammed the door shut. For a moment, Constantine just stood in front of that closed door, with his hands clenching and releasing. His body was too tight. Too tense. And too many dark longings filled his head—longings for Juliet. He wanted to stalk into her bedroom. To rip that dress off her. To stroke and taste every inch of her.

Then he wanted to drive into her until she was screaming his name as she came.

Another knock at the door.

*Sonofabitch.*

Jaw locking, he opened the door once more.

Holden waved. "Hi, there."

"You're pissing me off."

"I get it. Truly, I do. You might be surprised to learn this, but I actually get that reaction fairly frequently. Especially from partners at Wilde."

"You don't say."

Holden sucked in a breath. "Look, I get that you're some big mystery guy."

"Is that what I am?"

"And you've got all these connections, and Eric Wilde thinks you're a super star and that's why you were brought into Wilde and immediately given jobs with the VIPs." His shoulders squared. "I might not be former FBI or CIA or whatever else you are, but I am good at what I do. I know the press, and I know how to use them, and I'm telling you right now, we need them on our side. We need them to run with the story that you and Juliet are wildly in love. Fairytale romance shit. The beautiful princess who fell for her bodyguard. Don't let her ex mess up what we have going. Trust me on this."

"Juliet doesn't like the reporters." He'd never forget the scene of them swarming her behind Sal's.

"And you *clearly* don't like whatever it is that Juliet doesn't like. She hates something and you do, too. Got it."

Constantine prepared to slam the door again.

"I'm just saying that *maybe* you are not being one hundred percent unbiased in this situation. You're trying to make her comfortable—and that's cool. Totally cool. But, sometimes, in order to protect the client, we have to do things that the client doesn't necessarily like."

"I know how to protect her."

"Yes." Holden looked away. "Apparently, it's by killing her ex," he mumbled.

"Say again?"

"Apparently, it's by ignoring her ex." Holden flashed a smile, but it didn't reach his eyes. "Five minutes with a reporter will smooth this over. Five minutes will make sure that Dr. Christian Hale doesn't have a leg to stand on."

Constantine opened his mouth to reply—

"Okay," Juliet said from behind him. "Make it happen. We can talk before the plane leaves."

*Fucking hell.* He'd heard her behind him, those soft, hesitant steps that the carpet had almost completely swallowed. *Almost* being the key point. Constantine had been planning to slam the door on Holden again, but, now it was too late. With his brows lowering, he asked his partner, "Happy now?"

"My mood is improving." He retreated. "I'll set things in motion, and I'll, ah, be on my merry way."

"Fantastic."

And, again, he shut the door. Shut it, locked it, then swung toward the client who had *not* followed his orders to stay in the bedroom. "What in the hell were you—"

He stopped. Had to stop because she was so incredibly beautiful. Still in the dress. But with her lips plump and red from his earlier kisses. With her hair a sexy tangle around her face. With her eyes gleaming.

Looking at her, he remembered having her silken legs spread for him. He remembered tasting her core. He remembered how she'd come for him.

"I'm not in love with Christian."

"Good to know." Also, something he'd discovered, he didn't like talking about her asshat ex.

"I can talk to the reporters and say that he's lying. That's, ah, I overheard you and Holden. That's why I came out."

He kept closing in.

She swallowed but held her ground. Points for the princess.

"Uh, Constantine?"

"You didn't follow orders."

She didn't like that—he saw it in her eyes. "I just came out of the bedroom because you were talking about me."

"I'll often be talking about you. You're the target."

Another flash in her dark eyes. Again, she hadn't liked what he said.

He stopped right in front of her. "I don't know what situation we'll find in Lancaden. You could have enemies on every single side, or you could be greeted with open arms. Either way, I have to know that you'll follow my orders. Your safety matters more than anything else."

"I just walked about ten feet out of the bedroom in order to talk to you and Holden. Hardly a dramatic situation." She sucked on her lower lip.

He wanted to be sucking that lower lip. "Go to your bedroom."

"Another order? You sure are tossing those out like mad tonight." She rose onto her toes. Peeked over his shoulder. "I don't hear Holden pounding at the door. Why do you want me fleeing this time?"

"Because I'm trying to keep my hands off you. Trying not to fuck you."

She fell back down as her feet flattened. "I see."

He saw that she wasn't heading back into the bedroom. "Juliet..."

"I thought you were going to come into the bedroom with me. After Holden left, I thought we'd—" She stopped.

"Finish where we left off?" Nothing would make him happier. "That will make things complicated as hell."

"Sex can be complicated." Her gaze fell to the floor.

"I'm not just talking about sex."

And her stare flew up to his face. "Love?"

"I'm talking about the kind of fucking that makes you nearly insane."

"Ahem." She cleared her throat. "Right. Sure. Yes, that kind of fucking. Absolutely."

She wasn't getting it. "You haven't been with a lover like me."

Now she did take a step back. "I suppose you know every detail about the relationships I've had in the past."

He did, and he hated the bastards who'd been with her. Something he should probably analyze later, but, screw it. He'd just hate them and not care too much about why. "You haven't been with someone like me," Constantine repeated.

Once more, she sucked on her lower lip. "Is this your way of saying you're like...kinky?"

His teeth snapped together. "I'm saying I don't fuck in the dark for five minutes." He wanted to put his hands on her. Wanted to haul her close. Wanted to take her against the nearest wall. "I'm not a safe lover. I'm demanding and intense, and when I get in you, I won't be done fast. I'll come, oh, yeah, I'll come hard and deep in you, but I won't stop. I'll want to keep going and going. I'll want to have you come over and over. Until you can't think of anyone but me. Until you forget everyone who ever touched you *before me*."

He should stop. He was probably scaring her. So why the hell did he open his mouth and keep going? But he did, and he said, "You want my deep, dark secrets?" Because she'd asked for them before. "*I'm* deep and dark, sweetheart. I'm not some safe lover that you can play with because you're scared of all the attention you're getting. Because you want an outlet. An easy release."

She flinched. "Is that what you think I want?"

He didn't know what she wanted. A walk on the wild side? A fuck away from prying eyes? "You're the woman who gets serious. Who dates her lovers and has a two-month rule about not sleeping with them too soon."

Juliet sucked in a sharp breath. "It's—it's not a rule. I like to get to know someone first. Not like I look at the calendar and then magically, bam, two months have passed so I decide it's okay to have sex." Her words were muffled. Hurt.

Because he was the guy who would hurt her. "It's a rule. Your rule. But you're changing it for me? Why? Because I'm convenient?"

She thrust back her shoulders. "I think you might just be the most inconvenient man I've ever met."

"I'm the most dangerous, the baddest, and the deadliest bastard you've ever met. I can guarantee you that fact. Because that jab Holden made about me being an assassin? Really not too far from the mark." The floodgates had opened, and it was time for the princess to get scared. *Before I take her and can't let go.* "I grew up with nothing, but I studied everything I could. Wound up in the FBI with some idea that I'd change the world. Instead, my team sold me out, and I would have died if one of the worst criminals out there hadn't come to my side. The guy had a reputation for being an untrustworthy prick, someone with whom you did not screw, and Remy became my best friend."

Juliet froze as she watched him.

"The Feds had turned their backs on me. The team I'd had was dirtier than hell. So I went into my new friend's world. And it was no longer about being undercover and trying to fit in. That was the new life for me. And I stayed in that life, and I broke the law."

"Constantine?"

Yep, her rose-colored glasses were shattering right in front of him. "Bet you wish I'd never put my mouth on you, huh?"

She trembled.

Now that he'd started, the words wouldn't stop. "I did things that had to be done. I worked with some of the worst scum out there, and I stopped a lot of those bastards. I stopped them *my* way." He'd never revealed so much to anyone else. "By that point, Uncle Sam had me and my buddy pulling dirty deeds. In order to erase the sins from our pasts, we were pulled in when the government needed our particular brand of expertise."

"Wh-what was your particular brand of expertise?"

"My friend had lots of specialties. Remy's best talent was with painting. Never seen a better forger in my life. But he was also a thief, a con man, and someone who was not afraid to pull the trigger when a mission went to hell and back. And our missions? They were typically always hell."

She shook her head.

"Yeah, baby, they were. Not like I was dealing with some white-collar bullshit. We're talking about international criminals. Drug rings. Gun running."

Her eyes had grown huge. So stark. "What was your area of expertise?" Again, she'd gone back to that. "Not your friend's. Yours. Were you a forger, too?"

"I can't paint for shit." Something Remy cheerfully told him all the time. Though Remy had offered to teach him more than once over the years. "But I'm a pretty fabulous chameleon. I can blend in anywhere, with anyone." This was what she needed to understand. He slid even closer to her. "I can be the worst criminal you've ever met. I can spend months with gangs and have them making me their leader. I can adopt a new accent, change my walk, change my appearance, and if you met me again, you wouldn't even realize you'd known me before."

Juliet shook her head. "I would know."

Mocking laughter spilled from him. "Would you? Because others haven't." Remy had always been able to tell. Remy had helped train him, after all. "I can become a millionaire Italian businessman who flies in to seal a deal that results in everyone at that meeting getting busted by the CIA because the meeting is a front where the real exchange is government secrets. I can be a hero. I can be the villain. I can be everything in between." He wanted to touch her. Because he wanted it so badly, Constantine kept his hands at his sides. "At my core, I'm dangerous. I like the adrenaline. I like being on the edge." It was all he'd known for years. "I don't get afraid. I don't hesitate."

"Must be nice, not ever being afraid."

"It has its moments." Why the hell was she not running back into her bedroom? "I've done things that would make you wake up screaming in the middle of the night."

She wet her lips. That was it. One nervous gesture. What. The. Fuck? The princess should quake.

Determined to keep pushing, he said, "Right now, I'm being a bodyguard. I'm showing you someone who protects, but I can just as easily be someone who hurts. You don't want me getting close to you."

"Who hurts...you mean, someone who eliminates the threats that come to me? Isn't that what you were saying with Holden?"

"He's my partner, and he worries that I'll cross lines. Doesn't that tell you anything?" *I am not good for you. Don't let me have you. Don't tempt me with what shouldn't be mine.*

"It does tell me something, yes." A fierce nod. "It tells me that he doesn't know you very well."

Constantine rocked back a step. "What? *That's* what you just got from our talk?"

"You're trying to be good right now."

"The hell I am. I'm trying to not pick you up, shove that dress out of the way, and take you against the wall." Guttural.

"Yes. Exactly. Trying to be good." A brisk nod. "You're attempting to scare me away from you."

Attempting? Did that mean he wasn't succeeding?

She stepped toward him, eliminating the space he'd just created. And Juliet put her hands on him. "I wait two months so that I can get to know my partner."

"It hasn't been two months, and I had my mouth on your—"

"I trust you."

*Fucking fuck.*

"It's not just about the attraction, though, yes, it is certainly there. You make me feel safe."

"Because that's how I want you to feel. Didn't you get the whole part when I just told you my skill is manipulation? I make people see what I want them to see. I make people feel what I want them to feel."

"No."

"Juliet, *yes.*"

Her fingers curled around his arms. "You're attempting to scare me because you're intent on protecting me, even from yourself. Constantine, do you really think you're that dangerous to me?"

*I think I'm that wrong for you.* "I'm not some polite lover. I'm rough and possessive. I will make you come apart for me."

"And do I get to make you come apart for me?"

The impression of his zipper would probably be permanently imprinted on his dick. He was so aroused that he ached, and having her so close, having her touch him and ask that tempting question just made the situation even worse. Or rather, it made his wicked need even stronger.

Constantine could only shake his head. "Why won't you fear me?"

"Because I want you more than I can fear you. Because I'm not buying the camouflage. Because I'm looking deeper than what you want me to see." Her fingers pressed harder into him. "Because you just told me all of your secrets and you only did it so I would run away from you."

Yes, he had. Well, get her to run *into* the bedroom and shut the door, anyway. "Can't run. I'm the bodyguard, remember? I'd just chase after you."

"I'm not running. I'm standing right here."

"I can see that." Growled.

"I don't think Eric Wilde would hire some dangerous criminal."

*You'd be surprised on that score.* The agents at Wilde came from some very interesting backgrounds.

"I'm sorry you've known so much betrayal and pain. I'm sorry you've had to go to so many dark places over the years."

Dammit. Why did her words make his chest feel funny? "I don't mind. I'm comfortable in the dark."

Her lashes lowered, shielding her gaze. Then, soft, "Sometimes, so am I."

*What?*

Her lashes lifted. "The dark doesn't always have to be a terrible thing." She pulled her hands away.

He instantly wanted her touching him again.

"By the way, pushing me away *is* you being good, not you being some badass bastard. It's like Psych 101, but it's still cute to see."

No, the hell, *no,* she had not just called him cute. And she was analyzing him? Seriously? A wrong analysis, by the way. Completely off. He excelled at being a badass bastard. Ask anyone.

"We're moving fast," she said.

Fine. So she got that she needed to slow down. She was realizing that she needed to retreat. Good.

"For the first time in my life, though, I don't care about fast or slow. I get that I just met you. I get that you have some giant file on me somewhere so you know every detail about my life. But my emotions are out of control right now. Maybe you think that means I should play things safe with you."

Yes, she needed to be careful. They both did.

"But if you've spent as many years as I have playing it safe and holding back from what you really want...and then in an instant you lose everything—your home, your belongings, the life you'd known—if you lose it all that fast, then you realize that playing by the rules and holding back and being good all the time doesn't actually get you what you want most."

Her hands rose behind her back.

Aw, hell. "Uh, Juliet..."

He heard the hiss of a zipper. Staring straight at him, she rolled back her shoulders, and her dress fell. No underwear. No bra. No panties. Not anymore. He'd ripped those panties away earlier. Where the hell were they? He didn't even know and it didn't matter because—holy fuck, she was *gorgeous*. Her breasts were absolutely perfect. Her tight nipples thrust toward him, and he pretty much drooled. Constantine leaned forward because he wanted his mouth on her.

"I don't need to play it safe with you. You're my bodyguard. I'm pretty sure my safety is your top priority."

It was. Fucking her was also right at the top.

"But if you want to play things safe, I get it."

What? Him? Since when did he take the safe route on anything? But the answer was in his mind, pushing at him. *I'm playing it safe with her. Trying not to screw up with her.*

"I've never stood naked before a guy like this." She wet her lips. "But that was probably in your file. Some bit about me being a hesitant lover? Not very adventurous?"

She was naked, and he was sure she was talking but all the words weren't quite registering because...naked Juliet. "I'm not hesitant." What he was—Constantine was a man who had about five seconds of control left.

"No, I don't think you are. I think you are unlike anyone else I've ever met. If you don't want me, then this is probably all terribly embarrassing and I should go into the bedroom, and when the door closes, we will never speak of this moment again. And I—" She blew out a breath. "Okay, that's it. The end of my courage. Because standing naked in front of a man who is fully dressed and not touching me or reacting at all is incredibly hard." Juliet spun away.

Too late. Because that five seconds of control that he'd had left?

The time had run out. His arms closed around her. Around her warm, silken body, and he pulled her back against him. "Trust me," he breathed the words against her ear even as he lifted her body up, and, in that position, with her back to him, her lush ass rubbed right over his thick cock. "I am reacting." His tongue licked over the shell of her ear.

She shuddered. Her hands grabbed for his arms. "Constantine?"

"I'll still do the job." Gritted. Grated. Stark. "Still protect you and still give orders that you *must obey.*" Talking was way hard. All he wanted was to sink into her core.

"Yes," a moan from her because one of his hands had dipped down her body. He still held her with his other arm wrapped around her stomach, held her easily even while his left hand slid between her legs and stroked her.

*Wet for me.*

"Constantine." His name sounded so different on her lips. "I need you."

He needed her. He whipped her around, took those lunging steps toward the wall. He pinned her there with his body even as his mouth crashed onto hers. There was no more talking. He'd gone past the point where he could. Desire fueled his blood, and he wanted to devour her. Her hands struggled to shove away his shirt. He heard a button pop off, and he didn't care. He kissed her and tasted his Juliet, and lust roared in his blood.

When his mouth tore from hers, he just lifted her higher so that he could lock his lips around her nipple. In that position, she rode one of his thighs because he'd slid it between her legs to help brace her body. She rocked against his thigh as he laved and sucked her nipple, and the breathless moans that spilled from her told him how close she was to release.

*This time, I'll be inside her.* He lowered her. Forced himself to step back.

"Con?"

He stripped out of the rest of his clothes, pausing only long enough to yank a condom from his wallet. He tore open the packet. Her fingers tangled with his as she helped him to roll it on.

The bedroom wasn't far. The bed would be big enough for them both, easily, and they'd get to that bed—later.

This time, he was taking her there. No more waiting. No more playing it safe. No more trying to be good.

The bad guy got to fuck the princess.

He lifted her up again, his fingers sliding around her waist. His mouth took hers even as her legs wrapped around his waist and he drove into her, slowly, deeply, until he'd gone as far as he could. As deep as she'd take him.

*"You feel so good,"* she told him.

He withdrew, thrust again. Harder. Stronger. She was pinned between him and the wall, and she was so tight and hot that he knew he wasn't going to last. How could he last when nothing had ever felt this good? His teeth locked. His hand slid between them. Stroked her clit even as he pounded into her. And her sex squeezed him so tightly. Her body stiffened, and she cried out just before he felt the inner muscles of her core tremble around him.

She came and his name was on her lips.

He pounded harder, thrust in a frenzy. Constantine came, and her name was freaking burned on his soul.

***

Two hours later, she was asleep in the bed next to him.

Constantine should be sleeping, too. But he stared up at the ceiling and knew that a bastard like him should not be in her bed.

But he also knew one night was never going to be enough for him.

*I am screwed.*

He slipped out of the bed, being careful not to wake her as he grabbed his pants and hauled them back on. He couldn't help but notice the woman looked absolutely precious curled up with one hand under her chin. Way too trusting and innocent. Though, uh, after all the things he'd done to her, innocent didn't exactly qualify anymore.

*And I want to do those things again and again.*

Locking his jaw, he snagged his phone and crept out of the bedroom. When he was far enough away that Constantine thought he wouldn't wake her, he made his call.

Sure, it was the middle of the night. He expected his buddy to be sleeping, but if you couldn't wake your best friend up at three a.m., then was the man really your best friend?

*"Con,"* a growling, grumbling greeting.

"Hello to you, too, sweetness," he returned.

Another growl. But one that was slightly more awake.

"I may need some assistance on a case I'm working."

A rustle in the background. Then, "Would this have anything to do with a pretty princess?" His best friend yawned.

"Yes." *My princess.*

"How is that situation working out for you? A con man and a princess. Got to be interesting."

More like red-hot. He was pretty sure they'd singed the sheets. "It's fine. Totally professional."

And Rembrandt—Remy to his friends, the international art thief and all-around criminal that most people should never, ever trust—snorted out a laugh. "Whatever. I saw the video of you two. I know all about the engagement."

"It's cover. Nothing more. We're not really involved."

A squeak from the hinges on the door behind him. The door down the hallway. The door to her bedroom. *Fuck me.*

He whirled around.

Juliet stood in the doorway. So much for tiptoeing out and not waking her. She stared at him a moment, and because the bedroom was dark, he couldn't see her face, just the outline of her body.

He had the heavy, sinking feeling in his gut that he'd hurt her. Because he was a dick who'd just said the wrong thing. But not like he wanted to confess all on the phone in the middle of the night. Not like he had an *all* to confess.

Juliet stared at him a moment longer, then quietly shut the door.

Sonofabitch. Talk about a cluster of a situation.

"What do you need from me?" Remy asked.

He stared at that shut door. After a moment, he swallowed. "Potentially, backup. We're flying to Lancaden, and I'm not sure who I can trust there." *She shut the door. I hurt her.* Usually, he didn't care so much about people getting hurt.

But this was Juliet.

And he could still taste her.

Clearing his throat, Constantine said, "I need you to take one of your fake passports and hop on a plane for me. Can you do that?"

"Consider me on the way." A pause. "And I can't wait to meet your princess."

"Remy..."

"Quick question. Do you think I can get a peek inside the royal gallery while I'm there? I've heard they have some incredible artwork in that place. Even a piece or two from Rembrandt himself."

Hell. "Remy...*don't.*"

"Don't what? Don't be a good friend who leaps into action and immediately flies across an ocean to help you out? Don't be the awesome human being that I am—a person who is willing to watch your back and the back of your lovely princess without any question or hesitation?"

*"Don't be the jerk who breaks into her gallery and steals paintings."*

"Oh." Deflated. "Fine. If you must take all the fun out of the trip."

"Yeah." His hand swiped over his face. "I must. Get your ass on the plane, all right?"

A long suffering sigh. "I'm going first-class. And I'm drinking all the champagne."

"You always do." He hung up the phone. Walked toward the bedroom door. His hand lifted and hovered over the doorknob. He wanted to go back into that room. Wanted to get back into that bed with Juliet but...

*You have a job to do.* And that job wasn't to fuck her into oblivion. She'd shut the door. Passion wasn't reigning. It was the time for control. For cool heads.

He stalked to the couch. *Between her and the door.* Between Juliet and danger—that was where he was supposed to be.

Not *in* her bed. Not *in* her.

So why the hell had he given in? Why had he taken her?

And why was it taking all his self-control not to go into that bedroom and have her again?

# CHAPTER FOURTEEN

*Step Fourteen: Lowering your guard will get her killed. Is that what you want? So don't do it. Do not. I don't care how deep or dark her eyes are.*

"We'll be landing soon." The announcement slid over the intercom and had Juliet tensing. She'd slept some on the flight, mostly because she hadn't slept at all the night before.

Because she'd been, um, involved with Constantine. And then, after his mysterious phone call, she'd been pissed. Hurt. So confused even though they'd both been clear that it had just been sex. There had been no talk of emotions and certainly not love or commitment but...

*"It's cover. Nothing more. We're not really involved."*

When he'd been inside her, it had certainly felt as if they'd been really involved.

"A car will be waiting," Constantine informed her. "I would expect a crowd to be in attendance. Everyone in the country will want to get a peek at you."

It had been a twelve-hour flight, with one stop in Amsterdam. By the time they landed, darkness would have fallen in Lancaden, so she wouldn't be able to tell much about the area. When she looked out the window, all she saw was the night sky.

Holden snoozed a few feet away. Or, at least, she thought he was sleeping. Like her and Constantine, he hadn't chatted much during the flight. He wore a ball cap, and it was pulled down low to cover his eyes.

"You think they'll be out this late?" Juliet asked.

"Not that late on Lancaden time. So, yeah, I think plenty of people will be out."

She rubbed her sweaty palms on the front of her dress pants. "When do you think I'll see my grandfather?" Because she didn't know how much time he had left.

"First thing in the morning. Tried to get you in sooner." The faint lines near his mouth deepened. "But by the time we unload and get to the castle, it *will* be later. We'll be pushing midnight. You can go in and see him at first light."

She had so many questions. And mixed emotions. "Do you think I'll stop feeling like a fake anytime soon?"

"What?" He leaned toward her. The seatbelt flexed around his waist.

"A fake. A fraud." She waved one hand vaguely. "Like everyone is going to look at me and know—"

"That we're not really engaged?"

She stopped waving her hand. Stared at the ring. "I'd forgotten that part." She actually had. Juliet cleared her throat. "I wasn't talking about that. I meant that I don't feel like some lost princess. It's all surreal, and I'm scared that all those people you say want to see me—I'm scared they will all be disappointed."

He held her gaze. "They won't be." Certainty.

But he had no way of knowing. "If my grandmother really tried to kill the king, why would they want me back? Wouldn't everyone hate me?"

"*You* haven't done anything wrong, Juliet. No one has a reason to hate you."

And yet she had a bodyguard. Two bodyguards. And she was lying about her relationship to Constantine so he could stay close because he clearly thought someone would come at her.

"*It's cover. Nothing more. We're not really involved.*" Once more, the words she'd come to hate slithered through her mind.

"Juliet?"

She'd been silent too long. "Do you think my grandmother hired that assassin?" Constantine would have all those precious files to tell him about the case.

His gaze cut away.

So, yes, he did.

"Why haven't you told me more about her? About what happened?"

"You haven't really asked." He kept peering into the darkness. "And I didn't want to hurt you. Knowing that your grandmother was a would-be murderer who spent her whole life on the run because if she'd been caught and sent back to Lancaden—if she'd been sent to Lancaden she would have been put to death. I don't see how me telling you that right away would have helped anything."

She heard the thud of her heartbeat echoing in her ears. "Put to death?"

An exhale. His gaze returned to her. "That's the punishment on the books in the country. The attempted assassination of a sitting king or queen has a death sentence attached."

She blinked quickly. Shook her head.

"He was her lover, the assassin she hired. She gave him the ring and asked him to kill the king. If he had done the job, and it hadn't been tied back to your grandmother, she would have taken the power in Lancaden. While not in line by blood to rule, the laws still would have given her the throne. She would have ruled until her child—the child biologically linked to the king—had been old enough to take over the throne. In Lancaden, the bloodline is key."

The pilot made another announcement. They were about to descend. *To the place where they wanted to kill my grandmother.*

The place where her mother had said... "My mom told me that the people here wanted us dead."

"Probably because your grandmother once told her that if *she* ever came back, she'd die. And your grandmother wasn't wrong about that. It's the reason she invented a new life and stayed hidden so long."

She could feel the plane shifting as they descended. "Why didn't her lover kill the king?"

He held her gaze. "Because someone killed the assassin before he could get the job done. Your grandmother mistakenly believed he'd betrayed her. That he'd taken the ring and run, but the truth was that her assassin was murdered. His body was hidden, and the truth only came to light recently."

Her breath choked out. "Where was he killed?"

The plane's engines seemed to rumble in the descent. "Right here in Lancaden. His body was found walled in the castle during some recent reconstruction."

*OhmyGod.*

The plane dipped a little more.

"Welcome home," Holden said, as he tipped back his ball cap. "To the place where they seal you in a wall and you claw at the bricks until you die."

She could not *breathe.*

"Sorry," Holden added with a roll of his shoulders when Constantine glared at him. "Was I supposed to leave that bit of the story out? Figured this was the part where we were putting all our cards on the table for the pretty princess. After all, isn't it our job to make sure no one walls her up?"

"I think I'm going to be sick," Juliet said as her stomach rolled and churned.

Holden snagged a paper bag from the seat beside him and tossed it to her.

Constantine kept glaring.

They landed.

\*\*\*

Constantine had been right. There was a crowd waiting outside the little airport. People with signs. People with flowers. People who were waving and bundled up in coats because the temperature was biting.

Juliet saw them all in a blur. Constantine was at her back, with Holden walking a few feet in front of her.

People of all ages were there. Kids, grandparents. They seemed so excited.

*And I feel like the biggest fraud in the world.* She didn't get why these people were happy to see her. They'd left their homes, gone out into the cold, and they were greeting her with a warm enthusiasm that made her chest ache. She found herself walking toward the crowd. They were behind some ropes, and men and women with dark uniforms seemed to be maintaining security.

"Juliet." Constantine curled his hand around her shoulder.

"I just want to say hello." Wasn't that the least she could do? Say hello? Stop for a minute when these people had come out to see her? This wasn't like the throng of reporters who'd cornered her outside the bar in Baton Rouge. This was different.

She tried a tentative smile for them. Spotlights seemed to be everywhere. "Thank you for coming out." What else was she supposed to say? *I'm excited to be here*—that was a lie. She wasn't excited to meet a grandfather who was dying. She was terrified and scared and a dozen other twisted emotions that burned in her heart. "Thank you." That was all she could manage.

*Thank you for being here. Thank you for smiling and not glaring. Thank you for not hating me the way I feared.*

One boy rushed beneath the rope and pushed roses into her hands. The thorns pricked her, and she could feel the blood welling, but she held the roses even tighter as she bent toward him. His mother cried his name, and Juliet nodded to him as she kept the smile on her face. "These are beautiful. Thank you, Pierre."

He beamed.

Juliet wished that she had something to give him, but she didn't even have her purse. Everything had been taken and handled by someone else. *"Merci pour ces belles fleurs."*

He bobbed his head and ran back to his mother.

Constantine's hand curled under her arm. "Sweetheart, we need to go."

She rose with him.

His head turned and his mouth brushed along her ear. "This is a security nightmare. Anyone can be hiding in that crowd, and if a slim rope can't keep an eight-year-old back, it sure as shit won't keep a killer back."

The thorns dug deeper into her palm as her hold tightened even more on the flowers. Her gaze swept the crowd. At first, it had seemed that everyone was happy to see her, but now...

In the back, she caught a glare on one woman's face. To the side, a man watched her with stone-faced intensity.

Juliet took a step in retreat. Another. With an effort, she kept the smile on her face. Her heels clicked on the cement and then she was in the back of the waiting car. She was safe. She'd made it and she could take a breath and let the fear out.

"Welcome to Lancaden, Juliet," Alexandre said as he lounged inside the limousine. His words made her jump. He lifted a drink and saluted her. "May it be your home for the rest of your days."

Constantine had entered the limo, too. "What the fuck are you doing in here?"

"Acting ruler, remember? I go where I want." His gaze slid down to Juliet's hands. She'd taken a seat on the side opposite him. "Lovely flowers, but..." His eyes narrowed.

There was plenty of light in the back of that limo. Plenty of light for her to see the faint smile that tilted his lips and for him to see—

"You've spilled blood, princess. Barely in Lancaden for ten minutes, and you're bleeding for your country. How incredibly noble." He winced. "Though I certainly hope it's not a portent of things to come."

Yes, she rather hoped it wasn't, too.

*** 

"The princess will be staying in these royal chambers." Alexandre made a flourish with his hands. He'd stayed with them after they'd arrived at the castle and acted as their escort.

*An actual, honest-to-God castle with turrets and a moat. A big, dark moat that circled the whole stone structure.* Granted, the moat had several bridges that had been designed so traffic could cross it, so the castle wasn't exactly in isolation, but still...*A real castle.* And to actually be there...

To hear the echo of her steps as she'd climbed the stairs. To see the heavy tapestries, the paintings of her ancestors, the rich rugs and the antique furniture that she knew had to cost an absolute fortune...Stunning. Breathtaking.

Overwhelming. Insane.

A dream.

A nightmare.

Alexandre was flanked by two men and one woman, all in black uniforms. Black, with gold embellishments. Swirls that shifted with their movements. The same sort of uniforms that the security personnel had worn at the airport. Alexandre hadn't introduced her to them when they'd entered the castle, so she'd introduced herself.

They hadn't responded.

"Protocol," Alexandre had chided. "That's not quite how things are done here."

Well, it was how she did things.

But the guards had kept stony expressions the whole time. They'd seemed on alert. They'd also seemed eager to do Alexandre's bidding. *His personal guards?*

And other than the guards, the castle seemed so quiet and empty. Echoing. Cold. "Where is everyone else?"

"Asleep," Alexandre assured her smoothly. "Did you really want us to wake everyone for your arrival?"

No, of course, not, and now she felt silly for—

"Yes," Constantine drawled. "Absolutely, we did. Because she is the princess and you're just some placeholder, so how about you stop acting like your shit doesn't smell to hell and back, huh?"

She was pretty sure that Holden snorted from his nearby position. He'd been a quiet shadow following their movements through the castle.

Alexandre stiffened. "Did you call me a placeholder?"

"Sure. I did, and I don't like that you brought her here without allowing us to meet every person who is in this castle tonight. That's what I call a security threat. A major one. Now I don't know who belongs and who doesn't. An intruder could walk down the hall at any moment, and as long as he has on one of your fancy royal uniforms..." Constantine motioned toward the silent guards. "He'll get full access, won't he?"

Alexandre's chin lifted a good inch. "There will be no intruders here." He pointed to the man on the left. Blond hair. Green eyes. A carefully trimmed beard that hugged his jaw. "Antoine is in charge of security. He makes certain the castle stays safe."

"Then maybe Antoine should have said that when Juliet introduced herself to him. Instead of standing there like a statue and not making a peep."

"Protocol," Alexandre enunciated.

"Or maybe he was following orders." Constantine shrugged. "Maybe you told him to stay quiet. The same way you told everyone else to stay in their rooms and not come out. Because you want Juliet to feel alone and isolated. You want her to feel lost. You want her to need someone who can help her out, and you really, really want that someone to be you."

Alexandre's nostrils flared. "Your room in down the hallway, Mr. Leos. I assume that you would like to be close to Juliet—"

"For someone who is so crazy about protocol, you keep calling her by her first name all the time. Seems a breach in etiquette to me."

"She has not officially received the title of princess. It is one that would have to be bestowed on her in a ceremony that *I* would perform after her lineage has been verified—"

"She's the princess, we both know it, and something else we should both know? I'm not sleeping down the hallway." Constantine peered inside the open doorway. "Looks like that bed will have plenty of room for two." His fingers twined with Juliet's as he lifted them to his mouth and brushed a kiss over her knuckles. "Right, princess?"

There was no way she'd be staying alone in that room. She'd peeked inside and knew it was massive. "Right." Everyone was watching. "Darling."

"Cool." From Holden. He exhaled on a long sigh. "I am tired, and I think I'll take that room you've got set up for Constantine. No sense in me being too far away from my client, am I right?"

A muscle jerked along Alexandre's jaw. "I told Eric Wilde that once she was here, the princess would be under royal protection. We do not need your services, Mr. Blackwell. I have arranged for you to stay at a hotel nearby where I am sure you will be quite comfortable."

Juliet's brows rose. "You have an entire castle, and you're sending him to a hotel?"

"*You* have a castle, my love," Constantine corrected even as he frowned and turned over her hand. "And you're still bleeding. What the hell?"

"I—just scratches. From the flowers." Flowers that Alexandre had taken from her in the limo. She wanted them back.

"Come on. I'm getting you cleaned up." He kept his careful grip on her hand and pulled her toward the open door of that room. Without looking back, he said, "By the way, *I'm* the client Holden just referenced. He's being paid to protect me, not Juliet. And I want him close, so he's getting my room. Thanks for preparing it for him."

Juliet turned to look back. Holden had already sauntered down the hallway.

As for Alexandre...

"I know," Constantine said before he kicked the door shut. "That shade of purple is alarming, isn't it?"

It wasn't the purple color coating his features that was alarming. It was the absolute fury on his face that scared her. A fury that seemed directed completely at Constantine.

# CHAPTER FIFTEEN

*Step Fifteen: The closer you are to the princess,
the safer she will be.*

The warm water washed the blood off her palm. Constantine's fingers slid carefully along her skin as he inspected the tiny wounds.

"It's really nothing," Juliet assured him. "Just a few scratches. I hardly felt them at all. They just, ah, they just came from the thorns in the roses."

"You shouldn't have stopped to take the flowers." He turned off the water. Pressed a soft, clean cloth to her hand and hated that she'd been hurt. They were in the giant bathroom connected to her assigned bedroom. Opulence? Double check. More like overkill. He barely batted an eye at the surroundings, though. Not his first time in a castle. Not his second. The castles he'd stayed in before had been different. One had been a decaying, supposedly haunted castle in Ireland. Then he'd spent some time in Windsor. But you want to talk about opulence? Well, he'd seen things when he visited a palace in the Middle East that still had him scratching his head and wondering why the hell anyone would really need a throne made out of gold.

"I didn't want to hurt the boy's feelings." Her head tilted forward as she stared at the small cuts on her palm cut. And there was something about her voice...

*Shit. You didn't want to hurt his feelings the way I hurt yours?* Because they hadn't talked about it during the flight. *It*—the insane sex. *It*—the way she'd caught him being a complete dick right after said insane sex when he'd said that unforgettable bullshit line of, *"It's cover. Nothing more. We're not really involved."*

"Juliet." He wanted her to look at him.

Instead, she pulled her hand away. "All better."

No, he didn't think it was. "The boy could have been a distraction. Someone could have paid the kid to slip under the rope. Most people don't see kids as threats, so he would have been the perfect tool to use."

"Pierre was a kid, not a tool."

"You haven't seen the things that I have." Kids were used as weapons all the time, and it was freaking heartbreaking.

Her head whipped up. Now her eyes were on him, but they were filled with pain. Confusion.

*Lost princess.*

"He could have been a distraction," Constantine repeated because she needed to start looking for threats everywhere. "When you stopped for him, when you bent down, someone could have shot you from the crowd. You could have made a perfect target when you hesitated right there. Or the shot didn't have to come from the crowd. It could have come from a sniper who'd positioned himself on the nearby roof." They'd been in the open, and all he'd wanted to do was grab her and *run* to that limo. "You think people are good, but they're not always. You have to follow my orders."

She licked her lips. "Pierre was just a little kid."

"Follow my orders," he rasped.

Her eyes flashed. "If some sweet kid wants to hand me flowers, I'm taking them."

"And if some sweet kid has a knife stashed in the flowers and he stabs you in the chest with it, what then?"

Her mouth dropped open.

*Fuck.*

"I—" Juliet stopped, seemingly at a loss.

*Way to scare her to death, asshole.* But maybe Juliet needed to be more afraid. Because when she trusted the world, the world just had the chance to hurt her. "Your house is gone. Someone is after you."

"I'm an ocean away now." Quieter.

"Doesn't mean a threat isn't here. I'm being paid to protect you." Actually, he wasn't being paid a dime. He was doing the paying.

"Yes, of course. You're doing your job. All cover. Nothing more."

Damn. He felt that hit right in his heart.

She turned away. Stopped. "You must have seen a lot of terrible things in your life. Things that make you think innocent boys can be killers."

Boys could be killers. Anyone could kill.

"I hate that you've had to see all that darkness, and I really, really hope there's been some light to balance things out." Her shoes clicked on the old stone as she headed back to the bedroom.

He watched her walk away—watched the little bit of light that had recently come into his life.

Yeah, he had some light all right. And he'd fight dirty and hard, and he'd take out all the threats to her. Because there were some things— some people—in this world who were worth protecting.

***

"You're staying in the chair? That's where you intend to sleep?" Juliet had pulled the mountain of covers up high. A fireplace waited to her right, a massive, crackling fireplace in the middle of a long wall that seemed to be made out of stone. She'd needed to climb up a small stool in order to get on the giant bed. Heavy, ornate curtains were tied to the bed's four posters. She'd changed into her pajamas, silk pajamas that the mystery person at Wilde had purchased for her. "There's plenty of room here." She glanced at the other side of the bed. "You don't even have to touch me the bed is so wide."

"Because you don't want me touching you?" Low. Guarded.

They'd turned out the lights in the room. Technically, was it two rooms? The bedroom and a sitting area and then the bathroom to the side. Three? She shook her head because it didn't even matter how many rooms were in her temporary chambers.

Constantine sat in a chair about five feet from the bed. He hadn't changed. He still wore his blue suit, but his tie had been jerked away.

"I...I just meant that you didn't have to touch me." This was awkward. "There's enough room for like, four people—not that I'm saying four people should be in this bed." Jeez. "I'm just saying—" *Stop this.* "You don't have to stay up all night in the chair. You need sleep. You can sleep here with me. Besides, if someone comes in tomorrow, and your side of the bed hasn't been touched, don't you think that will look a little suspicious?"

Silence.

"Look, you can get the side that will put you between me and the door, and I know how you like being between me and doors." Yes, she was trying for humor, and the attempt failed. "I'm hardly going to force you to sleep in the bed with me." Brittle. "I just thought you'd be more comfortable."

"Will *you* be comfortable?"

"You're here. That means I'm safe." Simple.

He swore. Low, deep, and inventive. "Did you feel safe when I was fucking you last night?"

Okay. That had certainly turned the conversation. "Yes." Her hands fisted on the covers. "I felt safe and good, and I felt so much pleasure I thought my whole body might shatter apart." A pause. "Am I supposed to regret what we did? Is this why you're in ultra-bodyguard mode? You think that because we're here in the castle now, things have changed?"

"I should have kept my hands off you when we were in the US."

Wonderful. "The words every woman longs to hear," she muttered. *I should have kept my hands off you.* So much better than...*I can't resist you. You drive me crazy. I want you again and again.*

"I will be keeping them off now." A deliberate hesitation, she was sure, before he added, "Princess."

He was putting boundaries in place. Check. "Fine. Sleep in the chair. Protect that virtue of yours because clearly, you think that if you get within a foot of me in this *massive* bed, you will not be able to resist my incredible charms." She flopped back on the bed. Yanked the covers to her neck. "You try to do something nice. You offer a man a comfortable mattress so he doesn't sleep in a chair all night and he acts like you're attempting to jump him. FYI, my hands will be here, under the covers, not touching you. You don't need to worry about seduction from me." Her eyes squeezed closed. *"Good night."*

"Uh, Juliet?"

"I'm sleeping."

"You're not. You're talking."

"Fine. I'm trying to sleep and this bodyguard who thinks very highly of himself is interrupting that attempt."

He choked out a laugh. Her eyes almost opened so that she could glare at him. She didn't, though. Juliet kept her eyes tightly closed.

"You do not act like a princess."

Her back teeth clenched. "So I keep being told." Freaking protocol.

"No, I meant—hell, forget it. Get that sleep of yours, and just know that this bodyguard will be keeping watch."

"If you don't get some sleep, you'll be dead on your feet and no good to me or anyone else." Surely, he had to see the logic in her argument?

"If I get in that bed with you, sleep will be the last thing I want."

Oh, back to that, were they? "I'm not going to seduce you. I get that I made you break your rules before, and you're pissed at me."

"What?"

"You've been giving me the cold shoulder ever since you got that mystery phone call, and I get it. You don't have any emotional attachment to me. Understood. Not like I was asking you to fall in love with me. So you can take a breath, bodyguard." If he kept calling her princess, then Juliet decided she'd be calling him *bodyguard*. Maybe that would help to put some mental distance between them. "I'm not planning to pull you into my wicked web again."

"Not like it would take much pulling."

She cracked open one eye. The light from the flickering fire revealed and concealed as shadows and darkness chased across the chambers.

"Let me just be clear with you." His hands had curled around the lion-shaped ends of the chair's armrests. "You breathe, and I want you."

Her breathing got a wee bit faster.

"You smile, and I want to slay a freaking dragon."

There weren't any dragons around.

"You tell a sarcastic joke and make me laugh, and I want to put the world at your feet."

That was...a lot. The whole world?

"And you can pull me into your wicked web any day of the week. Consider me a willing victim."

Now both of her eyes were wide open. Did he really mean those things? She needed more light to see his face. Dammit!

"I'm not in the bed with you because if I'm in the bed, I'm in you two minutes later. Wasn't sure you still wanted me. I get that things are real now. You're here. You've got a crowd waiting to chant your name. So maybe you don't want to be screwing the bodyguard when all too soon, we'll be parting ways."

She didn't want to be parted from him. "I can't imagine not wanting you." A stark truth. "Because..." Juliet sat up. "When you breathe, I want you."

He leaned forward in the chair. *"Juliet."*

"When you touch me—even if you're just cleaning some scratches that I have—my whole body seems to electrify. A charge fills me, and all I want is for you to keep touching me. Because when you touch me, everything is all right. No, better than all right. I need you, I want you, and there is no fear or any doubt for me." There was just Constantine.

He surged out of the chair and took a quick step toward the bed.

"And when you smile..." She swallowed the nervous lump in her throat. "You have these little dents that appear in your cheeks, and I think they might just be the cutest things I've ever seen. You still look dangerous and tough, don't get me wrong, but there is something about those dents that, I swear, melts my heart."

His mouth crashed onto hers. A deep, drugging kiss as he loomed over her. She didn't even know if he'd used that little stool to reach her. He was just suddenly in the bed with her. Kissing her. Using his lips and tongue and making her wild because she acted that way with him. Restraint vanished in a blink, and her hands grabbed for him. She clutched him as tightly as she could. No one had ever made her feel the way he did. She knew, in the depths of her soul, that no one else ever would again. Whatever they had, it wouldn't last long. But while it did last, she didn't want to let him go. Not ever.

Except, he'd just let her go. He'd jerked back as if he'd felt some sort of jolting, electric shock.

Her mouth was still open. She could still taste him, but Constantine had yanked out his phone, and he glared at the screen. "Nine-one-one." Sharp. Tense. "Fuck." He flew off the bed.

Her mouth closed, then opened again.

He rushed to his luggage. The bags had been delivered shortly after Constantine had kicked the door closed on Alexandre, and the bags waited just inside the open door of a small closet. Constantine shoved his hand in his black duffel bag and froze. "Sonofabitch. Someone took my gun."

His gun?

He whirled back toward her. "The room is secure. I searched every inch while you were changing in the bathroom. Bolt the door behind me."

She'd noticed the gigantic, rather old-fashioned, almost dungeon-like bolt when she'd entered.

"Do not open this door for anyone but me, understand? Not a soul. I don't care if your grandfather hauls his ass out of his deathbed—"

She flinched because, wow, that had been harsh.

"You don't open the door."

Juliet climbed from the bed. "What's happening?"

He had his phone to his ear. "Holden texted me nine-one-one, and now he's not answering. I need to check on him, but I don't want to leave you."

Easy solution. "Take me with you." Her toes curled over the stone.

"No, because if he's in trouble, you can't be exposed to danger. Lock the door. Stay *here*. Promise me, Juliet."

Her arms curled around her stomach. Barely in the castle any time at all, and already, the first threat had come. Maybe her mother had been right. Maybe death was the only thing that waited in Lancaden. "I promise."

\*\*\*

He heard the bolt slide into place behind him, and Constantine's head jerked in approval. Good. At least Juliet was safe. He'd searched every inch of her quarters himself. No one had been in there, and they were so high up, it sure as shit wasn't like someone could scale the castle wall in order to get to her.

The long corridor was lit with faint light. Not torch light because they weren't that old school, but carefully designed flickers that were supposed to *look* like candles danced from their mounted position along the walls. He rushed down the corridor. To the right, an open door led to a library. Walls and walls of books. On down a bit more, and he saw a small kitchen. Another door waited just past that kitchen, and when he slammed his fist into it, he heard the echo of the pounding in the hallway.

He also heard a grumble from Holden. *This is his room.*

Constantine pounded again. Harder.

The door opened with a screech of its hinges. "I swear, I think they shoved my ass in a storage closet," Holden grumbled. "Though since this room was intended to be yours, I think we can both be assured that they were *not* rolling out the royal welcome for you."

Constantine glared at him. "That was the emergency? That you don't like your room?"

Holden's brow furrowed. "I'd call it more of an inconvenience than an emergency, but thanks for your concern." He poked his head out of the room and looked down the hallway. "Shouldn't you be with the princess?"

"Yeah, I should be, but my partner's fool ass texted me a nine-one-one, so I came running and left her securely locked in her quarters."

Holden whipped his head toward Constantine. "I didn't text you."

"Uh, yes, you did." Constantine held up the phone. "Your number, your text."

"*I didn't text you.* I was searching for my phone when you started pounding. I swear, I left the thing on that wobbly nightstand before I went in to shower, but when I came out, it was gone. I thought it had fallen under the bed or something, so I was looking but—"

Constantine had already whirled away. He raced back down the corridor, cursing himself.

# CHAPTER SIXTEEN

*Step Sixteen: Be prepared to tear down the world for her.*

Juliet paced back and forth near the foot of the bed. She'd grabbed a robe because even with the fire crackling, a strange chill had seemed to enter the room. Juliet could have sworn that the temperature had dropped ten degrees in the small length of time that Constantine had been gone. She'd turned on the bedside light because those flickering shadows cast by the fire had made her even more nervous.

The bolt secured the door. She was safe, she knew that, but she worried about Constantine. If he could just hurry back, maybe the weird chill would leave her bones.

Juliet inched toward the door. She wanted to peek outside and look into the hallway just to make sure that everything was all right.

*"Juliet!"* A bellow that reached her clearly even through the thick door. Constantine's bellow. That bellow was probably going to wake up the whole castle.

She closed the last bit of distance between her and the door and reached for the bolt.

And she felt something—someone—grab her from behind. The touch was so shocking and sudden that Juliet opened her mouth to scream. But a hand covered her lips before she could. A gloved hand slapped against her mouth even as she felt a jab in her back.

"That is a gun, princess." Low. Muffled. "His gun. Loaded with his bullets and currently pressing into your back. If you call out to him, I will shoot you right here and now, and he won't be able to open the door in time to save you."

Her breath shuddered out. *How is he in the room?* It had just been her. There was only one door, and it was in front of her, and it still was bolted.

Constantine pounded on the door. "Juliet! Open the door for me. *Now!*"

With every bit of her being, she wanted to rip that door open, but the gun pressed to the middle of her spine. If she tried to rush forward, he'd pull the trigger. She'd die or be paralyzed at the very least when the bullet ripped its way through her spine.

"Come with me now, and I swear, *I* will not hurt you."

She was supposed to believe the man jabbing a gun into her back? *Lie, lie, lie.* If she went with him, she was dead.

But if she fought him or screamed...*I'm dead now.*

Maybe acting like she believed him would buy her more time.

The door shook beneath Constantine's fist. "*Juliet!*"

"Shout back to him," the rasping voice ordered. "Tell him that you want to be alone. Say anything else, and the bullet will fly through your spine."

His hand lifted from her mouth. She wet lips that felt bruised. "I want to be alone." A whisper.

"He can't hear that."

"I want to be alone." Had she just heard an accent in his words? Not American.

"*Louder.*" The gun jabbed harder. Hard enough that she knew there would be a mark.

"I want to be alone!" Juliet screamed.

Constantine stopped pounding. "Move away from the door, sweetheart." Low, but she still heard him.

But she didn't get a chance to move away, not before the whole door *shook* as if a sledgehammer had just been shoved into it.

And then it shook again.

Her attacker cried, "The fool is breaking down the door!"

Yes, he was. She could see the hinges loosening and a smile spread over her lips. *My bodyguard is gonna kick your ass.*

The hand that had been over her mouth grabbed her shoulder. "Too bad you won't be here when he gets inside." He yanked her around, moving at the same time so that he remained behind her body, and, in the new position, her eyes immediately landed on the window. Was he going to force her to jump? Not happening. She'd take a bullet long before she hurtled to her death. But maybe she could get the gun away from him. He was distracted now by Constantine, so she might have a fighting chance.

Except, he wasn't pushing her toward the window. With that hand on her shoulder and the gun still shoved to her spine, he sent her toward the elaborate fireplace. "This room belonged to your *grand-mère*," he told her. "Her lover slipped in and out all the time."

What?

He let her go long enough to shove his palm against one of the stones on the fireplace mantel. And when he let her go, she lunged for the fireplace poker. Her fingers curled around it.

"I don't have the safety on this gun. I squeeze the trigger, and you are dead. I can make my getaway and leave your body for the boyfriend to find."

She still gripped the poker.

"I said I wouldn't hurt you. I stand by those words."

Those lying words.

"Let it go, or I will have to shoot you. Our deal will be off."

They didn't have a deal.

But she saw that when he'd pushed in that stone on the fireplace, some of the elaborate rocks on that wall had shifted. No, not shifted. *Opened.* A section of the stony facade had pushed outward, like a door swinging open.

Cold air blew from that opening.

No wonder the temperature in her room had chilled. He'd let the cold air in. He'd been in the room with her, watching her, and she hadn't even noticed. *When did he come inside?* When she'd rushed to the closet for her robe? She'd only been in there a moment.

"Go in *now*."

She only saw darkness beyond that small opening.

Behind her, she could hear Constantine trying to break down the door. How much longer until he succeeded? How much—

"Maybe I should just fire a shot through that door and shoot the boyfriend. Will that convince you of just how serious I am?"

She went into the darkness without any other hesitation.

***

*"What is the meaning of this?"* Alexandre bellowed as he rushed down the hallway.

Constantine barely spared him a glance. The jerk looked like some playboy wannabe in his black smoking jacket. Constantine went right back to ramming his shoulder into the heavy wooden door.

Holden helped by slamming his shoulder against the door, too.

The wood splintered.

One more hit and that door *would* break.

"Stop!" Alexandre thundered. "Stop him, now!"

And the guards who'd just been gaping at Constantine surged forward to grab him. One of those guards was the prick head of security, Antoine. Before Constantine could kick that guy onto his ass, Holden intervened. He leapt forward and threw a hard jab at Antoine. The head of security staggered, seemed absolutely stunned, and his body trembled as he appeared ready to topple. In the next instant, Holden swiped out with his leg in an effortless takedown and had Antoine falling onto the floor.

"Head of security?" Holden snorted. "Head of security, my ass. If it's not this joker's first day, I'm stunned."

"You can't break down a door just because the princess kicked you out!" Alexandre latched onto Constantine's arm.

Oh, fatal mistake.

Constantine looked down at the arm, then up at Alexandre.

Alexandre swallowed. "You hit me, in front of all these witnesses, and you will be locked in a Lancaden jail. I promise you that." But his words quivered with his fear.

Rage coursed through Constantine's veins. He leaned close so that Alexandre and only Alexandre could hear his next words. "I can kill you, in front of all these witnesses, and you will be dead so fast that no one ever has the chance to help you. I promise you that."

Alexandre let him go and leapt back, a good five feet. "She kicked you out! Stop destroying property! If you are no longer her consort, then you are—"

"The princess is in danger, dumbass!" Holden snarled. "Stop being a prick!"

Constantine shoved into that door one more time, and it splintered. Chunks of wood went flying as he kicked and shoved his way past the remnants and into the room. *"Juliet!"* He'd heard her voice moments before. Heard the fear in it and that fear had gutted him.

The bolt had partially come out of the wall. He didn't care about the bolt. What he cared about was her, but as he ran through the quarters, searching for her, ice spread over his body because she wasn't there.

She wasn't there, but the door had still been bolted from the inside.

She wasn't there, but there was only one door that led into her quarters.

She wasn't there, but she'd been inside moments before, calling out to him.

"What the hell?" Holden spun near her bed. "Where's Juliet?"

More broken wood fell onto the floor as Alexandre—or rather, Alexandre's royal guards—poked their way inside. One of them—a woman with close-cropped, red hair—undid the bolt and swung open the door so Alexandre could enter easily.

Constantine stalked right past the female guard and locked his hands on the lapels of that Hugh Hefner smoking jacket. Using his grip, he hauled a gaping Alexandre forward. "Where's the passage?"

"The what?"

"Remember what I told you would happen five seconds ago?" Maybe it had been longer. Screw it. He didn't care. "If you don't tell me where the passage is right now, I will make sure my promise is carried out."

The female guard inched forward.

"You can't threaten me!"

He can. He had. "Juliet is *gone*. She was talking to me through the door moments before. She didn't just pull a Houdini. Someone *took* her. Someone in the castle you said was safe." He wanted to rip the bastard apart. "You gave her this room, deliberately, I'm sure."

"The room belonged to the princess's grandmother," the red-haired guard said. "Putting her here was a courtesy." Her delicate jaw hardened. "You need to release the counsellor at once."

"Courtesy, my ass," Constantine blasted, and he did *not* release Alexandre.

"It...it *was* her grandmother's," Alexandre rushed to say. "When she and the king began to fight, the queen was moved here. I thought Juliet would feel closer to her grandmother if she stayed in this area. I thought it would give her a connection to her past."

*"Where is the passage?* There's a secret passage into this room, and I want to see it, now."

Alexandre's eyes widened. "If there's a passage, I'm sorry, but I don't know a thing about it. I just put her in here because I thought she'd like to stay in the quarters her grandmother had once used. I was trying to be kind."

He didn't think the man had ever been kind a day in his life.

"Uh, Constantine?"

Holden needed to stop talking because Constantine was about to beat the truth out of a prick counsellor.

"Is it my imagination," Holden continued, voice sharpening, "or does it look like that fireplace poker is an arrow pointing to the stones?"

Constantine freed Alexandre and flew across the room. His gaze swept the fireplace. When he'd left, the poker had been on the rack to the left of the fireplace. He knew because he'd stirred up the fire a bit to make the room warmer while Juliet prepared for bed, and he'd put the poker back himself. It had been moved and now, yes, the sharp edge of the poker pointed up and toward an area of the stone just like an arrow.

*Juliet, I fucking love you.*

The thought had him stumbling. Holden grabbed him before Constantine could trip.

"Dude, you okay?"

Shaking him off, Constantine reached for the stones near the location indicated by the poker. He pressed his hands over the stones, one after the other after the other until the stones moved. Cold air wafted toward him. His head turned toward Alexandre. "No passageway? That was what you said?"

Alexandre's mouth hung open. "I-I...I had no idea!"

He'd get an idea, once Constantine kicked his ass. But first, he had a princess to find. *I'm coming, Juliet.*

\*\*\*

She almost tripped twice going down the twisting stairs. Total darkness surrounded her, and she clung desperately to the thin railing on her side. A railing that seemed ready to crumble at any moment. The man behind her remained close at all times, and his gun would shift from her shoulder to her spine, to her shoulder again. Always touching some part of her.

She wouldn't cry. Juliet refused to cry. Instead, she tried to figure out what she could do in order to escape. Would Constantine notice the way she'd left the poker? Would he see that it pointed up toward that section of stones?

Her foot slipped again, but only because they'd reached a landing. They'd gone down, down, down. Surely more steps than she'd taken to reach the third floor of the castle when they'd first arrived?

"Turn right." More a grunt than anything else.

Her toes were absolutely frozen, and as she turned, she tugged at the belt on her robe. She pulled it free and let it fall. It was so dark that she didn't think he could see the movement. How could he see anything? The only way for him to know where they were going... "You work here at the castle." The only scenario that made sense to her. "You've worked here a while, so long that you literally know your way in the dark."

"Stop talking."

No, she should have been talking sooner. Because the more she talked, the more she would seem *human*. Not some object he could eliminate. She needed him to relate to her. To feel for her. To feel badly about the idea of killing her. "I came to see my grandfather."

"You came to steal a crown that isn't yours." Definite accent now. That Lancaden mix that was a little bit flowing French and harder, rougher English.

"He is the only family I have left. I've lived my whole life without a crown, I can keep right on doing that forever. I came back to see him." *And to get the truth about my grandmother.* "He wants to see me, too. He asked for me to come home. If he hadn't asked for me..." Juliet's hand rose before her face because she was afraid that she'd slam into a wall at any moment. "If he hadn't asked, I would have stayed in the US."

"You want to hurt him."

*"No."* An instinctive denial. "I don't."

"You're just like her. She poisoned you. Turned you against everyone, so it's only fitting that you meet the same fate that her lover did."

It shouldn't have been possible for her skin to suddenly get colder, but it did. And her fingers touched stone in front of her at the same moment she felt the muzzle of the gun finally pull away from her back.

Her hands slapped at the stone. *A dead end.* No, no, please, she really, really didn't want it to end this way. Juliet whirled around. "Don't shoot me, please! I've never hurt you! I've never hurt anyone!"

"Liar." A breath. *"Poor lost princess."*

Those words...they seemed familiar. And she remembered being surrounded by reporters. Having everyone close in on her. Being pushed. Being on the ground and scared and that whisper had teased her ears.

Her shoulders bumped into the stone. There was no escape behind her. The only way out was through him. "Were you in Baton Rouge?"

She heard the sound of scraping. Stones scraping against each other. Her eyes strained in the darkness. She could just make out his shadowy form. Big. Menacing. "I thought you weren't going to hurt me!" Juliet shouted, a deliberate shout because maybe someone would hear her. Someone, somewhere in the castle.

A light flared. A sputtering candle. It lit his face—or, rather, the big, twisting mask that covered his face. Like a Mardi Gras mask that she'd seen parade float riders wearing when she visited New Orleans on Fat Tuesday. White and stark around his eyes and nose, the mask dipped low to slide just over his top lip.

He held the candle in one hand and the gun in the other. Staring at her, he slowly lowered the candle to the stone floor. "I won't put even a bruise on your skin."

Wrong. She was sure her back was already covered in bruises from his jabbing gun.

"The light won't last long, especially once you're closed in. But it doesn't seem right to leave you with just nothing."

Her whole body swayed because she feared she knew exactly what he was about to do. *It's only fitting that you meet the same fate that her lover did.*

He'd been talking about her grandmother's lover. Oh, God. Her lover had been sealed inside the walls of the castle. Hadn't Holden said that the lover had tried to claw his way out?

"Goodbye, princess."

*No!* "Do you have a mother?" Desperate words. "A sister?"

He'd been backing away, but now he stopped.

"Would you do this to her?" Juliet asked, as her voice cracked. "Would you leave her alone in the dark? Seal her inside to die from lack of oxygen or starvation or whatever it is that will take me? A slow death. Terrifying. Torturous. It would be kinder to just put a bullet in my head, but you're not doing that. You're picking the worst way to end me. A way that only a monster would choose."

"I'm not a monster."

*Keep him talking. Constantine will see the poker. He'll come down the stairs. He'll see the belt that you dropped and know to turn that way.* She just had to live long enough for Constantine to come.

"You just abducted a woman at gunpoint. You're going to leave me here to die. My last moments will be filled with terror and suffering. If that doesn't make you a monster..." She swallowed the lump in her throat. "Then what does?"

"*You're* the monster. You want to steal the crown—"

"You're Lancaden." She switched tactics. Fast, trying to keep him off-balance and uncertain. "And you're wearing the uniform of the royal guard." At least, she thought that was the uniform. Black and gold? "You're supposed to protect the royal family."

"I am." His voice hardened with determination.

*Uh, oh.*

More stones grated. He was shoving what looked like a large section of the wall closed. When he moved it fully into place, she would be trapped inside. Was this some old torture cell? Something left over from long ago? She knew the castle had been built back in the Middle Ages so there had to be secret, hidden remnants of its bloody past scattered in its depths.

He was trying to seal her away in one of those terrible places.

"*I* am the royal family!" Juliet leapt toward him. "You're supposed to protect me! Not kill me!"

The small candle showed him swinging the gun right toward her.

She stopped.

"Come at me again, and I will shoot you."

Fine. "I'll take a bullet to slow death, if that's my option, thank you very much—"

A roar broke through her words. A roar that seemed to shake the very stones around her.

A roar that she knew belonged to Constantine.

In that instant, Juliet dropped to her knees. The gun had been pointing at her, and when Constantine charged at her abductor—as she knew he was about to do—Juliet didn't want to risk a bullet firing off and hitting her in the chest or head.

Her knees slammed into the stone and the candlelight showed Constantine tackling her abductor in the same instant. Constantine hit the masked man with bone-snapping force. He hurtled his body right at him, and her abductor lost his footing and rammed into the nearby wall.

She heard a crack as his head hit the stone, but her attacker didn't go down. He shook his head and tried to swing up with the gun.

Constantine yanked the gun right out of his hand and flipped it around. Then he shoved the barrel of that gun beneath her attacker's chin.

"Juliet!" Holden rushed to her. His hands curled over her arms as he pulled Juliet to her feet. "Tell me you're not hurt."

"I—" Her heart thundered in her chest.

His hands flew over her. "No broken bones? No gunshot wounds? I didn't hear the gun blast, but I did damn near kill myself on that staircase because Con was running down the thing so that meant I had to run, too, and—"

"No bullets." Laughter.

Her head whipped toward her abductor.

Constantine still had the gun shoved under his chin.

"Told her I wasn't going to hurt her. I keep my word," the man continued. The white mask still covered the top of his face.

More pounding steps seemed to echo around them.

"*Where is the princess?*" Alexandre's screeching voice.

But she didn't look toward his bellow. She kept her eyes on Constantine and the man who'd forced her out of her room. "Is that true?" She pulled from Holden and took a lunging step toward the jerk who'd terrorized her. "That whole time, there were no bullets in the gun?" She'd only left her room because she'd been afraid he would shoot and kill Constantine.

"Let's find out," Constantine said simply.

And he pulled the trigger.

# CHAPTER SEVENTEEN

*Step Seventeen: Destroy. That's what you will need to do. Destroy her enemies. Don't hesitate. Don't stop. Do the dark deeds that must be done.*

His finger squeezed the trigger. *Snick.* But he'd realized the gun wouldn't fire even before he squeezed. Constantine knew his own weapon. He knew the weight, and he'd known the bullets weren't inside.

The wavering light from that stub of a candle let him see the smile on the bastard's face. "Told you. I never meant to *hurt* her. I keep my promises."

Constantine smiled back at him. "I keep mine, too." He drove his fist into SOB's liver. A direct attack that he knew would do fast, painful damage. The hit to the liver was an old, vicious technique, one designed to send blood pressure plummeting and to make the prick's heartbeat slow. Instantly, the jerk tried to curl into himself. A physical response he couldn't stop, and as Constantine's new worst enemy balled up, Constantine leaned in and promised, "You're a dead man." Because the bastard had taken Juliet.

Taken her away in the dark. Brought her into some kind of damn dungeon. For what purpose? If he hadn't been planning to shoot her, then...

"What were you going to do to my Juliet?" A lethal snarl.

"Guards, take him!" Alexandre shouted. "Put him in cuffs! Get him away from the princess!"

No, things didn't end that easily. They weren't going to take his prey.

Flashlights immediately swept toward Constantine and the man before him. The guards had come prepared. Constantine had just run straight into the darkness. He'd known there was no time to waste.

*The guards had lights with them. They knew there were passages in the castle that were consumed by darkness.* The guards...who wore black and gold uniforms just like the one the SOB in front of him wore.

Constantine grabbed the mask on the bastard's face and ripped it away.

The guy blinked blearily at him.

"Who gave the order?" Constantine demanded.

The sonofabitch's eyes flickered over Constantine's shoulder. *Oh, the hell, no.*

"He-he said he was going to seal me inside. Just like what had been done to my grandmother's lover." Juliet's voice shook with fear, and Constantine wanted to rip apart the man who'd taken her. A volatile mix of fury and fear fueled Constantine's body. He was used to fury. What he wasn't used to?

*Fear.*

But when he'd gone in that room and Juliet had been gone, fear had nearly blinded him. *Need her. Can't let her go. Can't let her get hurt.*

"She won't be queen." The fool smiled at Constantine once again. "Never will happen. She came home to die."

Screw that bullshit. Constantine slammed his head right into the SOB's face. He was about ninety percent sure he'd broken the guy's nose, based on the amount of blood that poured from it. As the prick howled, Constantine stepped back. He tucked his recovered gun into the waistband of his pants. Then he fisted his hands. "You're going to tell me everything."

The attacker swiped the blood from his face. Flashlights still focused on him.

"Constantine?" Juliet's fearful voice.

"Get her the hell out of here, Holden!" he ordered. *"Now."* Juliet needed to get out of the dark and back to safety. "Do not let her leave your sight for even a moment."

"Take him into custody!" From Alexandre. The pompous dick. "I am in charge here—I want that man in cuffs and locked up! He will not get away with abducting our princess."

The attacker's eyes flickered. He seemed confused. "But..." He swiped at the blood again.

Holden ushered Juliet away from that small, cold room. *A coffin. That's what this room is.* Because the SOB had planned to lock Juliet inside, and if that stone exterior had been slid completely back into place...

*Would I have found her?* Because all the damn walls down there—down in what was a real, honest-to-hell dungeon—were made of stone. Thick, heavy stone. Chamber after chamber and corridor after corridor of stone.

"She can't leave!" the attacker screamed. "She has to stay here! That was the order—she has to *stay!* She's too dangerous, she's too—" He tried to lunge and grab Juliet.

Not happening. *You will never touch her again.* Constantine drove his fist into the guy's kidney.

The man went down, slamming into the stone.

Constantine nodded at Holden. "Get her out."

"Constantine?" Juliet breathed his name.

His muscles locked. "Stay with Holden. Every minute." Because there was no one else in this castle that he trusted.

But Juliet chose that instant not to leave with Holden, but to run straight to Constantine. She threw her arms around him. "He said he was going to shoot you."

His arms closed around her. The thin, silk robe was icy. *She* felt icy. She was shaking and shivering, and his rage flared hotter.

"I only left the bedroom because he said he'd shoot through the door. He was going to shoot you—"

Alexandre's chief of security—that Antoine prick—chose that moment to sidle around Constantine and make a grab for the perp. Constantine tensed. The hell they were taking his prey away before he could get the truth from him. *I know when I'm looking at the muscle of the operation. I want the brains. I want the one who sent him after my Juliet.*

"Don't," Constantine bit off, as he pulled from Juliet.

His prey had been sprawled on the stone. Antoine bent near him, reaching out with a hand that had cuffs gripped in it. "You're being taken into royal custody," he announced. "You're—

The perp surged up. He grabbed for Antoine's waist. For the *knife* that the fool had strapped there. He whipped up the blade and sliced it across Antoine's chest.

Antoine fell back, crying out in pain.

And the attacker locked his eyes on Juliet. "I didn't want to hurt you." Blood dripped from the knife.

*Why the hell aren't Antoine's other guards charging him?* But they'd frozen.

Constantine didn't freeze. He stepped in front of Juliet. "You won't be hurting her. Because in order to do that, you'd need to get through me. That won't happen." His hands clenched. "Holden, get her away from here!" How many times did he have to say that? "Carry her out if she won't go—*take her, now!*"

Juliet gasped behind him, and Constantine was pretty sure that Holden was, indeed, carrying her, but he didn't look because he couldn't take his gaze off his prey. The bastard surged forward with his knife. He'd raised it high above his head, and his intent was clearly to stab Constantine. To stab anyone who got in his way. He wanted to get to his target, and he wasn't stopping.

The knife flew down toward Constantine. He lifted his hand and used his forearm to stop the attack. "Try harder," he challenged.

The attacker pulled back the knife. Breath heaving, he came in for another attack.

Constantine grabbed the man's wrist. He twisted, used all his strength because he was going to snap that wrist if that was what it took. He was going to—

The attacker's foot flew out and caught Constantine's. Hell, no, he wasn't going down. Constantine side-stepped and shoved the knife back at the bastard.

The knife found its target just as gunfire blasted. But the bullet didn't hit the attacker. It sliced over the top of Constantine's arm. At least, the first bullet did.

The second slammed into the perp's back. He gave a gurgle, a shocked cry. His body swayed.

A third bullet thundered. A bullet fired from Antoine's gun as he knelt on the stone floor. It hit the perp. He toppled. And when he fell, Antoine's gun was still up and aimed—aimed perfectly at Constantine's chest.

Because it sure as shit looked like Antoine was about to take the shot, Constantine threw the knife. It flashed, end over end, and sank into Antoine's shoulder. The man cried out in pain even as the gun dropped from his fingers.

"What in the hell?" Antoine grabbed his shoulder. And it was the craziest thing. His Lancaden accent slipped away in that instant. "I just saved your ass!"

*He's not Lancaden.* When in pain, even the best actors could lose their facades. Constantine took a step forward. His shoe crunched the white mask that the attacker had worn. "Reflex action."

Antoine glared at him.

Alexandre kept shouting orders. More of his men filled the tight space—even tighter with so many bodies crowding inside.

Constantine bent over the fallen bastard's body. He put his hand to the guy's throat. Still alive. But for how much longer? "Look at me," Constantine commanded.

The man's lashes remained closed.

"If you're really loyal to Lancaden, then you'll give me a name. Now. You'll tell me who ordered you to take her. *Tell me.*"

His mouth parted.

And Alexandre's other guards shoved Constantine out of the way as they surrounded the jerk.

"We need a medical team!" Alexandre cried out. "One of our own is down! He is *down!*"

Constantine locked his jaw as some of the guards hurried to Antoine's crouched form. The female with the short red hair grabbed for the hilt of the knife. The weapon was still embedded in Antoine's shoulder. "Wouldn't do that," Constantine warned.

But she didn't listen. She yanked out the blade. Blood poured. Antoine screamed.

\*\*\*

Gunfire blasted. For an instant, Juliet stopped breathing. *No!* Then more gunfire. Three shots total. Three chilling shots that were enough to absolutely ice her heart. "Take me back!"

"Nope." Holden had her thrown over his shoulder. Actually *thrown*. One hand gripped the back of her thighs while the other held a flashlight he'd snaked off one of the royal guards. "Just so you know, it's not easy carrying you up the stairs, in the dark, while you're twisting so much. If you don't want us both plunging to our deaths, then how about you stop all that squirming?"

"Those bullets could have just hit Constantine!"

"Have a little faith. The man is a professional." He mounted more steps, but at a faster rate, as if he'd just become more nervous. "Though he is scarier than I originally thought."

"Holden, let me go! I need to get back to Constantine!"

"No, princess, you need to get to safety. You need to get out of the scary tunnel to hell and back in your room."

He kept mounting the steps, and he was so much stronger than she'd initially realized. He held her easily as he rushed up those steps, and Holden didn't even seem mildly winded.

When they reached her room, the stone wall was wide open. He needed to crouch to get them through it, but then they were back in her chambers. All the lights had been turned on in there, and she had to blink so her eyes could adjust to the sudden, fierce illumination.

"The princess!" Hushed, but excited.

"She's alive!"

"He brought her back!"

And, as she hung over Holden's shoulder, with her hair streaming everywhere, Juliet realized that they'd returned to a bedroom full of people. Her hands slapped against his back as she pushed herself up so that she could see them all. Men, women. All in various states of night dress. Robes. Pajamas. Gowns.

And all slowly lowering their heads and bowing to her.

"I think..." Juliet cleared her throat. "I think you should put me down now."

"Probably a good idea." Holden eased her off his shoulder and back onto her feet. Juliet stood there, with all those people crowding her room, and she was so scared that she couldn't stop shaking. What if Constantine had been shot? She needed to see him.

"Got a dead man!" A shout as a guard burst from the opening near her fireplace.

Juliet frantically shook her head. "No, no—*no!*" She lounged for the guard. No, for the opening because she was getting back down there. No one would stop her.

Strong hands caught her, wrapping around her shoulders. "I'm not the dead man, sweetheart."

Constantine. Emerging from the darkness. Looking grim and dangerous and so incredibly gorgeous to her because he was safe. Alive.

"The bastard who took you is dead."

Her breath shuddered out.

Whispers drifted around them.

"And I may have driven a knife into the head of security," Constantine added.

Her lips parted.

He shrugged. "Whoops."

She could only shake her head.

"In my defense, I thought he might be preparing to kill me." His eyes glittered as he stared down at her. "And that wasn't going to happen." His head lowered. "Because *no one* is going to separate me from you. No one."

Her breath heaved. She shot up onto her toes. Grabbed tight to him. And her mouth slammed up to meet his.

*** 

"New room." A large, white bandage wrapped around Antoine's shoulder as he led Juliet and Constantine into their new quarters. He looked a little ragged around the edges and sweat slickened the hair near his temples. "I will have guards stationed on the other side of the door. And Holden is being given the quarters right across the hall."

Antoine appeared to be on the verge of toppling at any moment. "Shouldn't you be resting?" Juliet blurted.

"Yes," the woman beside him said. Katarina. The redhead had identified herself earlier. "But someone seems to think of himself as invincible when he is clearly not."

Antoine's lips tightened as he ignored her words. "A man tried to kill you tonight. A man dressed in the garb of a royal guard. I've identified him as Jean Biancheri." A muscle jerked along his jaw. "I recognized him on sight, as soon as his mask was removed by your consort, so the identification was simple. While Jean wasn't one of my guards, he did work at the castle."

"In what capacity?" Constantine demanded as he closed the door to their quarters.

Antoine winced as his fingers tugged on the bandages. Juliet could already see a bit of red soaking through them. The bandages were on his shoulder, but hadn't he been sliced on his chest, too? "You're still bleeding."

"I'll get stitches soon enough."

Katarina began, "You should get them now—"

"You're dismissed," he told her, voice curt. "Thank you for your assistance. Your services are no longer needed."

Her lips thinned, but she bowed to Juliet and marched from the room.

"I think she was right," Juliet noted. "You should get stitches now." That bloom of red was spreading before her eyes.

His gaze flickered to her. "Is that an order, my princess?"

If it kept him alive? "Sure, yes, absolutely consider it an order. Go get stitches. Stay alive." She didn't trust this man and wanted him away from her.

For the last hour—two?—she'd been surrounded by people. All the staff members who lived at the castle had come billowing out. There had been so many questions. So many whispers.

Her abductor's body had been carried from the castle. She'd watched the removal, and, from her window, she'd seen his body get loaded into the back of a black van.

The story would hit the news. Reporters would swarm from all over the world. She could already imagine the headlines. *Princess abducted during first night in castle. Man shot to death by security.*

A man she didn't know had wanted her dead. He'd been preparing to seal her away and let her die, like something out of an Edgar Allan Poe story. Her mother had definitely been right. Death did wait in Lancaden.

The red deepened on Antoine's bandage. "You should go," she said again. The last thing she wanted was for him to fall at her feet. Why the man was still carrying out his duties, she had no idea. Shouldn't he have been taken to a hospital? Why hadn't Alexandre ordered his transfer?

Moving his head in curt acknowledgement, Antoine started for the door. Only to have Constantine step into his path.

"Come on," Constantine chided. "You think you get to cut out so easily?"

A shrug of Antoine's non-injured shoulder. "I was just wondering when you were going to say something."

She frowned. His voice was wrong. No faint Lancaden accent. He sounded more... American?

"Wasn't sure if you wanted the princess to know or if you wanted to keep acting like I was a mortal enemy. Gonna let it all be your call." Antoine held his position near Constantine.

Her hands fisted at her sides. "What is happening here?" Other than the fact that Antoine and Constantine seemed to be locked in some sort of glaring contest. It was too late for this crap. She was too tired and far, far too near the end of her rope.

Constantine didn't answer her, but Antoine glanced back over his shoulder. "We have a mutual friend." His lips pursed. "Maybe more like acquaintance? He's definitely Constantine's friend, though I am not so sure he always considered himself my friend."

Who was he talking about? Did it look like she was in the mood to solve a mystery?

"In fact, dare I say...he and Constantine are thick as thieves."

"Watch it, asshole," Constantine growled.

"Or what?" Mock fear entered his voice—his *American-accented* voice. "Will you..." A gasp. "Stab me? Again?" He shook his head. "And to think, I was always told you didn't strike first. You didn't go for the attack *first*. Such lies."

"You had a gun pointed at me," Constantine snapped back. "I'd just had a bullet rip down my arm because of you."

He'd *what?* Juliet stumbled forward. "You never said you were hurt!" Where? Where was the wound? He'd said his arm. Juliet reached for him.

He pulled away.

His retreat hurt. Her hands froze in mid-air.

"A scratch," Constantine dismissed. "I slapped a bandage over it while you were watching the body get hauled away. Not a deal. Some of us don't cry like bitches when we get a small wound."

"Oh, seriously?" Antoine puffed out his chest. "Now you're saying I'm a bitch? You *stabbed* me."

"Gun. You had it pointed at me. And you *killed* the man I needed to interrogate."

"Whatever. Like you weren't planning to kill him yourself? Save me the lie, I saw the truth in your eyes. I saw—"

*"Stop it!"* Juliet lunged between the two men. With her back to Antoine, she focused on Constantine. "I want to know what is happening, and I want to know now."

"Is that a royal order?" Constantine asked, voice silky.

Why did these men keep asking her that question? Her response was the same as before. "Yes." A hiss from her. "Consider it a royal order if you must. *Tell me* what's happening!"

# CHAPTER EIGHTEEN

*Step Eighteen: Lies are necessary. They get the job done. They twist and churn, and they can hurt and destroy. And it's a really good thing I am a natural-born liar.*

"Fine." His hands flew out, curled around her shoulders, and he picked her up and moved Juliet to his side. Then he took a protective step to place his body partially in front of hers. "But don't give that man your back. I don't trust him."

"Uh, what do I need to do in order to have your trust?" Antoine demanded with a wiggle of his brows. "Say the magic word? Fine. Here goes. *Remy.* Or maybe you prefer *Rembrandt.* Does that do it for you? Will you stop wanting to kick my ass when you get that I am on your side? Just what is it that I have to do in order to prove my loyalty? You know, other than killing to protect you."

*Remy.* That was Constantine's friend. The, uh, shady one he'd told her about. "What does Remy have to do with this?"

Antoine's stare locked on her. "Remy found out that I was already in position with a cover here. When your boyfriend—or bodyguard or whatever the hell he is—called for backup, Remy instantly notified me. Remy knew it would take him longer to get here, even with his shadowy resources, and he didn't think there was time to waste. He wanted to make sure that if shit hit the fan, I would have your back. And Constantine's." He blew out a breath. "Thus, me bravely saving everyone from the madman charging with the knife."

"First," Constantine's voice had gone even colder, "he only got the knife because your dumb ass was too close to him and didn't have it properly secured. Second, I needed the man alive so I could find out who was pulling his strings."

"You're welcome," Antoine assured him. "Happy to save your life. Would do it again anytime."

Constantine growled.

Juliet rubbed her temples. "You're not Lancaden."

"Nope. I'm CIA." He stuck out his hand for her. "Real name is Ty."

She took his hand even though Constantine was still making that weird growl. She had the feeling that Constantine's control wouldn't be lasting much longer. Fair enough, hers was more than frayed around the edges, too. "Why is a CIA guy working undercover as head of security?"

"Because we believe that someone plans to assassinate the king."

"He's already dying," Constantine muttered. "All the person has to do is wait. No assassination required."

She flinched.

"Cold bastard," Ty noted, and he sounded admiring. "You and Remy have lots in common, don't you?" A shake of his head, but his gaze remained on Juliet. "The king's health took a very dramatic turn six months ago. Some in positions of power believe that turn came with help."

She backed up. "Wait. Are you telling me that you think someone is what—poisoning the king? Making him sick?"

"Possibly. My job is to get close. To find out. But so far, I've turned up jack. Contact with the king is limited to a very closed circle. Few have even seen him since he's taken to his deathbed. No pictures or even videos have surfaced because anyone entering his room is typically searched."

And Juliet realized that he was right. When she'd been researching Lancaden, she *hadn't* seen any recent photos of the king. Of course, she hadn't discovered that her grandmother had been suspected in an assassination attempt, but that seemed like common knowledge to plenty of others.

"There was also the worry that someone at Lancaden was getting into the business of illegal weapons." Ty added the last bit almost casually, as if it was not a big deal.

She needed to pick her jaw off the floor. Because it was a very, very big deal. "Weapons?"

"Not a business your kingdom ever condoned," he continued carefully. "In fact, Lancaden has a long history of avoiding such ventures. Tourism is your game. You keep this small spot on the map alive because so many people want to come and see the castle. They want to sample the wines. They want a safe place to visit and snap pics for their social media accounts. You keep up your image of being some fairytale spot, and your people get their livelihoods. But you switch things, you start dealing in weapons and making deals with people with whom one just should *not* fuck...and then your whole kingdom crumbles into the dust." His expression darkened. "Wouldn't it be a shame if that happens?"

Juliet sucked in a sharp breath. "Are you threatening me?" Not just her, but all the people of Lancaden. What was he saying? That he'd destroy the country? What was happening?

"He isn't threatening you. He better *not* be." Constantine moved to stand fully in front of her. "Or it will be the last mistake he makes."

She peeked around Constantine's broad shoulder and saw Antoine—or Ty or whoever he was—raise his hands, palms out, toward Constantine.

"Remy was right," Ty said. "You are an untrusting bastard with a very, very big protective streak. Especially where the princess is concerned."

"I'm her bodyguard," Constantine tossed back without missing a beat. "Being protective goes with the territory."

"So it's bodyguard and not boyfriend?"

Juliet cleared her throat. "They hardly have to be mutually exclusive."

Constantine whipped his head to stare at her. His eyes blazed.

What? What had she said that caused that reaction?

But his attention had already shifted back to Ty. "She belongs to me." Flat. "There is no one in this world I would guard more closely."

"Right. Figured as much considering you were ripping the castle apart to find her earlier. So, here's the deal. I can't hang out in here much longer or people will get suspicious. By people, I mean Alexandre. I don't like him. He's a prick, yep, straight away, and I don't trust him. I especially don't like the fact that I discovered he just paid for someone named Christian Hale to fly on a private jet to Lancaden. Hale arrived shortly after you two did, and then he vanished."

Shock held her immobile. "He brought Chris here?"

"Dammit." A disgusted shake of Constantine's head. "Holden warned that he'd be a problem. Now I will have to listen to his I-told-you-so bullshit."

"Who is Christian Hale?" Ty demanded.

"Don't you know?" Constantine returned. "Shouldn't your CIA buddies have made a giant profile on him that they delivered to you?"

"Asshole, I'm undercover. No one should be communicating with me, not unless it is on a super secure channel. I still don't know how Remy managed to contact me, and maybe it's best if I don't find out." A sniff. "As far as Hale is concerned, like I told you, that fellow *just* arrived hours ago. So let's save me some time and share intel, got it? You know who he is, obviously, so bring me up to speed."

"He's my ex," Juliet explained softly. "Hardly some major security threat. I don't know, maybe

Alexandre thought Chris could say that Constantine isn't really my consort or something." She was tired of peeking around Constantine's shoulder. Ty didn't seem to be a threat. He was on their side. Whatever their side was. He knew the mysterious Remy and he was offering his help. She'd take it.

She moved to a position beside Constantine and held out her hand. "It's nice to meet you, Ty."

He looked at her hand, then up at her face. "Circumstances are shit, but it's sure a pleasure meeting you, too." His fingers curled around hers. "Never met a princess before."

"I've never met an undercover CIA agent before, either." A real-life spy.

"You've changed your appearance," Constantine noted. "Small changes. But they had a big impact."

Ty kept holding her hand. "I don't remember you meeting me before."

"Really? That's the story you're gonna sell? You're good at disguises, I'll grant you, but not that good. By the way, you can let go now." Constantine sighed in disgust. "And you can go and get those damn stitches before you leave a trail of blood in your wake."

He wasn't dripping blood, yet.

Ty slowly let her go. "Any other intel I need to know about before I make my big exit?"

"You need to know that we *will* be meeting with the king at first light. After that meet and greet, if Juliet wants to leave, I'll have her vanishing within the hour. If she goes dark, that's why."

Ty's eyes widened. "You already have the plan in place?"

"She was nearly killed tonight. If I had my way, I'd be carrying her out right now." He gazed at her. "Then she'd never be in danger again."

"I can't go," Juliet whispered. "I need to speak to him." She'd come all this way. No, no she couldn't leave yet.

Constantine dipped his head toward her. "That's why I haven't stolen a princess and vanished into the night with her. But that situation can change at a moment's notice."

"Guessing you won't be leaving her side again?"

"Not for anyone or anything."

"Thought so." Ty pointed to the little chest of drawers on the right. "Since your gun was confiscated—"

"And that was some bullshit."

"No, it wasn't. Even Lancaden has protocols to follow when there is an international incident like the matter of, oh, say a princess nearly being *killed.*" He rolled his eyes and pointed again. "But because I am amazing, I stashed a new weapon in that drawer for you. You can thank me later." With that disclosure, he strolled for the door. But right before he yanked it open, he turned to pin Constantine with a hard stare. "Oh, and don't tell your Wilde partner my real identity, got it? It's called being a *secret agent* for a reason."

"I trust Holden more than I trust you."

"Doesn't matter, he still needs to be kept in the dark. There is more riding on this mission than you realize." His gaze flickered to Juliet before returning to Constantine. "Try not to lose her again, would you? Because I can always take over consort duty if you'd rather someone else handle the job."

"You sonofabitch!" Constantine lunged for him.

Juliet grabbed his arm.

The door shut with a click.

"He was just trying to agitate you," she whispered. "You didn't lose me. Don't let him get to you."

He pulled from her. Stalked to the door and threw the heavy bolt into place. Then he proceeded to search every inch of the room, even shoving his hands against the stones near the fireplace. As she watched him, Juliet stood near the bed, with her arms wrapped around her stomach. All she wanted was for him to pull her close. To wrap his arms around her and tell her that everything was going to be all right.

Except, he wasn't doing that. He stalked like a caged lion, and there was a terrible tension that clung in the air around him. That tension stretched and stretched, and she was the one to finally snap and speak again. "I think it's safe."

His back was to her, and Juliet saw his shoulders stiffen.

"You're in here with me, so I know it's safe," she added.

Slowly, he turned toward her. "I fucked up on keeping you safe."

"You didn't. You got an emergency text from Holden. You went to help your partner." Her feet shuffled quickly toward him. Feet covered in slippers so that her toes no longer felt like little popsicles. "You were doing your job." She put her hand on his arm because she had a desperate need to touch him. Even if he seemed to be avoiding touching her.

His gaze dropped to her hand as it pressed to his arm. "You are the job."

Right. Like she needed that reminder.

"We found Holden's phone on the dead man's body. Did you know that?"

No, she hadn't.

"The whole thing was a setup to get me to leave you. I should have known better. The point of being your bodyguard is to guard you, not to run off chasing Holden."

"He's your friend," she returned as her hand lingered on him. "You wanted to make sure he was safe."

"And you nearly died because I messed up."

Anger hummed through her. "Stop saying that! You didn't mess up! You left for like, two minutes, and I'm the one who went with him when there weren't even any bullets in the gun!" How was she supposed to know that? She'd never been around guns before. Yes, yes, plenty of people in Baton Rouge had them, but she hadn't been one of those people. "I went with him because—"

"Because of me." A rumble.

She swallowed. "He said he'd shoot through the door. You were on the other side, trying to break it down in order to get to me."

"I did break the bitch down. You were already gone." He still stared at her hand. "That was when I lost my mind."

A nervous laugh slid from her. "You didn't. That was when you came rushing to my rescue." Just in the nick of time. "I knew you'd come. He was trying to seal me up, but I kept talking to distract him." And she just kept talking right then, too, her words tumbling too fast because adrenaline still poured through her veins, and she felt so jittery and unsettled. "First, I tried to make him empathize with me. See me as a person. Not just some *thing* that he was going to lock away. I needed to be humanized for him. But he was too mission focused. Too intent on believing that I was going to destroy Lancaden."

"You should stop touching me."

Her chest ached at the brutal rejection. "I— sorry." Juliet snatched her hand back. "I just kept talking, saying anything that came to mind because I knew you'd come and find me."

"You left the poker pointing to the stone."

A nod. She had, yes.

"And you dropped the belt of your robe, so I'd know which way to turn when I reached the bottom of those twisting stairs."

Another nod.

"And then you *asked the bastard to shoot you.*" His eyes glittered as his hands fisted and released.

Her head jerked. Not a nod. "That was—that was a distraction technique. He was sealing me inside, and I had to find a way to stop him."

"I heard your voice, Juliet. You said…'I'll take a bullet to slow death, if that's my option, thank you very much.'" Guttural. "You *thanked him*. For killing you."

"He didn't kill me." A breath. "Because you got there. You're my bodyguard. I knew you'd come. I knew—"

"You put too much faith in me."

"No, no, I don't. I *trust* you because you have never let me down. You're a good man—"

A snarl broke from him, and suddenly, his hands were on her. Tight and hard and gripping her shoulders as he pulled her toward him. "I'm not good. I was ready to kill him in an instant." His nostrils flared. "He was dead the minute he took you."

"N-no." A tremble. "You knew the gun wasn't loaded when you pulled the trigger." She'd thought about this, over and over. "You could tell a weight difference, couldn't you? You were trying to scare him. Intimidate him into telling you if he was working for someone else."

"He *was* working for someone else. I know a lackey when I see one."

He hadn't answered about the weight difference with the gun. "You were trying to scare him."

Constantine smiled. This smile was different from any other she'd seen him give before. His eyes seemed different. His whole expression different. All the warmth that she associated with Constantine vanished, and she was left with only the danger that clung to him. Her breath caught.

"I would have killed him in an instant. I planned to kill him once I had my answers, but that jerk Ty beat me to the punch."

Her head shook. "No—"

"I've killed before, Juliet. Holden wasn't far off the mark when he said I was an assassin. I've always done the dirty jobs. The jobs that leave my hands covered in blood." His voice was off. Too flat. Too cold. "These hands should probably never touch a princess."

A shiver slid over her.

"You're not cold," he stated. He leaned in closer, with that faint, almost cruel smile still on his sensual lips. "You're shivering because you're afraid of me."

"I'm not."

"You know I was going to kill him. You know I would kill anyone who hurt you, and I wouldn't hesitate. I was sent for this job—"

"Because you're a chameleon," she rushed to say. He'd told her this before.

"Because someone who isn't afraid to be brutal needed to be at your side. I'm one of the most brutal bastards you will ever meet. With my life, my past, there is no way I could ever be anything else."

She would not believe this. "You're not brutal with me."

"No. Just with everyone else."

Not true. There was so much more to him. "You're trying to scare me."

"You're already scared enough. So scared that if some bastards weren't plotting your murder—"

No way she couldn't wince at those harsh words.

"You'd be running from me as fast as you could," Constantine finished.

"No." Adamant. "I would be running to you."

His lips parted. Surprise flickered in what had been coolly emotionless eyes a moment before.

"To you," she said again. "That's where I want to run." So it was what she was going to do. "I'm not scared. I went with him *to protect you*. Doesn't that tell you how I feel?" If it didn't. "Fuck it. I'll just show you."

"Dirty language from royalty? Better watch out, I might be rubbing off on you."

Ignoring those taunting words because she *knew* what he was trying to do, Juliet just became all the more determined. "Basic psychology. You push away the ones that matter most." Her fingers curled around his head, but he was already swooping in to take her mouth. Their lips met. Their tongues. They kissed in a flood of furious, desperate, aching need. A kiss that marked Juliet to her very core. His kiss chased the cold away and turned the quivering adrenaline she'd felt before into burning need.

But his mouth pulled from hers. "What the hell makes you think that you matter? It's a job. You're a job."

Brutal. Painful. Her breath sawed in and out as she stared at him. She could feel her skin prickle. The drumming of her heart filled her ears. No, no, he was lying to her. Had to be. Right?

Except his expression was unyielding. *He doesn't care.* She had made a terrible mistake and pain pushed away the need and there was only a tight ball in her chest as the world seemed to spin too fast around her. Round and round and round in a blur.

"Damn *lie.*" His hands flew up. One sank into her hair. The other curled under her chin as he tipped her head back more. "You are *everything.*" He kissed her again. A different kiss. No fury. Only a possessive, consuming need. Deep and hard. Demanding.

Juliet shoved at the clothes that were in her way because she wanted him naked. Wanted him *in* her. Wanted the passion to block out the pain that still singed her soul.

Her hands pushed between them. Yanked open his belt. Jerked down his zipper. Snarling, he backed away, but just long enough to strip.

She should strip, too. Juliet knew that. Take off the robe and the pajamas. They were already dirty from her trek down the stairs and into the darkness.

The memory of that dark and of the grating stones filled her mind. *Sealed inside. Left to die.*

"Juliet?"

She took two quick steps back to him. She needed that memory *gone.* Her fingers reached out and curled around the heavy length of his cock. She stroked. Squeezed. Enjoyed the way he groaned for her.

But she needed more.

She lowered to her knees before him.

"Juliet, I can't hold on. I *need you.*"

She understood need. And she was going to take what she needed. Her lips opened over the head of his cock. Her breath whispered over him and then she was licking him. Sucking. Taking him. She'd never done this before. Been too nervous. Too awkward.

Now, there was nothing to stop her. Everything felt savage and primal. She licked and sucked and wanted him to come in her mouth. Wanted to break right through his control until the only thing left for them both was the lust that couldn't lie.

*No lie. What I feel isn't a lie. What I need isn't a lie.*

And what she wanted? *Everything.*

"Juliet!" He hauled her up.

"I wasn't finished!" A fast protest.

He whirled with her. Sat her on the edge of the bed—one that was just as high as the last one had been. He yanked off her robe. She kicked away her slippers. Then they both hauled down her panties and the pajama bottoms.

She blinked and found herself flat on the mattress. Constantine loomed over her. Her legs were parted, her hips arching toward him, and he slammed deep within her. A gasp tore from her because he felt so good.

"Juliet?" Hesitation. Worry.

She found his stormy gray gaze on her.

"Did I hurt you?"

"You did," she whispered.

His arms locked on either side of her as he pushed up and began to withdraw.

"No!" Her legs curled around him. "You hurt me when you lied. Don't lie. Not to me." He felt so good. She clenched her inner muscles around him.

He erupted. Pistoning his hips against her. Driving into her and retreating in a fast and furious rhythm that had pleasure careening through her as a sudden, intense orgasm blasted through her body. There was no buildup, just a mind-blowing release that sent her spiraling. Limp, weak, she tried to hold onto him.

Then she felt his explosion. A hot surge inside of her just as his mouth pressed to hers. A kiss of passion. Desire that wouldn't be checked.

A need that would never end.

And then she heard his words. A rasp. Words she would never, ever forget. Not a lie. The truth.

"I fucking love you, Juliet."

# CHAPTER NINETEEN

*Step Nine—oh, screw it. I'm in too deep now. I can't let her go.*

He'd more than fucked up. He'd lost his sanity, lost his soul, and he'd given the woman his heart.

Constantine checked his new weapon. Ty had even left him a shoulder holster, and Constantine slid it into place, before pulling on a suit coat that *mostly* hid the bulge.

Juliet walked out of the bathroom, and morning sunlight poured through the window to hit her hair, making it seem like absolute gold. She glanced his way, and a soft pink filled her cheeks.

Nervous with him? Now?

Or nervous because of what happened? They hadn't talked about it, but they needed to before she walked out of that room and went to meet the king. "I'm clear, Juliet. You don't have to worry."

Her head jerked. "Excuse me?"

"I didn't use a rubber last night. I don't want you worrying because..." Because that shit had never happened before. Because he'd never been so beyond control that he'd been that careless. "You're not at risk."

She took a hesitant step back. "I'm clear, too." Her lips curled down. "Though I suspect you knew that, didn't you? All that background checking you did on me. You probably had access to every doctor's report I've ever had."

All the way back to birth, but he didn't mention that, not then. Because the thought of birth... *"Hell."*

"Oh, no." Her lips curled in a faint smile. "What new calamity do we suddenly face?"

He didn't smile in return because the last thing he felt like doing was smiling. He marched toward her. His hand reached out, but he caught himself before he actually did something completely dumbass like *touch her stomach. Imagine her with my child growing inside.*

No, no, no. "You're on the pill." From his reports. They should be fine. "You have a prescription."

Her eyes widened. "You have been thorough. Points to Wilde."

*Don't imagine a baby. There won't be one. She won't be tied to you. Stop it.*

"But I had the flu about two months ago, and I stopped taking the pills. Since I wasn't exactly having the wildest personal life in the world, I didn't start them up again."

A dull ringing filled his ears. "You don't seem worried."

"I'm not." She blew out a breath. "Okay, fine. I am. I'm worried about meeting the king. I'm worried someone else is going to attack us. I'm worried that everyone will see I'm a fraud."

"You are *not*." He was. The fake consort. The guy who couldn't claim the heart of someone like Juliet.

"I'm worried about lots of things, but I'm not particularly concerned about being pregnant with your child."

He couldn't move.

Her hand moved. Dropped to her stomach. "I think that would be quite wonderful, in fact."

That ringing had gotten a whole lot louder. "What?"

"After my mom died, I was so alone. Didn't think anyone would ever make the ache I felt inside go away."

What was she saying?

"Then I met you, and nothing has been the same since."

"I am a *bastard*."

"You can be, yes. Especially when you lie to me." She stepped closer. Moved her hand from her stomach to his heart. "But when you tell the truth, like you did last night, you can change my whole world."

*I fucking love you, Juliet.*

So she'd heard him. She hadn't said a word back. Instead, she'd fallen asleep in his arms. All trusting and sweet. Like she hadn't faced a real-life nightmare such a short time before. Like she trusted him to keep the monsters at bay.

"Here's the thing, Constantine." She kept her hand on his heart. "I knew you didn't have a condom on. After all, I'd just had my mouth on you."

His dick jerked eagerly at the fabulous memory.

"And I knew you hadn't exactly brought condoms with you when we were given the new room. Everything got transferred in a rush. Our clothes weren't even brought in until this morning." She shrugged one shoulder. "I didn't care. I wanted you." She bit her lip. "Lie."

His brows lowered. "You're not the one who lies."

"I just did lie. Because it wasn't about wanting you. It was about so much more." Juliet's gaze held his. "I knew you'd find me when I went into the dark because I trust you. And I trust you because I love you."

He couldn't move. Not an inch. This was an important moment. Life-changing.

And some asshole was knocking on the door.

"That will be our appointment with the king." A slight hesitation. "Do you think my knees will stop shaking before we have the meeting? Because I don't."

The knocking continued. Dammit. He whirled away. Marched for the door. With one hand, he reached for his gun, with the other, he undid the bolt and opened the door a few inches. Just enough to see Holden's smiling face.

"Morning, sunshine," Holden greeted as if they hadn't been through the night from hell and instead had all gotten a glorious eight hours of sleep. "Running a little behind, are we? Not supposed to keep a dying king waiting."

Seriously? Talk about a dick thing to say. He glared at his partner. "*Tact.*"

"What? Are we all supposed to be surprised he's dying? Like that's a big reveal or something? I think we established that early on. That's why time is of the essence. Tick, tock and all of that."

"We're ready," Juliet said. Crisp. Cool. As if she hadn't just blown his world apart with three little words.

*I love you.*

Did she? He'd told her the same thing, and Constantine knew with utter certainty that he loved her. When you'd been without love for as long as he had, you knew that shit when it hit you with the force of a sledgehammer.

He looked back at his beautiful sledgehammer. She was poised and perfect in an elegant blue dress. Her eyes gleamed. A soft, glistening red gloss coated her lips. She had small pearls at her ears and black heels on her feet. She seemed completely calm even though she'd told him her knees were shaking.

Told *him* when she presented such a perfect front to the rest of the world.

Because she believed that she loved him.

How in the hell was he supposed to walk away? *If she's pregnant, I can't walk away.* And that was the truth—the dark and bitter truth that made him an utter bastard. No condom. The tantalizing image of Juliet and his baby tormented him. If there was a child, maybe she'd want him to stay.

He walked back to her. "You deserve better than a con man who wants to knock you up so you can't leave him."

"Oh, Jesus." Holden choked. "You did not say that—tell me you did not *do* that—"

Juliet smiled at Constantine. "You really can become anyone or anything, can't you? Quite impressive. I noticed it last night when you made your eyes go so cold and you sounded quite unlike yourself. For a moment, I thought I was looking at a stranger. Then I realized, you were trying to scare me away."

"Ahem. The clock—ticking and tocking and all of that," Holden prompted.

"You're trying to be brash and crude now. Trying to act like you're nothing more than a con man, but it just won't work." She reached up and patted his cheek. "But don't feel badly. I'm sure someone who didn't know you as well might believe the mask."

*Fuck.*

"Want a secret?" She rose up, pulled him close, and her lips feathered over his ear. "I really, really hope I am pregnant, but if I'm not, there's always next time."

His body shuddered.

Juliet eased back down. Her gaze turned serious. Maybe it always had been. "I want you at my side. Not because you're my bodyguard, but because you're my Constantine, and I need you with me."

He offered her his arm. "My princess, there is no other place I ever want to be."

When she took his arm, she sealed both their fates.

As they passed Holden, he said, "That's really sweet. I think I'm teary."

"Working with you is a rare pleasure, buddy," Constantine tossed back because he wanted to lighten some of the tension already cloaking Juliet as they left the room. "Rare. Maybe the rarest pleasure in the whole world."

Juliet slanted a look his way.

"Damn, man, that is the nicest thing you ever said to me." Holden's chest puffed out.

And Constantine almost felt bad for basically calling the guy a real prick. Almost.

But like Holden had said, a dying king waited, and the clock was ticking.

\*\*\*

"There are absolutely no weapons allowed in the king's chambers." Alexandre stood at the bottom of a carpeted flight of stairs.

Ty—still pretending to be Antoine—was at his side, once more wearing the uniform of a royal guard. The king's quarters were at the top of the stairs. So close. The big moment was finally at hand, and Juliet was using all of her willpower to project a calm facade. On the outside, she needed to appear composed even if, on the inside, she was a quivering mass of nerves.

"I can see the holster you're wearing." Alexandre motioned to Constantine's coat. "Leave it."

Leave it? But Ty had been the one to give Constantine the gun! Now they were taking the weapon away? That made zero sense to Juliet.

Ty stepped forward. "Not like you'll face a threat in there. The king is bedridden." His gaze slid to Alexandre. "So I've heard. This will be my first time to have face-to-face access to the king since assuming my position." He extended his hand toward Constantine.

After a brief hesitation, Constantine surrendered the gun.

"I'm afraid you won't be joining us for this meeting, Antoine." Alexandre clasped his hands together and nodded toward two other guards who waited nearby. "This is a private meeting, and no one will disturb this momentous occasion."

Why did those words make the hair on the back of her nape rise?

Ty's face darkened. "After the attack last night, I think we need to make sure the princess is covered—"

"I'll be backup," Holden said immediately. "I'll go in with them."

"No." Sharp. Once more, Alexandre inclined his head toward the guards. "They will make sure you stay here as well. The royal doctor does not want a flood of people entering the king's room. The king can't be exposed to so many germs, and too much excitement is not good for his condition." There seemed to be a faint tremble in his voice even as he instructed, "You will stay out here, as well, Mr. Blackwell, and that is not something up for debate."

A few more guards slipped into the room. Katarina was in the group, and a slightly confused expression flickered on her face.

Alexandre smiled. "As you can see, this part of the castle is exceedingly secure. Once we enter, you can rest assured that no one will disturb us. The princess will be able to have a private conversation with her long-lost grandfather. A family reunion that is long overdue."

"I'm coming with her," Constantine announced. "And *that* is not up for debate. I'm her consort. Where she goes, I go. If you're not down with that, then the meeting is not going to happen. Too bad for the dying king."

Katarina gasped.

Juliet looked around. The area they were in was actually fairly massive. The words seemed to echo as people talked, and she really didn't know why so many guards were appearing inside.

"If you were her consort, then perhaps your desires would matter," Alexandre said.

*If?*

Juliet's gaze snapped back to him.

"But I don't think you are." Alexandre snapped his fingers. "I have been told that position belongs to this man."

And the curtain on the right parted. Juliet had thought that curtain just covered a window, but instead, it seemed to lead to another hallway, and from that hallway, a familiar figure emerged. A figure that she had not seen in months.

Christian Hale grinned at her as he rushed forward. "Juliet! My darling!"

"Warned you," Holden muttered. "Said that asshole would be trouble."

Christian hurried toward her with his arms outstretched. He surged in to hug her.

And instead got to wrap his arms around Constantine. Constantine had moved straight into his path. "You're gonna want to stop that," Constantine advised him in a lethal voice. "Now."

Christian snatched his hands back. "What— Juliet—"

"You don't approach a princess that way. Your ass bows to her. You ask her permission to come close. And you sure as shit don't touch without her okay."

Juliet felt rooted to the spot. "Why are you here, Christian?"

He craned to see around Constantine's form. "Because it's time for us to come out of the shadows. I told the counsellor about our relationship. He knows you and I are engaged."

Constantine reached back, caught Juliet's left hand, and lifted it up. "My ring on her finger. *Mine.*"

"And I have emails that we exchanged where Juliet declared her love for me! Where she told me that she couldn't wait for us to be together. Where we talked about our dreams for a new life. A life together!"

There were no emails. They'd never talked about a new life. "You're lying."

His handsome features appeared stricken. "Darling, there is no need to pretend. Not any longer."

"I'm not pretending. You are." She slanted a glance toward an avid Alexandre. "I don't know what you think is happening, but I want this man escorted away from the castle immediately. He is not my consort. He has not been in my life at all for the last seven months." And this entire situation was making her very, very afraid.

"I've seen the emails," Alexandre replied. There were dark shadows under his eyes, as if he hadn't slept at all during the night.

"Emails can be faked." An immediate dismissal from Constantine.

"This is such bullshit," Holden groused. "Kick his ass *out*. You heard the princess. Shouldn't people be scampering to obey her?"

Alexandre's face hardened. "I've seen the photographs he possesses of the two of you together. Photos, videos. Some taken as recently as last week."

Impossible. Her breath left her in a surge.

"Juliet knew the crown was coming to her," Christian explained into the thick silence. "She wanted to keep our relationship quiet until her coronation was complete. Because I wasn't Lancaden, she thought it best to appear unattached." His voice sharpened. "But then this ridiculous story about her and this *imposter* appeared, and I wasn't going to stay quiet any longer!"

Constantine looked back at her.

"He's lying," she said simply. "There can't be any videos. I haven't seen him in months."

"You can authenticate them!" A fast cry from Christian. "Get Wilde to do it—I've heard the company excels at things like that. Juliet is pretending, and she is breaking my heart." His voice dropped even as he put a hand to his heart. "I love you. You said you loved me."

Constantine stiffened. He was still staring straight at Juliet, not at Christian.

"I know you want the crown, darling. I know you want the castle and the money because you grew up with nothing, and I know we planned everything so that you would look like the perfect princess."

*What was happening here?* "Not true. We planned nothing. *Escort him out now!*"

The guards maintained their positions. Katarina bit her lower lip.

Ty slowly stepped forward. "You heard the princess."

But Alexandre waved his hand, and two other guards also advanced, only to put their hands on Ty's shoulders. "You've been relieved of your position," the counsellor said.

"What?" Ty barked. "Remove the hands, gentleman. Now."

They didn't. They did look nervous. So did Katarina as she gazed around in surprise.

"A royal decree," Alexandre explained. His throat clicked as he swallowed. "The king has put someone new in charge of security as of this morning."

Footsteps rapped on the floor as someone else stepped from that curtained corridor.

Alexandre exhaled on a low sigh. "I believe you will remember Emile from your meeting in Atlanta."

Her eyes widened. Yes, she knew him. He'd been one of the men who tried to take her from the elevator at Wilde.

"Oh, I remember him," Constantine rumbled. "So does my fist."

Emile's eyes narrowed. "I'm to escort the fake consort from the castle." Only he didn't march toward Christian.

He came right at Constantine.

# CHAPTER TWENTY

*Step Twenty: Fight for her. Battle with all you've got. Take down two men? Three? Ten? Done. Bring it on, bastards.*

Constantine rolled back his shoulders and got ready to take on the entire room of guards. A quick sweep showed him that ten guards had now entered the waiting area. But it wasn't ten against one odds. After all, he had Holden and Ty.

Hardly a fair fight at all. Ten against three. The guards were going to get an ass kicking in record time. And he wasn't certain, but he thought Katarina was gonna be on his side, too. She looked damn uncomfortable by the situation unfolding. But before the fun could begin—

"No!" A hard, commanding cry came from Juliet.

He glanced back at her to see that her eyes were lit with a hot fury.

"No," she snapped again. "Don't you *dare* put your hands on Constantine. He is my consort. He is my fiancé. He is the man I love."

He would never, ever get used to hearing her say those words. And he would probably never think he was worthy enough of her.

"I don't know what lies this man has told." She made a slashing motion with her hand toward

Christian. "But I want him removed from my presence immediately. And if you do not obey me, right the hell now, then *you* will be removed. As soon as I take the crown, I will have you removed from this entire country. Do not test me because I mean exactly what I say."

Wow. Color him impressed. She sounded cold and commanding and several of the guards had quickly lowered their gazes to the floor. No one was making any moves toward Constantine. Not even Emile.

But Emile's attention did cut toward Alexandre. The guard was obviously waiting to get an order from him.

"Why are you looking at him?" Juliet snapped. "I'm the princess. I'm the one with royal blood. I am the one who will take the crown."

She sounded like she already had power. Fucking beautiful, that was what she was.

"I gave you an order. Follow it. Get this liar out of here. *Now.*"

Katarina marched toward Christian.

Christian shook his head at Juliet. "You are the one lying, and I don't understand why. We have such plans. I did everything you asked."

Juliet spun toward Alexandre. "So it's my word against his. Who will you believe?"

Constantine didn't think it was a matter of believing. More like a last-ditch effort to get Juliet separated from her bodyguard. But that shit wasn't happening. "If I leave, she's going with me." A bluff. He would never leave, and he hardly expected Juliet to give up a kingdom for him.

"Absolutely," Juliet agreed at once. "Because we are a package deal."

A curse broke from Alexandre as he stormed toward Christian Hale. "You lied to me."

"I—"

"You gave me fake photos? Emails?"

"Juliet *loves* me!"

Juliet shook her head. "The only man I love is Constantine Leos."

He wanted to kiss her right then. So, he did. Constantine pulled her into his arms and pressed a hot, hard kiss to her luscious lips. "Love you, too, princess."

She smiled at him.

But then he turned back to the threat. The asshole ex. "This man should be placed in a holding facility. I suspect he has been stalking the princess. I think he broke into her home in Baton Rouge, and I think he may have even started the fire that destroyed her belongings there." Granted, he didn't have actual proof, but he had a gut full of suspicions and a bastard right in front of him who should have been an ocean away. A little one-on-one interrogation time should get him the proof he needed.

"Take him away, Emile," Alexandre ordered. "Get him to a secure area."

Emile's brow furrowed. "But the king wanted me inside—"

"The king cannot give orders right now. I am speaking in his stead. Take away Dr. Hale. Secure him. And make sure that Antoine is escorted from the castle." He looked at his watch. "Juliet is supposed to be with her grandfather now."

"Juliet and her consort," Constantine corrected. Not like he was going to be left out.

"I'll help secure Hale," Katarina offered.

Emile cut a glare her way. "You shouldn't be here. You were given the job of guarding the castle's main gate."

"But nothing is happening there—"

"Go!" he blasted at her.

Jaw locking, she backed away and turned on her heel.

A roomful of guards still remained. And Constantine noticed that the two guards who'd grabbed Ty earlier had still not let him go.

*"The hands need to be removed from me. Now."* An order from Ty.

"He can see himself out," Alexandre allowed with a roll of his shoulders. "He knows the way."

The guards released him, but their wary gazes remained on their former head of security.

"Come, Juliet," Alexandre urged. "It's time. Your consort may accompany you, but otherwise this is a private meeting."

Constantine watched as the guards had to drag Christian Hale back down the corridor. His yells echoed as he cried out for Juliet again and again.

"Bye, bastard," Constantine called to him. "I'll see you again real soon."

Holden brushed against him. "Listen to me next time."

At the moment, he was listening to his own instincts. This whole setup was wrong. They'd been delayed on entering, the ex had been brought out and paraded around, and Alexandre had clearly intended to get Constantine's ass kicked to the curb.

But Alexandre had changed plans. He'd seemingly redirected at the last minute. Why? Because Juliet had said she would bail without Constantine? *Nah. I don't think that's the reason. Something else is at play here.* Something that was not good.

What the hell *had* been good about this deal? From the very first, Juliet had been threatened. The knife at her home. The fire. The abduction. He'd thought the knife and the fire were designed to force Juliet to Lancaden. To get her to the castle.

But then she'd nearly been killed in the castle on her first night.

*What is happening?*

Now Alexandre was climbing the stairs and Juliet was following because she was so eager to meet her only family member. This was the big moment, and everything was wrong. A thousand times wrong.

And they'd taken his weapon.

He pulled Holden close. Slapped a hand on his partner's back in what would look like a hug to everyone else. "Glad you have my back." *And I now have your knife.* Because Holden always kept a knife tucked inside the pocket of his coat.

Constantine took the knife, hid it with his palm and the edge of his coat sleeve, and turned to follow Juliet. An attack was coming. He knew it. He had to stay close to Juliet.

As he climbed the stairs, yet another guard appeared from the curtained corridor. Just like all the others, this man was clothed in the black and gold royal uniform. But, unlike the others...

This guy wasn't unknown to Constantine. Though the guard stood at complete attention, with no expression crossing his face, Constantine knew the man was sending him a message with his steady gaze.

*I'm ready.*

Because that guard was his best friend, the master thief himself, Remy Stuart. Rembrandt had arrived just in time to join the party. A good thing because Constantine feared all hell was about to break loose.

Alexandre swung open the door leading to the king's chamber. He entered first, holding the door open behind him so that Juliet could follow. Constantine pressed in right on her heels, with the knife tucked in his sleeve. He fully expected some threat to be waiting, and he was ready.

But the only person waiting in that room?

A frail, elderly man, so thin that his skin seemed to sag on his bones. Tendrils of white hair sprouted from his scalp as he sat up in bed, and long tubes fed into his arms. Machines near him beeped and buzzed, and his breath came in heavy, labored heaves.

And when he looked at Juliet, a trembling smile curved his lips.

# CHAPTER TWENTY-ONE

*Step Twenty-one: Stand back when she does not need you. Surge the hell forward when she does.*

"You look...like her." His voice was low and wheezing, and Juliet's heart squeezed in her chest as she stared down at her grandfather. The room felt terribly cold, and the cold chilled her to the bone.

Was it good for him to be in such a cold room? And where was his doctor? Or a nurse? Or-or someone? Her head whipped toward Alexandre.

"A private meeting," he said, as if reading the question on her face. "No one else should hear this." His lips thinned. "No one," he muttered. The shadows under his eyes seemed even deeper.

"Beautiful," the king breathed. "She was always...so beautiful." He coughed. "Come closer. Let me see you better." Stronger. More like the command of a king.

She crept forward. She wanted to see him better, too.

"Same hair. Same eyes." He swallowed. "More pointed chin. You're smaller, too. Delicate. Doubt you'd survive a Lancaden winter." Rumbling, rusty words. More heaves in his breath. The machines continued their beeping. One seemed to be hissing, a long sigh that sounded every few seconds.

"You would be surprised at what I can survive." Maybe that wasn't the right response. Maybe she should be bowing. No one had gone over protocol, and she was still shaken from the scene outside. *Why had Christian been there?* And had Constantine been right...had Christian been the one to destroy her home?

"She surprised me, too." Her grandfather shook his head. "Never thought she would get away."

Her grandmother. She stared at her grandfather. So very frail. Weak. She could see the veins running beneath his skin. She wanted to ask about her grandmother, but her heart ached as she stared at this man. Her only family. And he didn't have long left in this world.

His gaze shifted away from her. Slid to Constantine. "Who are you?"

"The consort," Alexandre replied. "Constantine Leos."

Her grandfather blinked. "That's the wrong man."

Juliet stiffened. She took a step in retreat and felt Constantine's hand press to the base of her back.

"It should be the professor." Her grandfather coughed. "Hale. He's the consort."

How did her grandfather know about Christian?

"Hale was lying." A flat response from Alexandre. "Juliet disputed his claims in front of a roomful of guards. Hale has been removed. Taken into custody by Emile."

Her grandfather's head snapped toward Alexandre. "That was not my order."

*What is going on?* The cold in the room sent goosebumps rising onto her arms. Or maybe the goosebumps came from something else. "It was my order."

His glare left Alexandre. Moved to her. "You do not give orders."

"When it concerns my life, I absolutely do. Christian Hale is not my consort. He is nothing to me." She reached behind her and took Constantine's hand. "I belong with Constantine."

Her grandfather laughed.

A hacking, rumbling, chilling sound. And his eyes—eyes even darker than her own—seemed to harden. "You think so?"

She didn't like this scene. Not as if she'd expected him to throw open his arms and hug her or anything, but this was wrong. All wrong. "I know so." She squeezed Constantine's fingers. "I came to Lancaden because I was told you wanted to see me before you die."

"You think you'll..." More rasping. "Take my crown."

There was no crown on his head. No servants at his beck and call. Just machines that beeped and hissed. "That wasn't my intention. I was living a normal life."

"At your dirty bar." His lips twisted. "I know about you." His stare cut to Constantine. "I know about him."

"Do you know," Constantine demanded in his deep, dark voice, "that someone tried to kill your granddaughter last night?"

The king pushed himself up a little higher in the bed. "I do." His nostrils flared. "And you rushed to the rescue."

"I'll always rush to her side."

"Because you're the bodyguard pretending to be a consort."

No. "There is nothing pretend about our relationship," Juliet stated, voice firm.

The king crooked his finger at her.

She stiffened.

"Want to hear a secret?" he murmured. "My voice. So weak...come closer."

Shivering, she did. She crept to the edge of the bed. Slowly sat on the mattress and leaned in toward him.

"I have spies everywhere," he whispered. "I know it's fake. I know the ring was bought by someone who worked at Wilde, not by him. I know Constantine Leos would sell out his own father if the money was right, and I intend to offer him a great deal of money."

Her breath froze in her chest.

"Leave!" he suddenly bellowed, the shout blasting in her ear because she was so close to him.

She started to rise.

But his hand clamped around her wrist, claw-like. "Leave, Alexandre," he ordered. "And get my new head of security in here, *now.*"

"No," Alexandre replied. Just that. Simple.

She yanked her hand free of her grandfather's surprisingly strong grasp. She shot from the bed.

"Did you *refuse* my order?" the king demanded.

"Way back in 1611, the king of Lancaden was removed from power because he was mentally...unfit." Careful, calm speech from Alexandre. "As long as another of the royal bloodline is capable of taking control, the transfer of power can occur easily. All that we need is for the counsellor and the heir to both stipulate that the ruler is ill. Too ill to govern."

"I am *fine*," the king snarled. "My doctors have said I am fine. You cannot dare to—"

"Mentally unfit," Alexandre repeated. "That's why the ruler was removed in 1611. He attacked two maids, stabbing them because he believed they were servants of the devil. Deeper investigation revealed that he had already killed four other members of his staff and had ordered their bodies—"

"I am *not* the mad king!" He pointed a bony finger at Alexandre. "You think to take my crown. You think to wed her. You think to have it all."

"I think Juliet has her consort. I think you cannot buy him. I think *you* are a danger to Lancaden."

Her grandfather? She backed away from the bed. Retreated until she was with Constantine again.

Her grandfather's eyes followed her movements. "It's not as easy as he wants you to believe. There would need to be a competency hearing. My doctors would testify. They would all say exactly what I've told them to say." He smiled. A sickly smile that held a slightly cruel edge. "There are too many here who are loyal to me. I will never lose my power."

She wanted out of that room. She wanted away from him.

"Too many," Constantine said, his voice strong when the king's had been weak, "like the man who took her last night? The man in the uniform of a royal guard who knew this castle inside and out?"

The king's smile stretched, then quickly dimmed. "I heard he died." A long exhale. "So unfortunate." He looked down, then cut his gaze back up in the next instant. "Luckily, there are plenty of others."

*OhmyGod.* "You tried to kill me?" Juliet breathed.

He crooked his finger at her once more.

*What the hell?* "I'm not coming to you!" She was going to get the hell away from him. Juliet spun for the door.

"You cannot leave Lancaden." His wheezing laughter poisoned the air behind her. "All I had to do...was get you here. You cannot leave...You will *never* leave."

She looked up at Constantine.

"Yeah, baby," he said without missing a beat, "you can go anywhere you want. Guarantee it. I will make you vanish, and he'll never find you." He glanced toward the king. "Never."

"Two billion dollars."

Her body whipped around. Why was the king—

"Two billion dollars if you make her vanish so that *no one* finds her." The king's eyes burned with dark fire. "It's so much more than I paid her grandmother's lover. You kill her, you eliminate Juliet, you put her body deep below where it won't be uncovered, and the money will be yours. I have it in my royal coffers. Take it. Take the jewels. Take the paintings that you and your thief friend used to enjoy so much."

*He just offered Constantine two billion dollars to kill me.*

And...

*He knows about Constantine's past. He knows everything. This man who is supposed to be at death's door...*

*He wants me dead.*

Constantine pulled Juliet behind him. "We're getting the hell out of here."

"You—you said jewels." Her stomach knotted as nausea rose in her throat. "My grandmother never gave an assassin her ring as payment for killing you." She surged back to Constantine's side so she could see her grandfather's face. "You used *her* ring as payment for him to kill her!"

Sitting in that bed, with tubes feeding into him, with those horrible hisses coming from his machines, the king nodded. *Nodded.* As if confessing to hiring a killer was the most normal thing in the world. "She wasn't going to leave me."

"But—" But he'd had a younger mistress. He'd been planning to move on from her grandmother. He—

"She didn't like my plans for Lancaden. Didn't like what I wanted to do with *my* country.

Thought she could stop me. Turn the world against me." A shake of his head. A cough that shook his body. "So I decided to make her disappear."

*She saw you for what you are.* Juliet could see, too. A monster hiding in the sagging skin and old bones of a man.

"But her lover didn't have the stomach to kill her. He let her *go*." Disgusted. "And she enjoyed taunting me. Sending me pictures. Letting me know—*her* line was continuing. That her daughter was out there. That you were there. And I had no more heirs. None who were like me. Only betrayers like her."

*Paranoid. Delusional. Narcissistic.* She could see all of him in that instant.

And...

*A killer.* "You ordered her lover locked within the castle walls."

"That's what happens to my enemies."

*OhGod.* And this man was the ruler of a country?

"This is why people shouldn't inherit power," Constantine rumbled. "Because sometimes they are completely batshit."

The king's finger shook as he pointed at Constantine. "You don't have his conscience. You won't fool yourself into thinking you love her. You will take the money. You'll take her down into the bowels of my castle, and you will make sure she never comes back up."

"The fuck I will." Rage churned in his fierce response. "But I will make sure that you *never* get close to her again. That none of the fools who are mistakenly loyal to you get close to her. Juliet will not be hurt. She will not be threatened. I will put my own army between her and the rest of the world."

"*Why?*" Her grandfather grabbed for the tubes that fed into his right arm. He wrenched them free. Swung his legs to the side of the bed. Blood trickled down his arm.

"Because I love her, and I'm not for sale."

Her grandfather rose. His body quivered but he struggled forward as—

"Why don't you smile for the camera, your highness?" Alexandre asked softly.

They all swung their heads toward him, and Juliet wondered just when he'd pulled out his phone to film this reunion scene.

"What? *How dare you!*" The king rushed toward him with his staggering gait and wrenched the phone from Alexandre's hands. "I will destroy any video! I will *destroy* you!"

"Destroy away," Alexandre invited. "But you might want to roll with the times. See, you can destroy the video now. Delete away. But I was live, and thousands of people already saw your confession. You're not going to keep power in Lancaden. You'll be locked away for the rest of your days. It's your turn to see what it's like to be sealed up and forgotten." His chin jutted up. "By the way, that assassin? The one who protected the queen and got her the hell away from you? He was my great-uncle." His gaze swung toward Juliet. "For the good of Lancaden, I serve you. The country is what matters, nothing else." He swallowed. "Constantine, get her out of here. Get her far away. I don't know who is loyal to him and who is loyal to her, but until he's in a cell or a grave, you have to protect her. *Go.*"

Constantine pulled her toward the door.

The king roared, "My men are outside! Emile follows my orders—"

Yes, Juliet had already expected that he did.

She heard a crash behind her and looked back to see that the king had thrown his body at Alexandre. She stumbled, trying to turn around and help the counsellor.

"You're the priority." Constantine scooped her into his arms. "I think Alexandre has plenty of tricks up his sleeve, so don't worry about him." He burst out of the king's chambers and shouted, "Watch out for the guards! Some of them plan to attack!"

"Oh, we know." A bored response from Holden. He brushed his knuckles along the front of his shirt, as if cleaning off dirt. Or blood. "We took care of them."

Held tightly within Constantine's arms, Juliet gaped toward the bottom of the stairs. Unconscious guards littered the floor. The only people standing were Holden, Ty, and—

"Remy Stuart, at your service." A man in black and gold bowed ever so gracefully to her. "And, though this probably isn't the best time, if you should be in the mood to pay me back for my life-changing intervention here, I did notice that you had a wonderful Rembrandt painting in your gallery—"

"Not the time, Remy," Constantine snapped as he bolted down the stairs. "The king just confessed to being a killer, I think he's completely crazy, and I don't know how many people in this castle are coming for Juliet. I want her out of here *now*."

Remy leapt into action. As did the other men. They all ran for the door, surrounding Juliet and Constantine like a wall as they tried to get the hell out of there.

"Have a getaway car waiting," Remy rushed to say. "South side of the castle. Had it there just in case."

She could have kissed him.

"You jump in with her, and we'll follow."

They raced through the castle. Juliet didn't understand why Constantine insisted on carrying her when she could be running with him, but when she tried to get down, he just tightened his grip. A few stunned faces greeted them, and she saw some of the castle staff holding phones. Katarina was one of the staff members. She stared down at her phone with shock clear to see.

Juliet knew they'd all witnessed the king's confession.

*I came home to find my family. And my only family member is a killer.* One who had wanted her dead, too.

But she wasn't dying. Constantine was protecting her. As he always had. And they were bursting out of what she figured had to be the south side of the castle. Two royal guards ran at them. Holden punched one, while Remy took out the other. A black car with tinted windows waited up ahead. Twenty feet. Ten.

They reached the vehicle. Constantine put her down long enough to open the back door.

*Bam.*

The bullet blasted from the back seat. Constantine spun around, falling to the ground. "Run," he gasped as he reached inside his coat.

She grabbed for his shoulders because she wasn't running without him. Juliet could already see red pouring through his suit coat.

"Too late to run," a familiar voice said. "My Juliet will never leave me."

She looked up and saw Christian climbing from the back of the black vehicle. He had a gun in his hand, and he pointed the weapon right at her.

# CHAPTER TWENTY-TWO

*Step Twenty-freaking-two: Walk through hell to protect her. Burn, then do it again. And again.*

"Get in the car, Juliet," Christian Hale beamed at her. "We're going for a ride."

The hell they were. Constantine was fucking tired of people waiting in cars that were supposed to just be for Juliet. First Alexandre at the airport and now this prick. When he took over security in Lancaden, this shit would never happen again.

Constantine had palmed his knife once more, and when Christian took a step toward Juliet, Constantine sliced the blade across the back of Christian's ankle. He aimed for the Achilles tendon. The bastard went down with a scream, and as he fell, Constantine threw his body over Juliet, worried the prick might squeeze the trigger and fire again.

But he didn't fire because Christian was too busy screaming and grabbing his ankle. Too busy yelling that he was bleeding to death. That he needed help.

"Juliet, help me! *Help me!*" Christian shouted.

Screw that. Constantine twisted away from Juliet. He grabbed the gun that the bastard had dropped. Then he pushed the bloody knife into

Juliet's fingers. "Anyone else comes at you, you stab them, got it?"

Her wide, stark eyes met his. "You're bleeding a lot."

"Don't even feel any pain. I'm fine." He wasn't going to look at his wound. Juliet needed to get the hell away from the castle.

Christian rolled on the ground, still screaming. Dramatic much?

Holden raced up to the car. "What happened to—jeez, that's a lot of blood."

There was a whole lot of blood around Christian. Perhaps Constantine had cut more than just the tendon. Oh, well.

"You should apply some pressure," Holden advised. But his gaze had already moved to rake Constantine. And he gave a low whistle. "So should you."

"He was waiting in the freaking car." Constantine ducked inside and swept the vehicle. No one else was there. Good. "We need to go."

"You need a doctor!" Juliet shouted. "Constantine, you have a bullet in you!"

He actually thought the bullet had gone through him, so no worries on that score. What did worry him...

Emile had been the one to take away Christian. And Emile was clearly following the crazy king's orders. That meant the bastard had to be close by. Only Constantine didn't see him. He just saw the car. Ready and waiting.

"Get in!" Remy yelled as he hurried forward to join them. "Heard some insane commotion behind me. Sounded like a riot back there!" But his eyes widened when he saw Constantine's chest. "Dammit, not again! Can you *stop* teasing death for me? Seriously? Stop!"

Constantine was worrying about his blood loss, too. Because the blood was pumping like mad. And if he was driving the car, and he passed out...

His hand clamped around Holden's shoulder. "Drive the car. Take Juliet."

"I'm not going anywhere without you!" Juliet instantly argued.

He would slow her down. He could feel *his* body slowing down. "I'll meet you. Remy and I will...*go.*"

"No!"

But Holden had picked her up.

"Stop doing that!" Juliet yelled as she fought him. He put her in the front seat, but she just jumped right back out.

Juliet ran to Constantine. "I'm not leaving you! *I will not!* Get your ass in the back of that car!"

Swearing, Holden rushed to the front seat. He turned the key. The engine sputtered.

Remy's head whipped up. "Shouldn't sputter. The engine should be fine. Perfectly tuned. It shouldn't sputter—"

Holden's head had snapped up as well.

A sputtering engine...

They all knew what it could mean.

And, about thirty feet away, Constantine caught sight of Emile. Standing there, watching, smiling.

The king had said he had spies everywhere. Spies that had told him about Constantine's friendship with Remy. The king had known that Remy would appear to protect Constantine and Juliet. The king had been ready.

*Had the king warned Emile to be on the lookout for Remy?* Constantine bet he had.

*Emile found the car. He knew we'd try to escape in it.*

So he'd put Christian inside. And he'd left one other surprise, too. *Because Christian was a loose end that couldn't come back to bite the crown in the ass.*

"Get away!" Holden shouted as he jumped from the driver's seat.

Constantine grabbed Juliet, yanking her against him even as he spun so that he could protect her from the impact that he knew was coming. Ignoring the blood that coursed down his body, he pushed past the weakness and rushed forward with her.

He'd taken seven steps when the impact of the explosion hit him. A white-hot blast of heat that slammed into his back, lifted him up, and tossed Constantine and Juliet through the air. He held her tightly, refusing to let go, never wanting to let go, and when they hit the ground, he twisted so that he would take the impact.

Alarms were shrieking everywhere. Voices rose in a chorus of screams, and a whooshing filled his head.

*Boom. Boom. Boom.* His heartbeat? Bullets? What was happening?

Constantine rolled his body and put Juliet beneath him. She couldn't be hurt. She could not be.

Her mouth was moving.

He couldn't make out what she was saying even though Juliet was right there.

*Boom. Boom. Boom.*

"You are on fire!" she cried.

What?

Something hit him. Someone. Someone slammed into him and took Constantine away from Juliet as he and his attacker rolled on the pavement. But when he came up swinging, he saw that Ty was in front of him.

"I'm trying to save you, asshole!" Ty shouted. Then he slapped at Constantine's suit coat.

Constantine realized—shit, he was on fire. His clothes were burning. He jerked out of his coat and shirt and dropped to the ground. Rolling, he sent pain careening through his bullet wound. Smoke drifted around him even as his frantic gaze sought out Juliet. She was safe. On her feet. Not burning. Blood trickled from a cut on her cheek, but otherwise, she was all right.

His breath heaved out as Constantine sat up. The fire had been limited to his clothing. He didn't feel any burns on his body.

"Damn, man." Ty's hand settled along his shoulder. With his hand lifted that way, Constantine saw that he had a holster beneath his right arm.

Constantine had dropped the gun he'd taken from Christian when the blast hit him. Constantine's gaze jerked to the left. Christian was still on the ground, but now he was covered in ash, and he'd gone statue still as he gazed in shock at the scene around him.

But, behind Christian, another figure raced forward. Emile. He was running for them, and his eyes were on Juliet.

Constantine grabbed the gun from Ty's holster. Lifted it. "Stop!" he thundered.

Emile wasn't stopping. And he had a fucking sword in his hand. A *sword.* Where the hell had he gotten that weapon? *Does it even matter?* He was running toward Juliet with a sword and Constantine just fired.

*Bam.*

A hit to the chest. Emile staggered. His mouth opened. He gaped. Looked down at himself.

Holden and Remy grabbed him as he fell. *Holden.* Thank Christ he was okay. Looking more than a bit singed and completely pissed, his partner yanked the sword from Emile's slack grip.

"Damn." Ty seemed admiring as he appraised Constantine. "You're quick on the draw." He peered over his shoulder at the fallen man. "Guess that's why you don't bring a sword to a—"

Constantine shoved him out of the way because this was not the damn time for a joke. He needed Juliet. She was what mattered. Always what mattered. But when he tried to go to her, his body sagged with weakness.

Who was bleeding more? Him or Christian? Hard to tell at this point, but Constantine staggered forward anyway. He would not give in to the darkness pulling at him, not until Juliet was safe.

She threw herself into his arms. Held him so fiercely. "You were on fire."

They had to get away. Since their escape vehicle was in about a million burning pieces, time for a different ride. "We're going, baby." Somehow, he'd get her out. "We're going."

They'd taken a few steps when...

*"The king is dead!"* And, over the shrieking alarms, Constantine heard what sounded like a church bell ringing.

Ringing again and again.

"The king is dead!" More cries. More shouts.

Ty and Constantine shared a long look over Juliet's head. Then they all turned to see Alexandre marching from the castle, with guards at his back. Three men and Katarina.

*What the hell are we facing now?*

Constantine pushed Juliet behind him. His fingers were bloody, and he knew he'd smeared blood on her body.

"Stop it!" Juliet cried. "Let me help you!"

No, he would protect her until his dying breath. And if those guards were coming for a fight...

Ty moved to his side. So did Remy. And Holden. They formed a wall in front of Juliet. An army to protect her, just as Constantine had promised.

"Emile is out of commission," Holden said as he swiped a hand over his own bloody lip. He glared at the approaching guards. "Which bastard is gonna be our next target?"

Flames crackled. The guards continued forward. Alexandre led them straight to Juliet—or as close as he could get considering she had a four-man wall in front of her.

Then Alexandre dropped to one knee. "I regret to inform you that the king took his own life."

*What. The. Fuck?*

Alexandre lifted his head. "Overcome with remorse for all his actions, he leapt from the window of his chambers just moments ago."

*Bullshit. You helped get his ass through that window, didn't you?*

"For the good of Lancaden," Alexandre murmured. He put one hand over his heart. "I swear my allegiance to Juliet Laurent."

The other guards all followed suit.

People were spilling out from the castle, left and right, and they, too, dropped to their knees. Women and men rushed from alleys. From the bridges that led over the moat. Whispers rose to a roar as so many people came forward to kneel before the new ruler of Lancaden.

The king was dead. Juliet held all the power.

"They have to do what you say, Juliet," Ty told her. "The king can't control them any longer."

Juliet's fingers pressed to Constantine's back. "Whatever I say?" She didn't wait for a response. Instead, voice shaking, she called out, "Get my consort to a hospital! Immediately! Help him!"

*Dammit, he wasn't that bad off. Maybe a little singed. Some blood loss.*

"The threat is over." Relief filled Ty's voice. "Cavalry is here." He waved toward the right. Five black SUVs had just pulled up.

Now the CIA appeared? *Now?* Typical. "Always late to the party." He looked back at Juliet.

"Hospital!" she yelled as alarm flashed on her beautiful face. "Now!"

He smiled because she didn't need to worry. He was going to be just fine. Like a bullet and an explosion would stop him. Nothing would stop him from standing between her and any threat.

"Love you, princess," he rasped right before his mouth pressed to hers.

# CHAPTER TWENTY-THREE

*Final Step: Hold tight and don't ever let the hell go.*

"I wouldn't imagine that assassinating a king—even a crazy-ass, murderous, villain of a king—would be an easy task."

Alexandre raised his brows as he sat at sharp attention in the seat across from Constantine. "No, I wouldn't imagine that it would be." His gaze darted over Constantine. "You certainly recovered quickly. I expected you to be in the hospital for at least several more days."

"I'm magical that way." The stitches pulled and annoyed the hell out of him. He felt like his whole body had been beaten by hammers, but no way had he intended to be in a hospital bed when Juliet needed him.

"How wonderful for you." Alexandre pursed his lips. "The coronation will be happening soon. I'm sure the princess will want you close."

"Oh, I'll be close." He stared straight at his prey. "But you won't be."

"Yes, I rather expected as much."

"The plan was quite good, I'll give you that. But you put Juliet at risk, and for that, you're lucky I haven't ripped off your head."

Alexandre sniffed. "I don't know what you mean."

"Sure, you do. Holden and Ty did some digging for me. Turns out, the king was never, ever alone. He either had a small army of doctors and nurses with him, constantly checking his health status, or he had his handpicked guards surrounding him. People who were completely loyal to him, despite his being batshit crazy."

No expression crossed Alexandre's face.

"You didn't know how far he'd gone, not until you took over in the last six months. That's when you stumbled on the truth, wasn't it?"

A shrug. "This is a fun, hypothetical conversation." Alexandre leaned forward. "You know, there were several people who saw the king jump. All on his own."

"People who seem very fond of you."

Alexandre smiled. "I can be charming."

"No, you can't be." Just so they were clear. "But you can be cunning. You realized that you had to get the king alone. Not like you could kill him with his loyal sycophants right there. They'd stop you, or, if you succeeded, they'd kill you on the spot. You needed to eliminate him, but in order to do that, you had to set the stage just right."

And that stage setting had involved Juliet.

"The ring appeared," Constantine continued, "and the king became obsessed, didn't he? He wanted Juliet dead because she represented his failure with the queen."

A long sigh slipped from Alexandre. "Foolish. Like cutting off a nose just to spite a face. Juliet was his only heir, and only a madman would kill his only heir." He snapped his fingers together. "But I forgot, we *are* talking about a madman." His stare hardened. "A man who dealt with some of the worst scum on the earth because he had no conscience. He traded the resources of this country and never hesitated. He used his own people. He went after his own glory. He didn't care about who might be left to carry on after he died. He was too tied up with his own plans. His own vengeance. His own hate."

"He hated Juliet."

"She was the future. One that did not involve him. I think he would have rather watched Lancaden crash and burn than to ever allow it to be led by anyone else. Oh, wait, I don't just think that, I know it."

"And *you,* unlike the king, always do what's best for Lancaden." *So you set up the scene. You agreed to bring Juliet to him. You knew he'd want to talk to her without prying eyes on them. And you knew you'd have your chance.* "You realized he'd make me an offer to kill her."

"Yes, with your background, that was to be expected."

Sonofabitch. "Everyone assumes I'm the bad guy."

"Sometimes, that's what you need. A bad guy who will do anything to protect the woman he wants. You wouldn't be at all afraid to say...get your hands bloody."

No, he wouldn't. Constantine's head tipped forward as he acknowledged the point. Then he focused on the part that kept nagging at him.

"Christian Hale was there. At the last minute, were you trying to decide if you wanted me or him in that room with the king?"

"I had *nothing* to do with Christian Hale's arrival. The king did that. They knew each other. Hale is a history professor, and he came to Lancaden one summer for his studies." Alexandre hesitated, then admitted, "Hale was aware of Juliet's real identity for quite some time. The king knew where she was for far longer than I realized, you see. It wasn't just the ring, though when that appeared, things certainly sped up. No, Hale was with Juliet by the king's command all along. At least, at first it was by command, but I think he developed his own unnatural attachment to her later."

Hale had already confessed to the attacks at Juliet's house. "The world is full of assholes."

"Indeed." Alexandre nodded. "The king paid him to keep tabs on her. You watch something long enough, you realize just how valuable that *something* is, and you might decide that you can't let go of it."

"He's let go." Hale had been given a blood transfusion at the hospital. Stitched up. He'd recovered. He was waiting to be tossed into a jail cell.

It wasn't just Lancaden justice he'd face. Apparently, the CIA had plans for Christian Hale and for Emile Duparte, too. Provided, of course, that Emile continued to live. He was currently under guard at the hospital.

So many who'd worked with the twisted king were going down. One right after the other, dominos all falling and never getting up again.

"Yes, I suppose he has let go, now." Alexandre smiled at him. "Is that all? Because I wished to watch the coronation."

"Ty hasn't arrested you."

"Well, I certainly hope not. I've been cooperating with the CIA, after all. And *I* am the one who promoted him to the chief of security position here. I was fully aware of his true identity, even if he didn't realize I was in the loop, shall we say?"

Alexandre was a shady SOB. "Your great-uncle was the assassin hired to kill the king."

"No, he was the assassin the king hired to kill the queen." A patient correction. "But you know that. You're just baiting me." His head tilted. "Because you know something else, too, don't you?"

"I know the king was too weak to make that jump without a little help."

A shrug. "Don't be too sure. He came at me quite fiercely when you left with Juliet. He was determined to call all his guards and to have them tear her from your grip. I will confess that things got physical between us. But I didn't *throw* him out of the window. Hypothetically, though— because weren't we talking that way at the beginning? He *may* have slipped and fallen when I dodged his blows."

Uh, huh. "Your great-uncle was an assassin."

Alexandre nodded. "We've covered that."

"My friends at Wilde delved into your family tree. Your ancestors have a long history of working with the royal family."

"So we do."

"As assassins."

Alexandre didn't blink.

Constantine leaned forward. "You weren't made to be a counsellor, were you? Not exactly your type of job description."

Alexandre shrugged, all innocence. "My family has a history of protecting Lancaden. Protecting her rightful rulers and her people. My great-uncle died to protect the woman who should have ruled. And I just stepped in to make sure that the current princess lived to claim her crown."

Damn. A royal assassin. That was a new one for him. "She has new protection now."

"Glad to hear it." Alexandre rose. "Though I will always be but a phone call away, should she need me."

Constantine also rose. "I've got her."

Alexandre turned away.

"The CIA isn't going to lock you up. They wanted you to take him out, didn't they?"

"Let's just say, I don't think they're upset with me. In fact, I think they may want to give me a job." Alexandre stopped at the door. Glanced back. "See you in another life."

"I hope to hell not."

Smiling, Alexandre sauntered away.

Constantine blew out a breath. Damn. Court politics could be killer. But Alexandre had been right about him. Constantine didn't mind a little blood.

Not at all.

Not if bleeding—or, preferably, making others bleed—would keep his princess safe.

***

"We can stop pretending."

Juliet looked up when Constantine entered her chambers.

"The bad guys are gone. The kingdom loves you. You have the world at your feet."

She'd had her coronation ceremony less than an hour before. He'd stood at her side, looking dangerous and dashing, and when she'd trembled with uncertainty, he'd taken her hand and squeezed her fingers.

"You don't have to pretend I'm your consort any longer."

Juliet shook her head. "We stopped pretending that pretty much from the beginning." What she felt for him wasn't pretend. She looked at her left hand. "But maybe we can get a new ring," she said. "One that you pick out for me."

"I did pick out that one. Gave very specific instructions on what I wanted. Because I wanted you to have the perfect ring."

Her gaze rose.

"Because maybe I was saying it was all pretend," he added gruffly, "but the truth was that I fell for you the minute I saw your picture. I didn't care that you were some long-lost royal. I just wanted you. I knew even before Eric told me that

I would be your bodyguard—I knew I would do anything to keep you safe. Then I met you and I forgot my own name."

His words had a laugh spilling from her. "That's not true. When we met, the first thing you said was your name."

"Because I'd had to remind myself of it. I blurted it out fast in case I forgot it again."

Warmth bloomed inside of her.

"I looked at you and everything else slid away." The back of his hand brushed over her cheek. "I have a confession I need to make."

"Please tell me that you haven't found more enemies at the castle gate." Or, heaven forbid, within the gate.

"I'm the anonymous donor."

Her brow furrowed.

"The guy who paid for your protection? It was me. I wasn't letting you leave the US without me at your side, so I made up that story about someone else."

"You did?"

"I lied. But I don't plan to lie to you ever again. You're the one person who should always get the truth from me." He sucked in a breath. "So here goes. Full truth. I'm not the guy who should rule a country with you. But I am the guy who will eliminate any and every threat to you. I can stay in the shadows. I can be here when you need me. I can—"

"Be what? My secret?" No. Never. She stepped closer to him. "You *are* my partner, Constantine. The man I want at my side. The man who shields me from fire." Nope, way too soon for that reference. She still had nightmares. "You are the man who will be the father of my children. The man who will share my life." A life she hadn't expected.

There would be a million adjustments for them both. So much to learn. So much to do. But she wanted to make a difference for the people here. She wanted to do good things. She wanted to make up for all the pain in the past.

And to do that? She wanted Constantine with her. "Stay with me?" she asked.

"In a heartbeat."

She smiled. "Rule with me?"

"If you think the country can handle me."

Joy built within her. "Fight for me?"

"With every breath in my body."

"Love me?"

He leaned toward her. "Forever." His lips feathered over hers. *"Forever."*

And Juliet knew she'd found the love of her life. To her, the badass bodyguard with the smoldering gaze would always be better than any prince charming.

So much better.

# EPILOGUE

"He got the princess. That's cool. Really. I'm super glad my partner gets to rule a whole freaking kingdom and live some happily-ever-after lifestyle with the woman of his dreams." Holden raked a hand over the stubble that coated his jaw. "But I'd just broken him in, you know? Just got the guy to the point where he was a decent Wilde agent. And now, what? I'm supposed to start all over from scratch? The struggle is real." He slumped back in his chair.

His boss, Eric Wilde, lifted one eyebrow. "Do you need some time off? Maybe a vacation?"

Holden perked up. A vacation wasn't a half bad idea. He could totally see himself sunning on a beach. Drinking something with a little umbrella in it. "Perhaps..."

Eric tapped the file in front of him. "I can easily get another agent to take this assignment. Just because you have history with the client, it doesn't mean you would be the best fit for her. Especially considering the way things ended."

And that beautiful image of a beach vacation popped as Holden shot to attention. "What assignment?"

But Eric shrugged. "You should take time off. I have other agents who can handle this. She did mention your name, but, like I said, given your former relationship, I already had concerns about you being able to maintain a proper, professional—"

"I am *always* professional. Ask anyone. Ask the princess. I now come with a recommendation from royalty. How do you get better than that?" But his mind was spinning because these hints that Eric kept dropping were pretty damn specific. "No." A sharp snap.

Eric's eyes narrowed.

Ahem. Holden cleared his throat. "No," he said again, a little less sharp. "It *can't* be the person I think." His fingers inched across the desk toward the file.

Seeing that inching, Eric pushed it toward him.

Holden flipped open the file, sure he had to be mistaken. There was no way this case could possibly be about his—

Ex-fiancée. Her beautiful face smiled up at him as memories came crashing back through his head. "This some joke?" he managed. Because she wouldn't come to him, not after the way he'd hurt her. She wouldn't come to him...*unless her world is on fire.*

"I'm afraid not. She needs protection, and she came to Wilde, asking for you specifically. But, seeing as how you are about to go on vacation—"

He jumped to his feet. "I'm taking the case."

"Good," Eric said. "Because she's waiting in your office."

Without another word, Holden rushed for the door.

## THE END

## Holden's story will continue...in
## HOW TO HEAL A HEARTBREAK.

# ABOUT THE AUTHOR

Cynthia Eden is a *New York Times, USA Today, Digital Book World*, and *IndieReader* best-seller.

Cynthia writes sexy tales of contemporary romance, romantic suspense, and paranormal romance. Since she began writing full-time in 2005, Cynthia has written over one hundred novels and novellas.

Cynthia lives along the Alabama Gulf Coast. She loves romance novels, horror movies, and chocolate.

## For More Information

- *cynthiaeden.com*
- *facebook.com/cynthiaedenfanpage*

# HER OTHER WORKS

## Wilde Ways: Gone Rogue

- How To Protect A Princess (Book 1)
- How To Heal A Heartbreak (Book 2)

## Ice Breaker Cold Case Romance

- Frozen In Ice (Book 1)
- Falling For The Ice Queen (Book 2)
- Ice Cold Saint (Book 3)
- Touched By Ice (Book 4)

## Phoenix Fury

- Hot Enough To Burn (Book 1)
- Slow Burn (Book 2)
- Burn It Down (Book 3)

## Trouble For Hire

- No Escape From War (Book 1)
- Don't Play With Odin (Book 2)
- Jinx, You're It (Book 3)
- Remember Ramsey (Book 4)

## Death and Moonlight Mystery

- Step Into My Web (Book 1)
- Save Me From The Dark (Book 2)

## Wilde Ways

- Protecting Piper (Book 1)
- Guarding Gwen (Book 2)

- Before Ben (Book 3)
- The Heart You Break (Book 4)
- Fighting For Her (Book 5)
- Ghost Of A Chance (Book 6)
- Crossing The Line (Book 7)
- Counting On Cole (Book 8)
- Chase After Me (Book 9)
- Say I Do (Book 10)
- Roman Will Fall (Book 11)
- The One Who Got Away (Book 12)
- Pretend You Want Me (Book 13)
- Cross My Heart (Book 14)
- The Bodyguard Next Door (Book 15)
- Ex Marks The Perfect Spot (Book 16)
- The Thief Who Loved Me (Book 17)

## Dark Sins

- Don't Trust A Killer (Book 1)
- Don't Love A Liar (Book 2)

## Lazarus Rising

- Never Let Go (Book One)
- Keep Me Close (Book Two)
- Stay With Me (Book Three)
- Run To Me (Book Four)
- Lie Close To Me (Book Five)
- Hold On Tight (Book Six)

## Dark Obsession Series

- Watch Me (Book 1)
- Want Me (Book 2)
- Need Me (Book 3)
- Beware Of Me (Book 4)
- Only For Me (Books 1 to 4)

## Mine Series

- Mine To Take (Book 1)
- Mine To Keep (Book 2)
- Mine To Hold (Book 3)
- Mine To Crave (Book 4)
- Mine To Have (Book 5)
- Mine To Protect (Book 6)
- Mine Box Set Volume 1 (Books 1-3)
- Mine Box Set Volume 2 (Books 4-6)

## Bad Things

- The Devil In Disguise (Book 1)
- On The Prowl (Book 2)
- Undead Or Alive (Book 3)
- Broken Angel (Book 4)
- Heart Of Stone (Book 5)
- Tempted By Fate (Book 6)
- Wicked And Wild (Book 7)
- Saint Or Sinner (Book 8)
- Bad Things Volume One (Books 1 to 3)
- Bad Things Volume Two (Books 4 to 6)
- Bad Things Deluxe Box Set (Books 1 to 6)

## Bite Series

- Forbidden Bite (Bite Book 1)
- Mating Bite (Bite Book 2)

## Blood and Moonlight Series

- Bite The Dust (Book 1)
- Better Off Undead (Book 2)
- Bitter Blood (Book 3)
- Blood and Moonlight (The Complete Series)

## Purgatory Series

- The Wolf Within (Book 1)
- Marked By The Vampire (Book 2)
- Charming The Beast (Book 3)
- Deal with the Devil (Book 4)
- The Beasts Inside (Books 1 to 4)

## Bound Series

- Bound By Blood (Book 1)
- Bound In Darkness (Book 2)
- Bound In Sin (Book 3)
- Bound By The Night (Book 4)
- Bound in Death (Book 5)
- Forever Bound (Books 1 to 4)

## Stand-Alone Romantic Suspense

- It's A Wonderful Werewolf
- Never Cry Werewolf
- Immortal Danger
- Deck The Halls
- Come Back To Me
- Put A Spell On Me
- Never Gonna Happen
- One Hot Holiday
- Slay All Day
- Midnight Bite
- Secret Admirer
- Christmas With A Spy
- Femme Fatale
- Until Death
- Sinful Secrets
- First Taste of Darkness
- A Vampire's Christmas Carol

Printed in Great Britain
by Amazon